Noah Hunter faces the most dangerous investigation of his life as he goes up against Arrow Point's first serial killer.

Police sergeant Noah Hunter attends a colleague's funeral and finds a body hidden in the small town's cemetery. A killer buried the corpse underneath an open grave, hoping it would not be seen once the casket was lowered.

During the investigation, more bodies are discovered, and the community is devastated and in shock as he investigates Arrow Point's first serial killer case.

Following leads, Noah interviews some of his closest friends at the police station, placing him in the murderer's crosshairs as he draws closer.

Unmasking a monster hiding in plain sight reveals even uglier truths waiting to be unearthed.

Some secrets should remain safely buried—forever.

Grave Choices

Copyright © 2021 by David Darling

All rights reserved. No part of this publication may be reproduced, distributed, or transmitted in any form or by any means, including photocopying, recording, or other electronic or mechanical methods, without the prior written permission of the author, except in the case of brief quotations embodied in critical reviews and certain other noncommercial uses permitted by copyright law. For permission requests, write to the author at the email address below.

www.daviddarlingbooks.com

This novel is a **work of fiction**. Names, characters, businesses, places, events, and incidents are either the products of the author's imagination or used in a fictitious manner. Any resemblance to actual persons, living or dead, or actual events is purely coincidental.

Cover Design by Norm Jolin at www.ndesign.studio.com

Novels by David Darling

The Noah Hunter Series

The Tipping Point

Grave Choices

Course of Action (June 2022)

Hunters Gambit (Forthcoming)

Standalone novel

Serve in the Shadows: Recruitment

I want to dedicate this novel to those who have fallen, those who continue to serve, and the families who have supported them.

You will be remembered.

Author's Note

I started out writing as a hobby, and from there, it has progressed into a desire and a *need* to continue. There has been inspiration and motivation from all corners of the planet as people posted reviews or messaged me. Thank you!

I have always said that even if I were to win the lottery, I would wake up early the next day and continue to write. It has taken me nearly five decades to discover my passion, and I'm not letting go!

I would like to thank everyone that read and helped support my first novel, *The Tipping Point*. The crew at Best Thriller Books (James), Steven Hendricks, Troy Pool, Mark E. Elliott, Tom Dooley, Simon Gervais (for the great advice and your time), Jeff Clark, J Todd Wilkens, Wendy Visser, Paula Kennedy, and Marc Harrold: your help by reviewing, promoting and commenting did not go unnoticed. I firmly believe your efforts have made a difference. You have no idea how much it is appreciated.

Next, you have a chance to win an autographed copy of Grave Choices by doing the following. If you find an error within this novel (grammatical or otherwise), send me a detailed account of the issue. I will enter your name into a draw, and a copy will be mailed to the winner.

There is *also* a chance to win a large cash reward. How? Very simple! Get a copy of The Tipping Point and Grave Choices into the hands of a Hollywood producer (or Netflix/Amazon Prime Producer). If I get optioned, you will win! Too simple? We shall see.

You miss 100% of the shots you don't take.

I look forward to your reviews and hearing your thoughts on Grave Choices. The adventures of Noah Hunter are nowhere near complete. I hope you and your family are safe and healthy and thank you for reading.

David Darling

August 2021

Grave Choices

The Noah Hunter Series: Book Two

David Darling

Chapter 1

The headlights blinded, and the airhorn caused him to panic as they came straight for him. Steve Misevski stumbled back to avoid the transport and was nearly knocked down by the wind gust. After the curve of the road, the truck drove too close to the shoulder on the Interstate. The plume of dust that trailed behind stung his eyes. He had to squint and keep his mouth closed. The red lights of the trailer disappeared into the night as the driver continued west on the Interstate.

"Son of a bitch."

Steve had gone into the city to see a concert with friends to celebrate his eighteenth birthday, and he had missed the last bus home from Cheyenne. He turned down an offer to sleep on a couch, and instead stuck his thumb out to hitch.

The first ride in the back of an old pickup truck brought him right into Casper, and he was now on the shoulder of I-26 west at two o'clock in the morning as he tried to get home to Arrow Point. There were a few streetlights on the other side of the road, but they were not too effective.

The spring weather was nice for the end of April, and Steve had to open his jean jacket to keep cool. The walk along the road had warmed him up.

Soon, another car passed him, and the driver pretended not to see his thumb as he looked for a ride. When his hand dropped to his side, Steve felt the cell phone in his pocket. He was tempted to call his father to pick him up. His mother died of cancer five years ago, and since then, his dad hasn't talked much. To even start a conversation with him was painful. Often, a whole week would go by without speaking a word.

Steve shrugged at the situation and continued west along the Interstate. He had hitched home a few times over the past year, and he knew sooner or later someone would stop. It was just a matter of time.

Once the last vehicle disappeared, the night birds resumed their chorus.

An hour previous, the clouds had cleared and revealed a thin sliver of moonlight and a million stars. He kicked the gravel and tried not to scuff his new white running shoes.

Another transport truck roared by, and it didn't stop, but he was glad to see the brake lights from the car that followed and pulled over.

Running up, Steve saw that the passenger window was down, and he could hear someone calling out from the front seat.

"Steve Misevski? Is that you?"

He leaned down to see inside, and he chuckled in relief. "Ya. I missed the last bus. Can I get a ride home with you?"

"Sure, get in."

He sat in the front seat and buckled up.

The driver smiled. "I barely saw you in time. It isn't safe to be out at this hour hitchhiking."

"I missed the damn bus and wanted to get home so my dad wouldn't worry."

"No problem. Glad I saw you."

They pulled back onto the Interstate, and the miles passed as the radio broadcast the news and weather report.

"Home in ten minutes. I think that was a little faster than walking."

Steve continued to stare out the passenger window. "Thank you very much, I—"

Steve didn't see the syringe jabbed into his left leg until it was too late. The plunger was fully depressed before it was removed.

"What the hell?" He fumbled for his seatbelt, but had trouble concentrating.

"Relax, you'll be out in a few seconds."

He managed to push down on the seatbelt release and turn to the car door, but as his hand reached for the handle—it lost all strength and fell back down onto his lap. Steve tried to lift his head and look to his left, but it rolled around shoulder to shoulder.

His heart rate slowed, and soon, a thin line of saliva hung from the corner of his mouth as his face went slack. Steve's attempt at a scream came out as a quiet moan as he lost the battle and slid into unconsciousness.

The last thing Steve would hear was a cheerful whistling in the car before he succumbed to the darkness.

Chapter 2

Sergeant Noah Hunter stood ramrod straight with his heels together, and his highly shone boots pointed outward at a perfect forty-five-degree angle. With his shoulders back and chest out, he moved his fists slightly to line them up with the outside seam of his dress pants before remaining still. The white gloves stood out in stark contrast to the dark blue dress uniform.

Noah stood an inch under six feet, and at thirty-eight-years old, he was in great physical shape. His dress uniform couldn't hide the broad shoulders and deep chest. He kept his brown hair short, resembled a military cut, and he had recently regrown his short dark goatee.

At the first note of the bagpipe, his right arm snapped into position, parallel to the ground, with his forearm on a forty-five-degree angle toward his head. The fingers were straight and his thumb tucked in tight, palm down. The index finger barely touched the corner of his right eyebrow.

He held the salute for over four minutes while Constable Randy Finlay played "Going Home." Those gathered around the coffin gazed at the picture of Captain John Richardson displayed on top of the high-glossed casket. He looked sharp in his dress uniform with the American flag as the background, and he had a slight smile on his face that most remembered from the man.

A bagpipe's sorrowful and haunting notes washed over the gathered crowd, and continued throughout the Arrow Point cemetery. The weather was contrary to the solemn occasion. The early May breeze felt like that of the hot summer months. Last night's brief rain gave the grass and flowers a fresh look, which made the colors more vivid, and it had added a little humidity to the air.

When the last note faded, Noah's arm snapped back down to his side into the position of attention.

Police Chief Birch had a few police officers gather around him, and he pulled a handheld radio off his belt for the Last Call.

"Headquarters to Captain Richardson, please respond."

The silence was broken as the birds sang in the trees at the edge of the cemetery.

"Headquarters to Captain John Richardson, please respond."

The chief wiped away a few tears as they slowly made their way down his cheeks while waiting the full ten seconds.

"Headquarters, no response. Captain John Richardson, rest easy and stand down. Thank you for your many years of service—end of watch, the eighth of May, thirteen-hundred hours. Rest in peace, my brother. Headquarters out."

The casket was slowly lowered into the ground on nylon straps attached to an electric motor. The aluminum bars rotated on the frame. It descended silently as befitting the occasion and with perfect timing.

A few sobs could be heard as Noah stepped backward and performed a right turn, then waited. The eight pallbearers conducted their left and right turns respectively and slow marched off the gravesite. The last man stopped and faced Sergeant Hunter and handed over an American flag, folded sharply into a large triangle. He saluted the flag before he turned once again to join the others.

Noah held the flag firmly with two hands, and in turn, slow marched to the chief and reverently passed it over. Sergeant Hunter saluted once again, followed by a right turn, and joined the pallbearers off to the side.

The chief walked over to the side and presented the flag to a woman in a long black dress. She was doing her best to hold back the tears. "I'm so sorry, Eleanor. Please accept this token as our gratitude for his thirty-two years of service. He will be remembered."

The chief stepped back and gave a perfect salute before he walked off to join the others. The Arrow Point Police Department members filled the gravesite along with the fire services, as well as countless others. Richardson was well known throughout the community, and he had touched many lives. His recent heart attack had taken them all by surprise and it was still hard to believe.

Wanting to give the family time alone, Noah thanked the officers. They would meet up at the Tavern to hoist a few drinks in the captain's honor shortly. Within fifteen minutes, the parade of cars had left. Noah and Lieutenant Zane Piekenbrock hung back and waited until the area was clear.

The LT stood a few inches taller than Noah at six-foot-two, and at fifty-eight-years old, he was physically fit with broad shoulders and a deep chest. His hair had turned white at an early age, and he kept it short. Both men were solemn as it fit the occasion. Noah would grab the picture off the casket, bring it with them and rest it on the bar. More than a few drinks would be hoisted in the captain's memory this afternoon.

The widow was the last to be escorted to her car by her son, and the priest left in his vehicle. The caretaker walked over to the head of the grave and brought the coffin back up on the lift. He knelt on the fake grass that lined the hole and brought it up far enough that he could reach the picture.

As his fingers brushed the top of the frame, the angled prop folded flat. The large image of Captain Richardson hit the top of the casket, slid down the side, and rested at the bottom, over six feet down.

"Crap. Sorry guys, it fell. Give me a second."

"Jesus Christ." Piekenbrock took a step forward.

Noah held his hand out, palm up to forestall him. "Accidents happen. Do you need any help?"

The caretaker shook his head. "I'm good."

Henry had worked at the cemetery for over twenty-five years, and unfortunately, this wasn't the first time he had knocked things down under a casket. At forty-five years of age, he had a lanky frame that caused his clothing to hang from his shoulders like a scarecrow. No matter how much he ate, Henry always appeared in need of a good meal.

The caretaker raised the coffin fully at the control unit, then moved to the side and gave it a push near the head. Once it hit the aluminum bar, it easily pivoted, and it gave him a four-foot gap in which to drop. The gray coveralls he wore were dirty but essential in his line of work.

Noah watched him sit on the edge of the open grave between the nylon strap and the end, and smoothly drop from sight. Two seconds later, Noah saw the picture frame come out of the hole and rest on the artificial grass. Two hands grabbed the framed tubing, and Henry pulled himself back up. With a neat turn, he sat on the side with his feet dangling down.

Noah expected him to get up right away, but he just sat there as he stared down into the pit. With his gaze fixed below, he called out, "Hey guys? Can you come here, please?"

Noah turned to the LT and shrugged. When they stood beside the caretaker, Noah followed Henry's finger as he pointed down.

At the bottom of the grave, the toes from a white pair of sneakers pointed up through the dark soil. Farther down, they could see a small patch of denim jeans where Henry's foot had disturbed the dirt.

Someone had been buried below an open grave.

Noah cleared his throat as he tried to take in the scene. "It seems Captain Richardson isn't done helping us yet."

Chapter 3

Noah and a few others slid the casket back into the hearse, then the driver inserted a stainless-steel pin into the rail system to prevent rollback and lock it into place. For now, Noah stayed in his dress uniform while the LT directed the scene.

Henry had willingly jumped back into the grave and, using the sleeve of his overalls, lifted one of the white running shoes just enough to prove that it was attached to a body. Piekenbrock soon had cruisers on the scene, and the funeral director had the hearse remove the casket.

The remorseful occasion and farewell for a comrade had turned into a crime scene.

Once the yellow barricade tape was wrapped around several headstones and formed a perimeter, the LT came over. "Hunter, I want you to interview the groundskeeper. Forensics is on the way, along with the county coroner."

"Should I talk with everyone that was here?" Over sixty friends and family had attended the gathering, not including the members of the police department. It would take weeks to track everyone down properly and get statements.

Zane shook his head. "At this point, it isn't required. They wouldn't have seen anything. Start with the groundskeeper and take it from there."

Grabbing his notebook and pen from the cruiser, Noah made his way over to Henry. He watched the whole proceeding while sitting on a landscaping golf cart at the edge of the crime-scene tape.

He slid in beside him on the front bench and sat for a minute in silence. Henry's hands gripped the steering wheel, knuckles white as he stared straight ahead.

"I have to ask you a few questions. Are you okay?"

Henry let out a deep sigh and folded his hands in his lap. "I'm around the dead every day, but I don't see them up close. Not really. It kind of shocked me. I'll be good."

Noah remembered his first time seeing a body while on tour. It was certainly something you do not forget, and it stays with you for a long time. Nearly twenty years later, he could still smell the residue from the explosion and hear the screams.

"When was the grave dug out?"

Henry closed his eyes as he recalled. "Yesterday afternoon. I remember finishing just before the rain started." He glanced at Noah and nodded. "I'm sure it was four o'clock because I went home just after I put everything away."

Noah kept his notebook closed and pen on top. He would fill in the statement later. From experience, writing while some people talked made them nervous. They were worried about *what* he was writing as opposed to remembering certain details which could be important.

"What did you use to dig the grave?"

Henry jerked his thumb at the tools in the back of the cart. Three long-handled shovels and a rake lay next to a small white cooler. The handles hung out over the tailgate and were held in place with a bungee cord. Rolls of sod filled the remainder of the space. "I start with a spade and outline the area, then remove the grass. If you do it correctly, it'll grow back right away."

Remembering the size of the grave, Noah had to ask, "You dug all that out by hand?"

Henry shook his head, "No, I use a backhoe loader. I put sheets of plywood down, so I don't rip up the grass before driving on it."

Noah already knew the answer to the next question, but he wanted the caretaker to provide further information. He shrugged and pointed to the gravesite. "Is it possible that the body was already there? Maybe you missed it?"

Henry gave a single sharp bark of laughter. "Not a chance. You always finish off the hole with a squared shovel and make the bottom flat for the casket. That way, it won't tip. I was down there yesterday, finishing it off."

"What security does the cemetery have?" Noah had taken a quick look at the area but did not see anything.

"There isn't any out here, but we have a few cameras and an alarm in the main building. Nothing in the maintenance shed."

Noah saw the county coroner pull up in his white window van, then back up to the perimeter. "Do you remember seeing anyone here yesterday? In this area?"

Henry nodded. "There were a few families out here, visiting. It was a nice day before the rain started. Once it rains, people don't come as much."

"What time does the cemetery close?"

He looked at his watch briefly before answering. "Yesterday was Friday, so they would have left just after I did. Five o'clock, the offices lock up. However, anyone can still park and walk in."

Noah wrote down Henry's phone number and a few brief points to help him remember. "Okay, thanks. I'll get ahold of you if I have any more questions."

He was surprised at the strength of Henry's grip as they shook hands. Digging graves kept him in shape, and despite the lanky frame, he had the physical power of a much larger man.

As Noah walked toward the grave, two young officers helped the coroner and his assistant down an aluminum ladder. George held the position of county coroner for over forty-five years. He could have retired long ago, but the small man had no family and truly enjoyed his job. His usual reply of, *my golf game sucks. I need to keep working* made Noah chuckle every time.

Hunter stayed back while George confirmed that the subject was deceased. He was the only one who could legally do so in the area. Finally, after three minutes, a small black leather bag was passed up, and George climbed out. Lieutenant Piekenbrock waved for Noah to join them as the coroner brushed off the dirt from his khaki pants and dark blue jacket. *Natrona County Coroner* was embroidered across the back in white letters.

The county sheriff's forensic team chose that moment to arrive in a long black van with an array of antennas and a small parabolic dish on the rooftop. The Arrow Point Police Department did not have the funding or capabilities for a forensics team. Various departments, including the Highway Patrol, used the Natrona County resources.

The officers helped George's assistant lift the body. The thick black plastic body bag had six separate ropes attached to the handles, and it was gently placed on a spine board then off to the side.

"What can you tell us now?" The LT remained in his dress uniform. Neither man had time to return home and change.

George pushed his thick glasses back up on his nose with the back of his hand and shook his head. "Young male, between eighteen- to twenty-years old. No obvious sign as a cause, and unable to determine any time of death. The ground is still pretty cold that far down at this time of year. It's like a fridge and throws off the readings."

"How long before an autopsy?" Noah had pulled out his notepad once again, pen poised above the paper.

The coroner paused in thought as he recalled the workload. "Monday morning would be the earliest. I can shuffle around a few that are not a priority."

The LT nodded toward Noah. "Send the results with attention to Sergeant Hunter. He will lead the case."

Noah only raised his eyebrows slightly at this. "I'll look forward to your report, George."

Piekenbrock waved over one of the forensic personnel from the county. "You guys are cleared for the site."

Sergeant Hunter recalled the murder investigation he led last fall and how that ended. Hopefully, this case wouldn't result in him being shot, always a worthwhile goal. Instead, Noah was ready for an investigation that was a little less dramatic and low-key. Hopefully, the body was a prank gone wrong or something easily explained.

As the body was loaded in the coroner's van, a shiver ran across his back, and Noah knew that would not be the case.

Chapter 4

Before going any further in the investigation, Noah headed to the station and changed into his patrol uniform. Investigating while dressed in his formal uniform wasn't appropriate unless you were looking for photo opportunities with the press. A thought that made him shudder. He would leave that to the officers and the chief.

The Arrow Point police station was on the northwest corner of Main and Oak Streets downtown. A three-story brick building had public access through the main glass doors and the staff parking in the rear. On the first floor were the locker rooms and processing. The second floor was mainly offices. A large area of the third floor was allotted to dispatch, the new emergency call center, and the administrative offices for the station. The deputy chief and the police chief had their offices off to the back corner, overlooking Main Street.

When Noah arrived at work, the parking lot was mostly empty of civilian vehicles and only half a dozen cruisers. Right behind him, Police Chief Birch parked two spots over in his reserved spot. Noah waited and held the door before they went inside.

"Sergeant Hunter, I just got off the phone with Lieutenant Piekenbrock. Before you head back out, come upstairs to my office."

From the deadpan look on the chief's face, Noah had no idea of the intentions behind the order. Far as he knew, he hadn't done anything wrong, but still, he felt uneasy. "Yes, sir."

Noah considered various possibilities for the meeting but came up short. Regardless, he changed into his patrol uniform and adjusted the Velcro straps on the ballistic vest. He stored the dress uniform in the garment bag, and with a look in the full-length mirror, he was ready.

"Let's go see what this is about."

Noah took the stairs to the third floor of the station and avoided the elevator. A new habit of incorporating more exercise into his daily routine. A quick knock on the open door and Chief Birch looked up from the computer monitor, then came around his desk. He still wore his dress uniform and hung the jacket on a coatrack inside the door.

"I have temporarily assigned Lieutenant Piekenbrock as acting captain to fill the vacancy." He leaned over and tapped a stack of paperwork sitting on his desk. "I've looked through the pers files, and I think you are the most qualified for the lieutenant rank. We can have a trial position for a few months before making it permanent. What do you think about that?"

Noah's mouth opened slightly, and he wasn't sure what to say. "Umm …"

The rank of lieutenant was more of an administrative position. However, Noah liked being out on the streets and not behind a desk. He was about to explain his choices when the chief chuckled.

"Relax. You look like someone hit you over the head with a club. Take out your badge."

The chief opened the top drawer of his desk and pulled out a small cardboard box. Noah opened his wallet and flipped to his silver APPD badge.

"I literally have a foot-tall stack of paperwork from all levels of government for your actions last fall, congratulating you. We're going to do this later formally, but I thought it is fitting." Birch opened the small box and lifted out a gold badge.

Noah's heart sank. "I'm not sure—"

"I told you to relax. We know you wouldn't be happy as an LT. However, I have received permission for a new rank. Well, new to our department anyways. Well-earned Detective Hunter."

Arrow Point Police Department, while growing rapidly as the town expanded, never had a detective rank. The duties of a detective were always delegated to the sergeants by default.

"I don't know what to say, Chief. Shouldn't there be some testing or examination for the position?"

Chief Birch nodded. "There may be one day, but I already wrote you down as having completed the on-the-job training required. The rank and qualifications were approved by the mayor's committee and the governor's office last month."

Noah slid the silver badge out of his wallet and left it on the desk. He ran a thumb over the new tin and bounced it a few times in his palm.

Birch smiled. "You will find it gets heavier with time. Congratulations, Hunter."

Noah tucked the wallet away and shook his hand. "Thank you, Chief."

"Not a problem. Keep me informed on this current case. The chair for the police services board has already called me wanting to know more. He was pretty close to Richardson, and he seems to have his ear to the ground."

"Yes, sir."

As he was about to turn, the chief stopped him.

"Detective, before you head back to work, sign out a shoulder holster, then go home and change. I'm a firm believer in a nice suit and tie."

Noah felt like the jaws of a trap had closed on him. They were doing their best to get him ready for the lieutenant position. While he knew administration work was critical for those in the field, it was not something he would feel comfortable with.

He sighed. "I'll keep you informed, Chief. Thank you."

Last year Noah had split his time living in an apartment and a small cabin he inherited, an hour's drive north-east of Arrow Point. His previous home was gone. His ex-fiancée had used explosives to demolish the house in an attempt to fake her death from those hunting her, but most importantly, to protect Noah.

It didn't take long for Noah to realize that apartment living was not for him, and he bought a home on the eastern edge of town. The property used to be a dairy farm with the pastures sold off many years ago to a developer and turned into streets and homes. Ten acres remained on the original land with a one-hundred and fifty-year-old farmhouse and barn. Noah felt like he was out in the country with no houses in the immediate area while only fifteen minutes from work.

He turned up the driveway and passed a massive Douglas fir tree that covered most of the front lawn before parking. It was the tree and the solitude of the property that sold him on it. Noah had paid quite a bit to ensure his privacy, but he had the money.

A considerable amount was spent on upgrading the old house's interior while maintaining the original look. All new wiring and insulation were needed, as well as waterproofing and repairing the fieldstone foundation. The original oak flooring was redone, and the dining room wall was removed to give it an open concept. A few modern comforts were added as well.

He pulled out his phone and deactivated the primary alarm system. After what he had gone through last fall, one thing Noah needed was a sense of safety. Red Knight Securities had descended on the location with their carpenters and technicians and installed the latest technology. As a result, the old farmhouse was now capable of withstanding a sustained attack and contained quite a few surprises in case anyone tried to break in. As good as the upgrades for the home were, what they did to the barn was even more impressive.

Noah pressed on a wooden panel at the side door to reveal a hidden numerical keypad. There was no more need for keys, and after entering the seven-digit code, the door unlocked. Once inside, he punched a different code on the tablet mounted to the wall as the camera verified him against the facial recognition software. As great as the technology was, the steel core in the doors and bulletproof windows reassured him further.

Five minutes later, Noah looked in the bathroom mirror and checked his dark blue tie. He knew the guys were going to raze him, but the chief made it seem more than just a suggestion. After sliding his Glock into the shoulder holster, Noah then tried on his dark blue suit jacket. Turning back and forth a few times, he could see the bulge from the weapon. The new gold detective badge sat in the leather holder to the right of his belt buckle. After eighteen years of wearing a uniform, he would now be considered a *suit*. Sighing, he grabbed a protein bar and a bottle of water before activating the system once again.

As Noah was getting back in his truck, his cell phone rang.

"Noah, it's Jacob Park. I have an identification on your body. Steve Misevski." Jacob was a civilian who worked in the administration offices and coordinated with the state police and other authorities, mainly dealing with missing persons and public relations. "The coroner sent over the file and some pictures for us to send out."

"That was quick."

"He goes to the same school as my son. I've known him for years. I didn't need to look anything up."

Noah knew the body looked young, but he didn't think it was a high school kid. "Sorry to hear that. Can you send me a copy of the report? I'll go talk to his parents."

"His mother died a while ago, and he lives with his father, as far as I know. Funny thing, I've looked, and there isn't a missing persons report on him."

Something wasn't right.

"Send me the information, and I'll go talk with his father."

Chapter 5

Not wanting to waste time, Noah drove straight to the cemetery in his truck and parked off to the side, at the end of a long line of vehicles. Barricade tape had been strung up in a large perimeter around the open grave, and the forensics team was still working. To one side, the dirt-separators made it look like an archeological dig as they searched for anything left behind—someone dressed in a white protective suit sifted through several buckets of dirt.

Lieutenant Piekenbrock winked as Noah walked down the pathway. With a big smile on his face, he chuckled.

"Congratulations, Detective."

A few officers clapped and one wolf-whistled, and then the comments started.

"Do we have to call you *sir,* now?"

"Looking good in a suit. Is it date night, Hunter?"

"Do you have to go to court?"

Noah knew it was coming and wasn't too surprised. He would have done the same thing. Instead, he simply smiled and used his middle finger to rub his eye as he walked over to the LT. The artificial grass had been removed from around the grave, and the electric lift system was also gone.

Piekenbrock pointed down the hole. "With everyone here today, the only place that isn't contaminated would be down there."

From below the ground, brilliant white flashes made it a lightning storm as pictures were taken of the interior walls.

"Any new details?"

Noah filled him in on what Jacob had passed along. "I'm going to talk with the father, and I hope to establish a timeline."

Piekenbrock nodded. "Sounds good. I'll stick around here. They're almost done since there isn't too much to look over. I'll have the guys do a full sweep of the area before we turn it back over."

They chatted a few more minutes, and as Noah was about to head out, the LT stopped him. "I know things have been complicated since Bennett died. However, as acting captain, I'm responsible for approving the roster, amongst other duties. If you can't come up with a partner, I'll assign you one."

Officially, Constable Stewart Bennett was killed in a car accident after running a red light, but Noah knew different. He was in a hospital in Chicago, recovering from his wounds after hearing the news. He was not able to attend his former partner and friend's funeral. It had bothered him for months. The passage of time helped, but he never forgot.

"Yes, sir. I'll let you know by the end of the day."

With a little wave to the guys maintaining the perimeter, Noah got back into his truck. Going over the choices in his mind for a potential partner, he headed back to the station before going over to the Misevski home. He wasn't looking forward to informing him of his son's death. Mr. Misevski may not even know Steven was missing.

*****

Scott Appleton held the printed paper and reviewed the paperwork. Arrow Point Police had wanted a formal report but allowed him to drop it off. With the circus of events happening at the cemetery, Scott barely had time to write it out, let alone go downtown for hours in person.

He had locked up the cemetery at five o'clock that evening and had driven straight home. After talking with his wife, Scott confirmed he was home by quarter after the hour because Kathy had her usual Friday night roast beef dinner ready when he walked in the door. A meal he looked forward to all week.

When he was younger, Scott was in peak physical shape after eight years in the Navy. Twenty years later and mainly sitting at a desk, snacking had been his downfall. His thick short hair had prematurely thinned out, and his stomach was far over his belt as his weight nearly doubled. At fifty-one years of age, he didn't look well and easily confused someone much older.

After reading the short paragraph, Scott signed the statement and used the office photocopier. He would retain a copy for himself in case there was a problem. The cemetery offices were fairly simple. When you first walked in, the large room had a three-dimensional map of the twenty-acre property, spread out on a large central display table. When pre-arranging for a plot, people liked to see the layout, even what views were to be had. A small conference room was through a thick glass door, where Scott went over the financial obligations required.

Scott worked alone in his office, and Henry worked outside full time, keeping the lawn cut and trimmed and getting the sites ready for burial. The maintenance building was at the far end of the parking lot, along a pathway. It was kept out of sight of the public; they had enough worries when they arrived.

For the most part, running the cemetery was a two-person operation, but on occasion, Scott hired summer help with cutting the lawn and trimming around the headstones. At times Henry was backed up due to more residents moving in. Regardless of what people thought, death happened in waves.

Scott activated the security alarm and locked up. He swung by the south field and left his statement with one of the officers on his way out. He reminded them he'd be in early tomorrow to look after any footage the security cameras may have picked up.

Once inside his Toyota, the cemetery director headed home for dinner. It was a Saturday night, so his wife would be cooking a chicken casserole. Kathy was predicable with her menu choices, and the food was delicious. Henry would lock up the gates when he left. With the continued police presence, he was not worried.

*****

Fifteen minutes after Scott Appleton had set the alarm and left the property, the old air-conditioning unit rattled in its frame. With a light squeak, the window above it was raised. The heavy unit was easily lifted and lowered gently on the floor inside the director's office. The door to the office and building was wired into the alarm system, but the window had been disabled to accommodate the air conditioner unit over a decade ago.

The forty-inch wide-screen monitor for the security cameras was mounted on the north wall of the office. The display was divided into four separate windows, each showing a different view of the parking lot and the front of the building. No cameras were showing the cemetery grounds or the office interior.

A figure pulled themself inside and stood in front of the digital recording unit. He pulled out a small yellow-bodied Taser that had a charge of four million volts. Pressing the large black button caused an arc of electricity to dance between the contact points. Without hesitation, the Taser was pressed against the metal shell of the recording unit, and a gloved thumb pressed the black button.

It took almost fifteen seconds for the distinct smell of ozone to fill the small office. The display on the monitor flickered once then shut off. Beneath the Tasers, the metal darkened around the contact points as it was heated. Before the charge was depleted, a few pops could be heard inside the digital recorder, and a thin trickle of smoke rose from the rear vent. The security monitor showed a blank screen, and then the *lost signal* message appeared as the interior fan shut off.

The air-conditioner was returned to the frame a few seconds later, and the window was lowered into place. Seventy seconds had elapsed from the point of entry, with only the smell of burned electrical components to show for it.

Chapter 6

The first floor of the Arrow Point Police Station had two holding cells off the processing area. Further down the hall were the lockers and supply rooms, the armory, a staff lunchroom, and a small kitchen. Noah signed out an unmarked Ford Interceptor long-term for his use before heading upstairs.

The second floor was the heart of the station with conference and briefing rooms and a large area with over thirty desks and a few offices. The former chief wanted the officers to have privacy and had cubicle walls installed around each desk. It turned the area into a maze of mini-offices, and it resembled a vast geometric cube. By the time Chief Birch had all the walls removed and the open floor plan restored, the name had already stuck—The Cube.

Noah logged into a computer station and after a series of clicks and typing, walked over to the printer, and waited until the eighty-two pages were printed off. The half-inch file made a loud smack as he dropped it on the desk in front of Constable Angie Dickinson.

The front page caught her eye, and she looked up at Noah, confused. "What's up, Sarge?"

Angie wore the standard blue uniform with a vest and a baseball cap. Her dark brown hair was pulled through the back in a ponytail. Despite being just over six feet tall, she appeared to be much younger than twenty-six-years old. With a sprinkling of freckles across her face and dimples, folks would call Angie a kid until her forties. A problem most women wished.

Noah reached down and tapped the top cover with one finger on the APPD, Sergeant Examination Package. "Are you interested?"

Reading the page again, her eyes opened wide when it sunk in. "Just a little too soon, isn't it?"

"You've done the minimum four years at your current rank. However, if you are interested in being a partner for a detective, a sergeant's rank is preferred."

Angie grinned. "Detective? Seriously?"

Noah pulled back his suit jacket to show her the new golden badge. "Serious as a heart attack."

"Wow! Congratulations, I didn't think APPD was big enough for that rank." A big grin spread across her face.

"It was a little surprising to me as well." Noah quickly filled her in on today's events and his mandated requirement for a partner. "So, are you interested?"

Angie leaned back in the chair and thought it over. "Why me? There are more experienced officers that you could work with."

"Last fall, I found you to be resourceful and good at your job and quick thinking. Those are fairly good prerequisites in my books."

"That pretty much sums me up." Angie stood and shook his hand. "I would love to work with you, Detective Hunter."

"I'll inform the staff sergeant of the personnel changes. Then, later on, we can go over the exam requirements. It's mostly procedural law and not too bad."

"Do I have to wear a suit? Because that may be a game-changer. I don't even own one."

"That uniform is fine. Meet me downstairs in five minutes?"

"What would you like me to do about the B&E at Main Street Animal Hospital? The reports are all done, no leads."

"File the paperwork, and we can see if we can work it in, but odds are it will be turned over to someone else. A murder case takes priority."

"Roger, ready in five."

Noah gave Steve Hutchings a call to make the arrangements for Angie to be teamed up with him and off the normal roster. Staff Sergeant Hutchings was Noah's first partner when he joined APPD and helped finish his on-the-job training. They went back over eighteen years, and Noah wasn't surprised he already knew about the promotion to detective.

"You deserve it, and you have your chance now to prove they made the right decision."

"Thanks. I also want to book Dickinson's sergeant's exam for four weeks from now. That should give her enough time."

Hutchings laughed. "That's enough time for you, but I think we can move it up a few weeks for her."

"She's that good?"

"Yes. Clearly smarter than you, sir."

Noah groaned. "Don't you start."

"Is that an order?"

"I'm pretty sure that a detective doesn't outrank an old grumpy staff sergeant."

Hutchings laughed. "Good, don't forget it, rookie."

Noah hung up and went out to the back parking lot in time to meet Angie and toss her the keys to the Ford. Noah directed her to the western edge of town, past the outlet mall and The Tavern.

The parking lot was filled for those attending the wake.

"It looks like half the town showed up." Angie sighed.

"I wanted to stop by as well, but work comes first. If there is time, we could swing by later and see who's there." Noah had already said his goodbyes to the captain. It was time to take care of the living.

After a few side streets, they pulled into the visitor parking at 1333 Mary Street and stopped outside unit forty-one. The address was a townhouse complex with over sixty units. The complex could be considered a low-income area, with many families working more than one job each just to get by. However, there were many units where the landlords stopped caring. Bushes grew out of control, shingles were missing from some rooftops, and a few backyards had yet to cut the grass this year. Pride in a home had taken a wayside with a lack of effort. Noah recalled a drug bust a few units down a few years ago, and the inside had been converted into a grow-op. Unfortunately, the parents were too stoned to realize they were under arrest, and child services took the young children.

The location had been getting a reputation as the calls increased over the years.

A dark brown door opened into a small hallway with two doors facing each other on the lower level, and after walking up the four steps, there were two more units at the top. It was the same pattern throughout the complex. At the top of the stairs, Noah knocked, stepped back and waited. He was about to knock again when the door opened.

The man who opened the door looked like he hadn't slept in a month, with dark circles and bags under his eyes. His dark hair looked like it lost a battle with a pillow and needed a wash. He stood five-foot-eight and in his late forties, wearing boxers and a white undershirt. The blue terry-cloth robe he wore over the top wasn't tied and just hung loose.

"Mr. Misevski?" The stale smell of cigarette smoke filled the hallway and made Noah's nose itch.

He didn't answer, but he looked back and forth between the two police officers, not understanding what was happening.

"Mr. Misevski, I have some news about your son, Steven."

Those words seemed to sink in, and he cleared his throat. "I'll go get him. If he's in trouble—that's his problem."

The door closed in his face. Noah turned to Dickinson with eyebrows raised and mouthed, *what the hell?*

Chapter 7

Detective Hunter didn't have long to wait until the sound of footsteps gained in volume across the creaking floor and the paint-chipped door abruptly opened. Mr. Misevski stood just inside the door, a puzzled look on his face. "What did he do? Steven isn't home. I don't know where he is."

Noah cleared his throat before speaking. This moment was never easy, no matter how many times he had gone through it. There had been too many similar occasions over the years. He had to steel himself against the emotions and remain impartial. Distant. That was the only way to get through it.

"I regret to inform you a body has been found, and we're going to need you to identify your son."

This was the moment the police had been trained for—a sign of fear or horror after the news was imparted. Did they look guilty and ready to run? Was panic setting in, or were they prepared to flee? If so, Noah would then change up their line of questioning and push to get a reaction or force their hand.

However, Mr. Misevski shuffled from side to side as his eyes closed and a low groan was felt more than heard. When his shoulders slumped, and his knees buckled, Noah thought the man was about to collapse until his hand darted out and grasped the steel beige doorframe with a firm grip. The distraught father struggled to breathe. Such an instant response, while not impossible, would have been hard to fake.

It took Noah a split second to mentally switch gears. "Mr. Misevski, when was the last time you saw Steven?"

The distraught father ran his other hand across his face. "Call me Luka. His school left a message last week about his attendance, but I'm not sure … ten days or so."

"Why didn't you report him missing?"

He shrugged. "We don't talk much, and he's eighteen. He's allowed to do his own thing."

Dickinson gently smiled. "Do you mind if we look at his room and if he has a computer, we would like to borrow it? It may help us find out what happened."

Luka took a deep breath and rubbed his eyes. "How did he die?"

"We don't know yet. Mind if we have a look?" Angie had to repeat herself to get the message across.

Mr. Misevski stepped back and, with a nod, allowed them to enter. A small galley kitchen was to the left, and opposite the front door in the tight foyer was a door to the basement. Luka flicked a light switch. Hunter and Dickinson followed him down the stairs.

It was apparent that the basement had been turned into the domain of a teenager. An old white couch took up most of one wall with a double bed in the corner. A television sat on top of a long dresser opposite the sofa and a coffee table made of black plastic milk cartons and plywood. Piles of clothes were scattered over the floor, and there were a few posters of rock bands tacked up on the walls. An acoustic guitar sat at the bottom of the stairs, leaning in the corner. The small window over the bed had a partial view of the backyard and tall grass.

Angie produced two pairs of latex gloves from a utility pouch and handed a set to Noah.

"If you like to get changed, I can make the arrangements for you to go to the coroner's office to make the identification." At Noah's request, Luka nodded and slowly made his way upstairs to change. Once alone, they started a search. Noah worked on the pile of clothes on the couch and began a systematic examination. Always fearful of needles, he checked the pockets as his new partner started at the bed.

"Well, he's normal." She had lifted the mattress and found a few adult magazines hidden.

"I have a laptop." Hunter found it under the clothes. After ten minutes of looking around, they only found a few joints in the dresser and the computer. Nothing seemed out of place or gave them any indication of anything being wrong.

Angie opened the laptop on the makeshift coffee table. "No password required."

She went through the emails and didn't find anything besides spam. Once she opened his social media account, Angie gave out a little whistle. "Thirty-five hundred friends. How's that even possible?"

Steven had dozens of unopened messages, and found what she was looking for rather quickly. "He met up with some friends and attended a concert in Cheyenne on April twenty-nine. It was his birthday."

"Anything on what he has been doing in the last eleven days?"

"Nothing online. I can't find arrangements for the concert or anything after. Steve must have been using his phone."

"Our tech guys will have to go through the computer. We shouldn't have any issues with a warrant for the phone. Hopefully, we can trace it, or at least get the records."

Noah went over the basement one more time before they went upstairs. Luka waited for them in the kitchen, and Angie showed him the laptop. "Can we borrow this? It may help find out what happened to your son."

Mr. Misevski was still in shock and moved about in a fog, although he had taken the time to get dressed in jeans and a black T-shirt. "I didn't even know he had it … yes, keep it."

"Can you give me Steven's cell phone number as well?" Noah wrote it down and gave Luka directions to the coroner's office. "I'll call and let them know to expect you. I'd recommend someone driving you or taking a taxi. Any problems, or if you think of anything that we should know, please give me a call."

Noah handed over his business card with his cell phone number written on the back.

Once they were back in the Crown Vic, Noah's phone rang.

FSL flashed on the screen. The Forensic Sciences Laboratory handled APPD and the Wyoming State Police evidence and was located outside of Casper.

"Detective Hunter, go ahead."

"This is Dr. Leslie Singh at the lab. We've conducted preliminary testing, and you're going to want to come by soon as possible."

He heard the excitement in her voice, and he could not help but grin in response. "I can be there in just over half an hour."

"See you soon."

Noah turned to Angie. "Looks like we have a lead. Hopefully, it's good news."

Chapter 8

The forensic lab was in a large white building west of Casper, off Interstate 26. An eight-foot-tall security fence surrounded the hundred-thousand-square-foot facility with strict access control at the southern security gate. It did not take long for the Arrow Point officers to have their identification verified and allowed inside. The critical nature of the evidence within demanded the utmost precautions. Investigations would be thrown out of court for corrupted evidence, and individuals that should be incarcerated, would walk free should measures lax or issues arise.

Noah had been inside several years prior when the facility opened. There were various laboratories: fingerprints, firearms, toxicology, trace evidence, chemistry, and a biology section. Large bay doors over eighteen feet in height dominated everyone's attention on the south side as they drove through the gates. Vehicles of all makes could be processed, from the smallest car to a fire truck, and moved inside.

When an item required multiple testing, it would go through the various labs. An ax could be analyzed for blood and latent fingerprints within two separate areas while strictly maintaining the chain of custody. The ballistics wing could identify bullets and match the weapon, and moments later, epithelial tissue could be extracted down the hall. The building had the latest and greatest in technology and was considered a one-stop shop for law enforcement throughout the state.

The lobby was decorated in various tints of white, including the polished stone floor and long reception and security desk. *FSL* popped in six-foot black letters on the long wall behind the sign-in desk. Four gray plastic chairs opposite the desk were the only other dark objects. The small glass table held various magazines.

After showing their identification to the receptionist, Noah and Angie were each handed a visitor pass to clip on their front pockets. They had only sat for a few minutes when a door behind the desk swung open, and Doctor Singh arrived. She was in her mid-forties with dark-rimmed glasses, and her long black hair was back in a ponytail. Her white lab coat was not buttoned up, revealing a light gray suit and cream blouse underneath. When Noah stood to greet her, he saw that she was about five feet tall.

Her photo identification hung on a red lanyard around her neck and swung to either side with each step.

"Detective Hunter, pleased to meet you."

Noah introduced Constable Dickinson, and they all shook hands before she led them back into the building. The interior looked like a small city with various offices and testing centers within the larger building, and everything was color-coded. The toxicology wing was green, and it was next to the blue chemistry offices and laboratory. Her office was just inside the green building.

"Have a seat, please."

Two black plastic chairs were facing her desk. The large desk and a bookshelf mainly took up the office.

"I have most of the results. The coroner will submit his own report, but we focus on the science we can gather from the evidence."

With a few clicks, she brought up the complete file on the case and swung the monitor around so they could see a chemical chain that filled a page. "What was interesting is the compound that we detected within the hair and fingernail samples."

The doctor turned the second monitor to the side so they all could see the same chart. "The hair and nails act as a record, showing what was in the body and approximately when. A large dose of a synthetic opioid was in the subject's bloodstream, at a best guess I would say between eight to ten days previous."

Two charts representing various data showed a spike with a chemical analysis versus an estimated timeline.

Angie leaned forward and pointed to the bottom chart, where a second spike on the chart was color-coded differently. "What's this one, and can you tell me what type of synthetic opioid it was?"

Doctor Singh pointed to the bottom chart. "This one is common, identified as tetrahydrocannabinol. The second one is more complicated."

Noah smiled. "I believe the subject smoked a joint?"

"Yes, that is the THC compound. The marker shows up rather well in a follicle sample. The second is a synthetic opioid. It's known as etorphine, and it's considered a class-one narcotic. Its main use is for the sedation of large mammals by a veterinarian. I would estimate it is three-thousand times more powerful than morphine."

Noah whistled. "Isn't that a little overkill?"

The doctor nodded. "Yes, however, the effects are almost instantaneous. The wrong dosage will kill a human, so someone knew how much to properly mix based on age and weight to achieve the result."

"Detective Hunter?" Angie had a stunned look on her face as she processed the information and the possible relevancy. Her right leg bounced with contained excitement. "Two nights ago, the vet clinic downtown Arrow Point was broken into. I was working that case."

Noah knew actual coincidences were rare, something that had been proven several times over in his career. The B&E most likely was related. "Okay, we'll revisit your case and incorporate it with ours should it pan out. It will give us a good place to start in the morning."

"One last thing, Detective." Doctor Singh scrolled down to another chart. "This is the blood results. I believe the coroner will come up with these same findings independently, but he died from protein-energy malnutrition and dehydration. He had a lack of food and water for a week or longer."

Noah could not help but grimace and run a hand over his face at the kid's fate. That meant that not only was Steve Misevski drugged and taken, but he was held somewhere without food or water for long enough to kill him. *Poor kid.*

"Thank you, Doctor Singh. If there are any other findings, please send them to APPD for my attention right away. You can also call my cell any time of the day."

"I will, and one last thing. If someone is using etorphine to sedate people, naloxone may or may not help. There's been no testing the drug against those levels, but it may be better than nothing."

Naloxone had been issued to the state police and EMTs in an attempt to save someone from an overdose. However, it had been a slow distribution process over the last few years across the state. "APPD hasn't been issued any as of yet, but I'll see if we can get some from the Highway Patrol."

Doctor Singh swung the monitors back and smiled. "I think I can help. We have a small supply here. It won't take long to teach you both about proper dosages, when, and how to use it."

Right now, Noah would take any help he could get. Ideally, he would never need it. But better to be prepared and not use it than the reverse.

A few key cards had been laid upon the table, and they pointed to a specific direction. The familiar excitement of closing in on a case rose in his chest, and he held back a grin. *It's not over till it's over.* A saying Hutchings had drilled into him as a rookie, and he had never forgotten.

Chapter 9

At two o'clock the next morning, an early spring thunderstorm rolled through Arrow Point. Windows rattled in time to the rumble like snare drums. Lightning lit up the night sky across the horizon and briefly woke thousands across town. Noah lay in bed, eyes wide open, and listened to the rain pelting the roof. At times the old farmhouse shook with the wind gusts, and the timbers groaned in protest. He was more worried about the massive tree on the front lawn. If it blew over, it could easily take out the house. Despite the concerns, he didn't want to get rid of the old tree. It was one of the reasons he bought the property.

Sunday morning, five hours after the rains, Noah awoke. The joyful birds and blue skies gave no hint of the powerful storm. Instead, the sun was shining, and despite the interrupted sleep, Noah felt good.

After a quick shower, Noah stood in his closet and stared at the selection of suits. If he were going to wear one for work every day, he would need to buy a few more. So, wearing the same dark blue suit, he wore a white dress shirt and a dark blue tie. One thing he swapped from his utility belt was his handcuffs and a pouch that would hold a pair of latex gloves, as well as the two shots of naloxone that Doctor Singh had given him.

Noah grabbed a protein bar and a bottle of water and locked up the house. The truck windows were down, and the air had a fresh, clean smell which helped wake him up. But, contrary to the calendar, the day would prove hot and humid. Mother nature had skipped spring and moved straight into summer.

As he drove east on Main Street, Noah slowed and eventually pulled over before getting out. Two fire trucks were parked across the road blocking traffic as they battled a fire in two stores. The drug store on the corner seemed to suffer only minor damage, while its neighbor looked destroyed. The smell of burned wood filled the street and made his nose twitch as he stood to the side and watched.

The two-person crew had just finished putting the last flare out, and the fire captain told them to check the roof on the flower shop next door to verify no sparks had traveled.

As Hunter walked up to the fire truck, he waved for the captain to come over. "Hey, Frank. Everything okay?"

Noah had known Frank Tyler for over fifteen years, as they could not help but run into each other on many of the calls. A friendship of sorts has grown between the two men. The firefighter could easily pass as Noah's brother, standing an inch taller, and he had the same build. The large shoulders and chest gave him a tapered look of a quarterback.

"Lightning strike earlier on, all good now. Just the two stores were hit."

Noah had frequented the drug store that stood on the corner of Main and Maple many times. "What was the second store? Can't recall."

The business had the windows blown out, and the sign was down from the fire and effects of the water. Frank jerked a thumb over his shoulder. "That was the vet clinic. Far as we could tell, there were no animals inside. That's a good thing."

Noah got a sinking feeling in his stomach. "Frank, when the fire marshal comes to inspect, have him call me." He briefly recounted how he was going to check out the clinic today. "Right now, I'm ninety-nine percent sure this is no accident."

Frank's eyebrows rose. "That means you are pretty sure then. Any particular reason that I should know about?"

"I was going to investigate the veterinary clinic and see if there was any tie-in to a murder, but I don't need to anymore. However, I do not doubt that it *is* related, or there wouldn't have been a cover-up."

Noah surveyed the street and checked above each of the shops, then shook his head. However, he smiled when he looked across the road on the opposite corner and spotted the bank machine. "Be right back."

Noah's joy was short-lived at the ATM as his fingers ran across the plastic above the display screen. Black paint had been sprayed over the bubble camera housing. Otherwise, it would have had a panoptic of the scene. He looked down at his fingertips and saw the black paint residue. With the humidity from the rain last night, the paint had not fully set.

The fire captain had followed Noah. He raised his fingers and showed Frank. "I'm one-hundred percent that fire was deliberately set."

Jacob Park placed the thick binder on the conference room table for Detective Hunter and Constable Dickinson. The young man wore jeans and a rugby shirt. His hair was still wet from the shower.

"This is going back eight years. Anything older is digital now. All this is available on the computer system, too."

Noah had called Jacob and asked for the missing persons for the state going back ten years. "Thanks for coming in today. It's appreciated. Sometimes, it's better for a paper copy."

Angie started flipping through the thick book. Each page was a person that was reported missing within the state. Some pages had follow-up reports tucked in behind the clear plastic sleeves, but most were just single pages.

"No problem. Drop it off on my desk when you're done."

With a little wave to Angie, Jacob headed out. She never noticed. Noah pulled the conference phone over, looked at the list beside it, punched in the number, and waited.

"Natrona County sheriff's office, how may I direct your call?"

"Detective Hunter from Arrow Point, I'm looking to talk to someone about old B&E cases."

"One moment, please, while I redirect your call."

A few seconds later, it was picked up. "Sergeant Robinson, how can I help you?"

"Detective Hunter from APPD, just a few questions that hopefully you can answer."

"I will if I can, go ahead." Robinson had a deep voice that reminded Noah of crunching gravel.

"Do you have any break-ins for any veterinary clinics? Right now, I'm going back ten years."

Noah heard him pounding away at a keyboard. "I had one last year on the second of December and another, the same location three years ago in Casper. In both cases, nothing appeared to be missing. Files are still open."

No suspects have been apprehended.

Writing down the information, Noah slid the notepad over to Angie. "Okay, thanks. Possible tie-in to a B&E at a clinic in Arrow Point."

"Glad to help. If they are related, keep us informed. Good hunting."

"Will do."

Noah hung up, then dialed the Cheyenne Police Department and went through the same process. He wrote down five separate dates for three clinics within the larger city going back four years with one difference.

Sitting back from the conference table, Noah looked at Angie and tapped his pen on the table. "Nervous yet?"

Dickinson had a stack of sheets removed from the binder corresponding to the dates Noah had written down. In almost every break-in case at various veterinary clinics, a corresponding person was reported missing within that time frame. "My heart is tripping hard right now at the possibilities."

Noah nodded, almost in shock at the implications. "Same here. Start the documentation process, and I'll get the LT. He'll want to join us when we leave."

She took a deep breath and quickly turned to write up the findings while Noah went across the cube and knocked on the office door. The implications were going to be staggering if he was correct.

Unfortunately, his gut instinct kicked in—informing him to get ready. This was going to be the tip of the iceberg.

Chapter 10

Scott Appleton climbed the front steps to the cemetery offices as three police officers waited. Noah stood next to the locked door and nodded when he came closer. The cemetery director wore gray track pants and a Rolling Stones concert T-shirt that had seen better days.

Lieutenant Piekenbrock stood to the side along with Constable Dickinson. The LT wore a suit that was fairly similar to Noah's but with a bright yellow tie, while Angie wore her patrol class B uniform and vest.

"Thanks for coming, Scott." Noah shook his hand. "This is fairly important, or we wouldn't have called."

The larger man seemed slightly out of breath after the six steps. "Not a problem. Give me a second."

Before allowing them to enter, he unlocked the door and punched in the security code on the panel inside the foyer. Noah absently noted the code. He seemed secure enough with the three police officers that Scott didn't bother to cover it up. *33878*

He turned on the lights and led them into his office. "Sorry, it's rather small." The LT and Dickinson waited in the doorway while the director booted up his computer. When he looked on the side at the monitors, he swore under his breath.

Scott hit the reset button on the digital recorder. Nothing happened. He toggled the switch on the power bar and flicked it back on.

"Jesus, this was only a year old. It looks like the storm last night fried it."

Noah grew concerned, and the furrow on his brow deepened. Alarm bells were going off in his head. "Was the surge protector tripped?"

The director paused, then shook his head. "No, I just hit it now."

Noah looked at the unit. Two white marks stood out on top of the recorder. He rubbed his finger across them and felt a subtle difference in the metal. At the same time, the computer finished the start sequence, and it beeped once.

"If it were the storm, the computer would have been fried as well." Angie tried leaning into the small office for a better look.

Scott glanced up from the screen and nodded. "Computer's fine."

"Okay, just go back six years for now. Then, if we need to, we can get the records later."

He printed off the list and handed it over. "Is this related to what happened yesterday?"

The lieutenant cleared his throat. "Right now, we're unsure. However, we'll find out shortly once Henry gets here."

"Henry?" Scott looked confused. "What does he have to do with all this? Is he a suspect? Because I can tell you right now, you're wasting your time."

Piekenbrock pulled out his phone when it chimed, and he opened the email. He showed the director the screen and document.

"We now have the authorization to excavate from the county coroner. Technically we are not exhuming a body since the caskets will remain closed. However, APPD wanted to make sure that any legal issues were covered."

"Do you think …?" Scott Appleton looked like someone had scared him senseless. His eyes opened wide in horror, and his face turned pale.

"Hopefully, we're wrong, but we have to find out." Noah put a hand on his shoulder, offering some comfort.

Soon as Henry laid down the last sheet of plywood, he jumped into the cab of the small backhoe loader and drove forward along the pathway he created. The yellow paint on the equipment had long since faded, and the scratches and dents showed its age. But, most importantly, it still ran smoothly, and the four tires appeared to be new.

Noah and the others stood back and watched Henry work. He kindly turned down their offers to help, knowing it would slow him down.

Once the backhoe was in position, he lowered the stabilizing legs onto the plywood and jumped out with a spade shovel. It didn't take long for the sod to be removed and placed to the side, and a large tarp was stretched out.

Twenty minutes later, the plastic was covered in a large mound of fresh soil, and when a slight scraping noise was felt more than heard, Henry shut it down.

He jumped into the hole and finished the area by hand. When the shovel hit wood, the dull thud made everyone jump in anticipation. Unable to remain on the sidelines much longer, Noah stepped forward to watch Henry work up close. After six months in the ground, the once highly polished exterior showed definite wear on the casket. Cracks had formed on the lid, and the metal-work was coated in damp soil.

"Water will have gotten inside. The smell won't be bad once we start moving more soil, and it's up top. The decomp has long since been over. Pass down the straps, please?"

Noah lowered the thick blue nylon that was piled at the head of the grave. "Here you go."

Kneeling on the coffin, the caretaker slipped the straps under the carrying handles and linked the ends together. Noah held his hand out to help, but Henry smiled and shook his head. "No sense in getting you dirty. I'm good, thanks."

He tossed the shovel up onto the grass, then jumped and lay his hands flat on the ground, pushing himself off the sidewall with his boots. Seconds later, he climbed in the cab once again and lowered the bucket over the center of the open grave.

Once the nylon straps were set, Henry lifted the boom. At one point, Noah thought the backhoe was going to tip over until a squelching noise set it free. Then, the casket was lifted from its earthen embrace and swung back and forth like a pendulum.

Henry moved the casket off to the side and lowered it gently on an empty sheet of plywood before shutting off the backhoe.

Noah leaned down and looked at the bottom of the grave. The sun was high in the sky, and the bright light shone once again, to where it never was supposed to—six feet underground.

Much of the earth had fallen inward along the edges, and a large flat area could be seen where the casket once rested.

In the middle of the flat area, the earth had caved in again, outlining a five-foot oval. A blue winter jacket rested below the coffin impression, covered in dark soil and groundwater. It stood out, easily spotted.

At the same time, a fetid smell came out of the hole once the breeze shifted. Noah turned away as the implications rose. He met the eyes of the LT and nodded.

"It's as bad as I thought it would be."

Chapter 11

"Ian Lawrence, age twenty-two from Casper, Wyoming. A young army reservist. Reported missing November fifteenth last year. No leads."

Noah had three different pages spread out on the hood of the police chief's cruiser while they held them down against the breeze.

"How sure are you of the rest of this information?" Birch looked like he was going to be ill once the news had sunk in. The situation had everyone on edge. Especially when they only had questions and no answers—yet.

Noah tapped the handwritten notes with the veterinarian clinic break-ins across the state and showed Chief Birch the missing persons report for the same timeline. "They match up, give or take, a week to either side."

"Do you think that's Ian down there?" Jason Birch straightened and ran his fingers through his short hair. The chief was used to being called at all hours of the day and going into work when he was off. He arrived at the cemetery shortly after dropping by the station dressed in a golf shirt and shorts.

After six months of being underground, there was no way they could confirm by a visual. "I can't officially say for certain. However, I believe that it is. Sandra Wilson was buried on November twenty-second."

The chief picked up the paper with Kyle's picture on it and nodded. "I think it's more than likely. Shut down the cemetery." Then, after a look around at the acres of tombstones, he sighed. "We're going to need help on this."

Noah followed the chief's gaze over the monuments that blanketed the fields. He noted all the possible access points, and he mentally tried to figure out how to restrict access. Short of building a fence around twenty acres, he couldn't do it. He would have to close the front gate and turn people away that came to visit the graves of their loved ones. Hopefully, they'd understand. Patrols around the perimeter would be a logistical nightmare.

"Chief, who are you going to bring in? The feds?"

At this, Birch shook his head. "I'm *still* doing paperwork from last fall because of them. I'll call the sheriff's department."

By eight o'clock on Sunday evening, Noah had set up a command center in the parking lot of Arrow Point Cemetery. The police force had a long mobile travel trailer used for public relations events that he commandeered for the job. The twenty-eight-foot trailer interior didn't resemble a camper anymore, except for the kitchen counter and upper cupboards. The dinette and couch were removed, and a series of desks filled the space. The master bedroom was converted into a meeting room with a table in the middle and chairs on either side.

The sheriff's department and the APPD were working together in the small space, and an additional table was set up outside. The parking lot of the cemetery looked like a law-enforcement convention with over a dozen cars blocking access. A patrol was set up for both forces to walk the perimeter of the grounds.

The cemetery was twenty acres of pathways and gravestones, with large fields everywhere. Vehicles could drive to most of the property. However, the outside fence had too many potential access points. Surrounding the cemetery were homes on the north side with backyards along the shared border. On the east and west sides were a stretch of woods for hundreds of yards.

"Detective Hunter, how are you doing?"

Noah turned from the large whiteboard to see Lieutenant Piekenbrock approach. "Good, sir. The second dig produced another body. However, the third dig was empty. Henry just called as he finished the fourth dig. Forensics are heading over there now. It looks like there's something."

They both turned to the whiteboard to look at the notes and chart Noah had drawn. Piekenbrock followed the columns. "The fourth dig would be just over twenty-five-months old?"

"Correct. Carol Stringer is our best guess. Unfortunately, she was missing from Cheyenne two weeks before the burial."

The LT shook his head at the task. "There wouldn't be too much left of the body after two years."

"It takes eight to ten years for the skeletal remains to be consumed. So, we're going back thirty-eight months. Should this method prove viable, we'll go back further."

Noah picked up a pile of paperwork off the desk and handed it over to the LT. "With cross-referencing, I'm estimating between twelve to fourteen bodies have been hidden. It may be a little lower."

"Has anything besides the bodies been discovered?"

Noah shook his head. "So far, nothing. We're hoping the locations for the older bodies reveal something. When they first started killing, their technique may have been sloppy, and they could have messed up. We just don't know."

Piekenbrock flipped through the paperwork before handing it back. "You've done some good work so far, Detective. Hopefully, mistakes were made that will point us in a certain direction."

Constable Dickinson entered the trailer. She escorted a middle-aged man wearing dirt-covered blue overalls with FSL embroidered in white on the breast pocket. He looked shrunken and in his late sixties. The round glasses perched at the end of his nose, and his slightly curly white hair stuck straight out randomly. He held a camera connected to a large tablet in both hands.

Noah thought he resembled Einstein. "Doctor Galley, nice to meet you."

"Detective Hunter, you're going to want to see what we have just uncovered." Angie looked excited.

At this, the officers from the Sheriff's Department stopped talking and listened in.

The doctor arranged the tablet on the end of the desk so everyone could see. "Site four was slightly different than sites one and two. Nothing in number three." The camera and the tablet display synced, and the still pictures of the latest dig were visible. "These were taken less than ten minutes ago."

Using the camera controls, the doctor flipped through the pictures. The first set of images documented the area and showed lights on stands, illuminating the grave's inside. A series of letters and numbers were written on a placard next to the headstone.

The next series of pictures showed Doctor Galley removing dirt and placing it into a bucket to be raised.

"Here it is."

Once the bottom was cleared, the skeletal remains were half exposed—enough for the pictures to distinguish details. "The body was placed in the ground face down, with the arms secured behind the back."

The skin and muscles had long since decomposed, leaving only the leather-like tendons to connect the skeleton. Fragments of clothing were visible around the pelvis and the shoulder blades. The next picture was a close-up of the wrists.

Everyone in the trailer held their breath. Curses were mumbled quietly once the reality of what they were seeing sunk in.

Angie and Doctor Galley stood silently while everyone else processed the information. Dickinson had already gone through the same wave of logic and emotions.

Noah reached behind his back and pulled out his cuffs to have a good look at them. The Smith and Wesson black carbon-steel handcuffs had a double locking system to prevent anyone from squeezing them tighter. The model he held was specially designed and had the designation of *police issue only*.

They were an exact match to the set on the corpse.

Chapter 12

When Noah's cuffs dropped on the desk, the officers were jarred from their thoughts. He looked around the small trailer and did a headcount.

Seven people.

Three officers from APPD, the technician, and three men from the sheriff's office looked stunned as the realization sank in.

"Let me make this clear. The first person who talks about this to anyone outside this room will be in jail so fast that their head will spin. I'll start with obstruction and anything else that will stick. Regardless, your careers will be over."

Noah reached over and turned off the tablet. "You will not talk to your superior officer about this or even your spouse. If this information hits the press, your world is going to end. Understood?"

Staring each officer in the eye, Noah watched them all nod, including Lieutenant Piekenbrock. Then, he turned to Doctor Galley.

"I need you to ensure that this information will only be available to me. Can you do that?"

The small man nodded as he understood the implications. "I better get back out there then before my assistant starts removal proceedings."

Noah took a deep breath and then forced it to come out slowly, calming him. Surprises like this one made him feel older. "If everyone can step outside for a few moments, I need the room cleared." Noah gestured for Dickinson to stay with Piekenbrock. Despite him being lead on the case, he did not presume he could order the lieutenant around.

Once they left, Noah sat down at the desk, and stared at nothing for a moment. "It may not mean anything. Those types of handcuffs could probably be bought off eBay."

Zane sat down across the table on a fold-out metal chair and seemed lost in thought. Thirty seconds passed until he spoke. "Do you recall any instances of anyone not able to account for their cuffs? We have all lost them or exchanged them over the years. After twenty-four years, I must have gone through a few dozen."

Noah shrugged. "I know at times we exchange them during a prisoner transfer. Sometimes they get lost, especially when we are in pursuit on foot. I've lost a few pairs that way."

"The serial number can be tracked. However, there's no central registry for them. Once we get the number, we may find out they were issued to APPD or another force." The LT drummed his fingers on the desktop while he tried to think this through. "You're on the right path. Keep this information close and follow the leads."

Noah pointed over his shoulder at the whiteboard, then shrugged. "I think we have more people to dig up, and hopefully, there will be more evidence. But I can't see this getting any easier."

Early the next morning, Noah adjusted his tie and took a sip of water before he began with the briefing in the APPD conference room. Chief Birch sat at the table with the county sheriff and his deputy while he stood at the head of the table. His paperwork was spread out in a fan before him. Lieutenant Piekenbrock stood at the back of the conference room, ensuring no others could enter.

Looking down at his notes, Hunter began. "Since yesterday morning, thirteen bodies have been recovered. We have cross-referenced the break-ins from the vet clinics across the state with missing persons." Noah held up the two pages from the cemetery director. "I focused on the burials within a week to two weeks following the missing persons report."

Noah put the pages down, picked up a large piece of paper and unfolded it. It was a two-by-three-foot map of the cemetery that he had grabbed from the director's office wall. An X had been drawn at the location where a body had been found. "In thirty-two hours, eighteen graves have been dug up, and thirteen bodies have been located."

Even though they had been briefed on the actual numbers, the three men shifted uncomfortably in their chairs.

"I believe we're done with searching unless we get new information."

Noah folded the map away. "Now for the bad news."

At this, Police Chief Birch sat up straighter. "Finding the thirteen bodies was the good news? Oh shit …"

Detective Hunter picked up more sheets of paper and handed them out. "At the site of the fourth dig, these were found handcuffed on the corpse. I've looked up the serial number."

Tom Gardiner was an older man in his sixties wearing his tan patrol uniform and the gold star of the county sheriff. Patience was not a virtue he had, nor desired. His face was flushed, and he could not wait any longer. "Spill it! What did you find out?"

"The Smith and Wesson cuffs are serialized, and the lot batches were shipped to Natrona County Sheriff's Office and Arrow Point Police Department. We're the only police forces in the state that are using the black carbon cuffs. Unfortunately, the serial number on the cuffs isn't listed in either of our systems."

The sheriff collapsed in the chair as if the wind was suddenly gone from his sails.

Noah held up his copy and showed them the serial number. "This sequence was from the first run when they were issued five years ago. I've checked our supply and records. We're down thirty-two cuffs over five years. Each loss has been properly accounted for on paper. I'll now be investigating each of those reports."

Lieutenant Piekenbrock stepped forward. "Sheriff Gardiner, I'm guessing you also are probably down a few sets of cuffs over the years."

The deputy sheriff nodded while he continued to stare at the picture. "I'll conduct the investigation from our side of things."

Noah cleared his throat before continuing. "Right now, there are only a handful of people that know this information. Ten people, to be exact. This may be our only edge for a break. Now, this leads me to some more bad news."

Hunter took another sip of water. "The veterinary clinic in Arrow Point was broken into a few days ago. When I discovered a tie-in to the case, the building was burned down during the thunderstorm on Saturday night. The fire marshal blamed the faulty wiring, but I have evidence to suggest otherwise."

Noah pulled out another piece of paper with a picture of a long black metal box and held it up. "It's the digital recorder from the cemetery. The director believed that it was damaged in the same storm on Saturday, but I noticed something."

Noah pulled out a hand-held Taser from his jacket. It wasn't the model that either of the police forces used, but it was commonly found. Noah pressed the button, and the electricity arced from the two contact points. He held the Taser up to the picture, aligning the contacts with the light spots on the black box. "The digital recorder was intentionally sabotaged. I've tested this same unit on a similar piece of metal housing and recreated the effect." Noah tucked the Taser back into his jacket. "Someone is covering their tracks because they know they've made mistakes." He stared at his fellow officers. "I'm going to find them."

Chapter 13

It was close to midnight when Noah pulled into his driveway. Throughout the fifteen-minute drive, he had trouble keeping his eyes open and yawned every few minutes. After the meeting, he filled out dozens of reports and other paperwork, including media releases. It was only a matter of time before the press found out about the bodies. Lieutenant Piekenbrock and the chief were holding press briefings and were fielding phone calls from every major news outlet in the country. The smaller police force didn't have a public relations branch, so they were kept busy.

They had also garnered the attention of the feds. However, the chief assured them that the investigation was well underway with solid leads. If they needed help, they would call. Although, they could still intercede and take the APPD out of the loop, asking for all information to be turned over. It may still come to that, but Noah hoped the case would be over before that happened. The evidence will point him in the direction required—at least it better.

Noah's main concern were the handcuffs. Despite the limited number of people knowing about them, it was too many.

He stifled another yawn, and was about to get out of his truck when he saw the small orange light flickering like a turn signal above the side door of his home. When Red Knight Securities wired the house, they installed a visual alarm. He pulled out his phone and saw that he'd forgotten he'd turned off the volume for the last briefing and failed to hear the notification.

Thirty-five minutes ago, someone had physically attempted to get into his home.

Keeping the truck in gear, he drove past the house, followed the trail through the backyard, and headed straight to the barn. With the application, he opened the large barn door, and by the time he drove inside, it was already closing behind him. The heavy-duty hydraulics locked the door into place while the stainless-steel pins went deep into the wooden timber frame.

Last fall Noah had received a great deal of money into a few secret bank accounts that his former fiancée had appropriated from her uncle. The Luciano Family had their hand in various forms of organized crime in the Chicago area, and they were branching out across the country. Feeling guilty, Noah had been quietly donating funds anonymously to various organizations throughout the town. The monthly interest from his account alone had paid for the new renovations at the men's shelter and hired new staff members. Despite sharing some of the wealth, a lot was remaining—a ridiculous amount. Noah had spent quite a bit on installing the state-of-the-art security system for his new property.

The barn had been remodeled into a panic room of sorts, one that he could drive straight into. From the outside, the barn had not changed in the last sixty years. But the interior had a small house inside made of cinderblocks and reinforced with cement and rebar. After getting out of the truck, Noah moved inside the shelter and turned on the interior lights.

The first room had a single bed against the wall with a chair and coffee table beside it. A small room next to it had a chemical toilet if needed, and the third room had a large desk against one wall, opposite floor-to-ceiling shelves. It was stocked with water jugs, canned food, and items with a very long shelf life. The lower ledge was filled with various types of ammunition. The rack on the wall beside it had a 12-gauge shotgun and an AR-15 semi-automatic rifle. In addition, a loaded Glock 17 was in each room, including the bathroom.

If Noah locked the door to the bunker, the barn could burn down around him, and he would be perfectly fine. Ventilation was hidden through underground shafts that came up on the far side of the field. He had turned down the plans for an escape tunnel despite how cool it would be.

For the moment, he left it unlocked.

He sat at the desk, turned on the monitor, and punched in the sixteen-digit code that appeared on his phone for authentication. A few seconds later, Noah watched the recording of a man walking across the field toward his house. Unfortunately, despite having the latest technology installed, he couldn't make out many details.

The figure wore a dark coat and pants, and a black balaclava was pulled down over his face. The camera on the barn tracked the man as he slowly walked across the lawn and approached the house. There was a light on at the side, but it wasn't strong enough to give his position away.

Noah switched the camera feed and watched as the prowler tried the side door, then moved around the exterior and checked the windows before coming back to the side. When the man stood next to the door, Noah had a better idea of his height, which was approximately six feet tall.

After a flash of light from his watch, the intruder opened the screen door, then leaned forward for a brief moment. Noah could not make out what he was doing. Thirty seconds later, he was gone across the field and out of range of the cameras.

Noah had wished he'd tried the front door. If so, he'd be having a nice conversation with the intruder. Red Knight Security had installed a surprise. When someone looked through the window on the front door, it appeared to open into a foyer with a glass wall and door on the far side. However, it was a Mantrap Security room. When someone enters the front door, the heavy hinges close the door behind the intruder, and when they try to proceed farther into the home, they can't open the interior door. It looked like an old glass french door, but it was an inch and three-quarter thick ballistic Plexiglas, inserted into a steel frame. With the front door locked behind them and unable to proceed forward, they would be locked in a six- by five-foot room until released.

More curious than concerned, Noah got into his truck and opened the barn doors, then headed back to the house. He smoothly drew his Glock from the shoulder holster and had a quick look around before he walked over to the side door. There was a twelve-inch strip of masking tape across the window.

After he opened the screen door, Noah grabbed the end of the tape and pulled it off. Stuck to the inside was a single black-carbon handcuff key.

Noah stood there looking around at the shadows before he holstered the pistol. He wasn't sure if the key was a clue or a warning. Until he found the answer, he would assume it was both.

Chapter 14

First thing Monday morning, Noah was at the station when the sun came up and had just left the locker rooms when Angie arrived. She handed him a cup of coffee. "Hopefully, you take it black?"

"Perfect. Thanks." He already had three cups but would take another. After reviewing the security footage for hours, he found himself unable to sleep beyond a few catnaps.

Dickinson followed Noah to the administration offices on the third floor. There wasn't anyone working this early, and the sensor lights turned on when they entered. The station employed civilian staff for many administration aspects: payroll, human resources, and so on, and except for dispatch, they mostly kept the nine-to-five schedules.

Noah's security passkey granted him access, and he found the files he looked at the day before in the second cabinet.

"I only want to go back five years and compile a list of names, along with the incidents. There are only thirty-two, so this shouldn't take too long."

Angie nodded. "Then interviews?"

"Hopefully, everything checks out. The last thing I want to do is investigate one of our own."

There were three desks along the north wall, and on the opposite side was a fourteen-foot wall of filing cabinets. Along the east wall sat a floor-to-ceiling filing system of shelves that moved side to side on rollers. The movable shelves were full of folders, books, and stationery. In the middle of the floor was a small yellow table with four chairs.

Dropping the two folders of paperwork on the table, Noah and Angie sat down and started going through the old files. Lost or damaged equipment happened fairly frequently, especially as the items aged or were worn down from excessive use.

The N1142-1A forms were completed before anything was replaced, no matter how minor. At times Noah thought real police work was nothing more than filling out forms and reports. Such work took up a large percentage of time per shift. The newer cruisers even had a printer so more work could be completed out on the road.

Prisoner transfers were the reasoning behind the lost cuffs for the majority. There were not lost as much as they were exchanged. Regardless, the form was still filled out—with the new serial number. Noah placed all that paperwork off to the side. He had briefly gone through the stack the day before, and the serial number did not appear.

The second most popular reasoning behind the reports filed was from rookie police officers trying to apprehend a suspect. The common mistake of failing to keep the flap secured on the handcuff holder caused the cuffs to fall out when they were running.

Noah had learned that lesson the hard way a few times.

A few names came up more than once, and Angie wrote them down in one column with checkmarks. "It feels like half the force has lost a set of cuffs over the last five years."

Noah looked at the list and pulled out his pen. "I'll interview this group. You can do the others."

Angie looked at the list and nodded. "How many did you say were on the list?"

As he frowned, Noah looked at the list of names. "Thirty-two."

Dickinson counted one more time to be sure. "There are only thirty-one here."

Noah grabbed the stack of forms and went through them once again, then double-checked the names. "I swear I counted thirty-two yesterday."

Angie sat back in the chair, her mouth open. "Do you think …?"

Noah once again read the names on the list and tried to remember what was missing. He shook his head. "I'd like to say I was one-hundred percent positive, but now I doubt myself."

Hunter watched her gaze shift over his shoulder, then Angie got up from the table and walked over between two of the desks. "No one from admin has worked this weekend. Correct?"

Noah looked at his watch. "Right, they should be here in an hour."

Beside the photocopier was a shredder, and underneath hung a clear blue plastic bag. With the sensitive nature of the documents that need to be shredded, the department used a micro-cut shredder. Once per week, the shredded material was picked up by a company to be burned. Standard practice.

Inside the bag were the remnants of a single piece of paper. The particles had flecks of blue and black within, but mainly white.

"Don't touch anything."

Noah crouched to look at the bag. It *could* have been the missing N1142-1A form.

"Go grab a fingerprint dusting kit. Don't talk to anyone. Come right back up here. Use this to open the storeroom, not your pass."

Noah pulled his security card out and handed it over to Angie. She left while he continued to study the control panel of the shredder: the main power button, a reverse option, and a selector switch for automatic or manual. The staff would have cleaned the offices on Friday night. However, Noah couldn't tell when that one piece of paper was shredded. He wasn't taking any chances.

Angie was back carrying the small black case in less than ninety seconds, winded from taking the stairs three at a time.

"Thanks. I need you to stand outside the tech room, and no matter what, don't let anyone enter. I don't care if the chief wants in. No one."

With a single nod, she darted out the door and moved down the hall. The tech support room, domain of Bruce Taylor, was on the third floor, past dispatch. If someone shredded a document, there was a chance they used their own card to enter the offices. The computer would have a record of any card used, as well as a time-stamp.

Kneeling beside the shredder, Noah opened the case and slipped on a pair of blue latex gloves. There were several small canisters inside, along with a small stack of latent print cards and brushes. If a print were found, it would be lifted using clear tape and preserved onto the cards as evidence.

He grabbed a brown camel-hair brush, then opened the black container for the powder. There were two different colored powders (ivory and black) for other surfaces and to obtain contrast.

He started a gentle rolling back and forth movement with the handle using two fingers. The spin caused the bristles to flare outward. Then, tilting the brush, he let the sides of the bristles barely touch the powder. It was better to use just a little powder to start. He could always add more later, but he could ruin the prints if he used too much on the first attempt.

Using the lid from the tin can, he made sure the excess powder was off before dusting the power button on top of the shredder. With the side of the bristles, he started the gentle back and forth movement sweeping across the area. It took several passes before Noah could see the powder adhering to the surface.

Just above the power button, a fingerprint started to emerge, but it wasn't complete. The pattern looked like someone had wiped down the top of the shredder. They had missed just a little part. Maybe three-peaked swirls?

He grabbed a print card, peeled back the film and lowered it onto the surface. Once he lifted the tape and lowered it flat against the white card, he sat back and examined it. There wasn't enough to run a check. There wasn't enough to even call it a partial.

Noah smiled as an idea formed.

Chapter 15

The APPD watch commander started off each shift with a daily brief and handed out the assignments. Noah had much the same briefings when he was in the army for their daily turnout. However, they called it first parade. The Arrow Point Police Department preferred *roll call,* and everyone was ready at the time of the shift with a pen in their hand and notebook open.

Call signs and areas of responsibilities were allotted, and special assignments handed out. Depending on the watch commander or duty sergeant, uniform inspections were conducted or a five-minute brief on new procedures. Standing at the back, Noah waited until Sergeant Bydal finished, and then he walked up through the briefing room to stand at the front next to the podium.

The room had a standard whiteboard on the front and eight rows of tables and chairs. It resembled a classroom, including an American flag in the corner.

"I'm here to update you on the findings at Arrow Point Cemetery. We have located thirteen bodies that were buried underneath the caskets. Each killing was associated with a break-in at a veterinarian clinic within the state. Right now, we have one solid lead that was recovered from the damaged video surveillance, and a partial print recovered."

At hearing this, everyone shifted, excited at the good news.

"Stay aware while you're out there, and if anyone asks any questions, refer them back to the station for a statement."

Noah stepped off to the side while the sergeant finished up the briefing. Afterward, the officers were dismissed to go to the armory and equipment room to get the keys for the cruisers and start their shift.

As Sergeant Bydal picked up his clipboard, Noah stopped him. "Stan, I need to have a quick word with you."

Stan Bydal had been on APPD for twenty-two years and had worked with Noah hundreds of times throughout their career. Stan was a large man standing over six feet in height, and his arms were the size of most men's thighs. His bald head always seemed to have a furrowed brow that made him seem perpetually angry or displeased.

Sergeant Bydal followed Noah up to the second floor, and they went into the conference room, just off the cube. "What's up? Something to do with the case?"

"I'm going over the lost inventory reports. I just needed to ask you a few questions about your handcuffs."

Bydal raised his eyebrows in surprise. "You're working our first serial killer case, and you want to talk with me about handcuffs? Spill it."

Noah sighed. This wasn't going to be easy. "The records show you've lost three pairs of cuffs over the last five years."

Stan leaned back in his chair and drummed his fingers on the conference table. His eyes narrowed as he stared at Noah. "I'm not too comfortable with where this is heading. How's this related to the cemetery killer?"

Stan looked like he was about to walk out. If Noah couldn't get a proper answer, maybe he'd get a reaction. Noah pulled out the picture of the cuffs recovered from the fourth body.

He unfolded the paper and slid it across the table, studying Bydal intently. "These were found with one of the bodies."

"Jesus Christ …" Sergeant Bydal looked down at the picture then back up at Noah. "Issued?"

Noah nodded. "I think so. We can't tell."

Stan's face reddened, and he leaned forward, staring Noah straight in the eyes. "All my cuffs were accounted for, and paperwork properly filed. Is *that* clear enough?"

After a moment, Noah nodded. "Yes. You know why I have to ask these questions, even if you don't like it."

Sergeant Bydal stood and slid the picture back across the table. "If you're following that lead, good luck. There must be hundreds of cuffs lost over the years."

"According to the records, there are thirty-two since this model was issued." Noah watched him closely at this revelation, but he never blinked.

"Anything else you would like to ask me? I have to go out and confirm a few rookies are set up off the Interstate."

Noah could tell Stan was pissed. "Sorry, yes. No problem."

The notification on his phone chimed, and he saw a message from Constable Dickinson. *He's here.*

Bruce Taylor was the glue that held the computer systems together and running at APPD, and at twenty-six-years old, the young man had pretty much guaranteed that he would always have a job. There wasn't anyone else at the station who knew the system as well as he did.

Angie stood outside the tech office talking with Bruce when Noah arrived. The technician seemed to be enjoying the company. Despite them being the same age, she looked younger and was several inches taller. From a glance, it seemed the attention was only one way. Good luck, Bruce.

"Good morning Mr. Taylor. I need you to check on something for me."

"Anything I can do to help. If you'll allow me to enter …."

Angie stepped aside, and then followed them into the office.

A single desk with five monitors was inside the door, with four server towers against the far wall. It was also freezing inside.

"How do you work here with it that cold?" Angie tried to see her breath, but it was too warm for that. But not by much.

Bruce shrugged. "Helps with the servers, and you get used to it. Besides, I like sweaters, so it all works out."

Noah pulled out his notebook. "Bruce. I need to see the entry logs for the administration room from Saturday morning until now."

"Easy enough, just give me a second."

The technician sat down at his desk and turned on the monitors. It looked like the console from a spaceship with all five screens activated and Bruce typing away. The captain at his helm.

"Each passkey has a number associated with it in the system. Here is your access for that area." Bruce tapped the lower-left monitor. It had a list of codes with a date and timestamp. "And here are the entries for this morning."

He pulled up the list of passkeys on another screen with a list of names for each one. "You are the only one to have entered the room in the last twenty-eight hours."

Noah had gone into the offices before the meeting and again this morning. "Shit …"

"I hope that helped."

"Sorry, yes. Not exactly what I was looking for."

"No problem."

Noah gave Angie a shrug. "It's possible I'm wrong. Let's head back and look at the paperwork again. Thanks, Bruce."

As they were heading out the door, Angie turned back. "What if a keycard wasn't used? Does a physical key still work for the doors?"

Bruce nodded. "That doesn't come up on the scan log. The system isn't set up for doors opening and closing, just electronic entry. Although, if the system were forced, an alarm would sound."

Angie turned to Noah and frowned. "You may be right after all."

Chapter 16

Noah conducted seven more interviews throughout the day while the officers were on patrol, or he would stop by their home if off duty. Each session went much the same as the first, with resentment and confusion at the hidden accusations. In every instance, they wondered about the tie-in to the bodies. Noah felt the knot of tension build and a headache from lack of sleep hovered at the edge throughout the day. But he had to beat the rumor mill and conduct the interviews.

When Noah walked into the cube, Angie was already working on reports. He sat across from her. "Any luck?"

"Nothing." She sounded as weary as he felt. "Everyone was a little defensive, and it didn't go over well. Only three people were working this shift."

"This will take some time, despite wishing we could wrap this up in a day. I want to go over the employees at the clinic as well and see if we can tie them into other clinics in the state. Full background checks."

Angie went through her notes while Noah logged in and pulled up the coroner's report on the first body. Steven Misevski died from severe dehydration, and there was no food in his system. A human can go between twenty and thirty days without eating if they have access to water. Unfortunately, it seemed Steven never had that chance.

The coroner had also included a chart based upon starvation and the estimated time of death. The young eighteen-year-old may have been placed within the ground while he was in a coma. Poor kid. Not a good way to go by any means. The readings from the ground temperature acted as a refrigerator, throwing off the data they may have captured.

"I'm just going over the employees at the vet clinic. There's one you should see." Noah turned around at the excitement in her voice.

Dickinson turned the monitor, and Noah quickly read the email. Doctor Gary Nelson was the assistant vet, and he seemed to have a checkered background. Thirteen months in the state correctional facility, released three years ago.

"Aggravated battery and grand theft."

Leaning forward, Noah quickly read the file. The forty-nine-year-old had permanently injured a mechanic, placing him in the hospital, and he was charged with stealing a vehicle. He was sentenced to twenty-two months and released early on good behavior. His probation period was without incident, and he is now a free man, albeit with a permanent record.

"Any work history with the other clinics? It's fairly close."

Angie shook her head. "Not that I can tell."

Noah sat back, trying to remember the case, but he kept coming up short.

"Good job. If Nelson was released three years ago, it falls into the timeline. Do you have a current address?"

She just smiled and slid a piece of paper across the desk. Noah winced when he saw the location, an hour northeast of Arrow Point. "Okay, I'll get permission to work outside of our city and inform the county sheriff."

Wyoming states that territorial jurisdiction is paramount. Should a felony be committed within the officer's immediate jurisdiction, they have a legal right to arrest or pursue a suspect outside their city. Since they were heading out of Arrow Point, they would be operating outside their jurisdiction and allowed to question a suspect but not arrest. Any arrests made would be a citizen's arrest and only if they witnessed a felony taking place. The same powers of arrest any citizen has.

Since they would be within Natrona County, it was courtesy to inform the sheriff's department. So that was who they'd call if they needed assistance.

"Ready for a road trip?"

Angie nodded. They both logged out and headed downstairs. Noah hoped that this lead would pan out. He didn't like the direction this case was headed. Victims deprived of water and food, then possibly buried alive. Capturing the one responsible and giving the families a sense of closure was motivation enough.

The traffic on Interstate 25 north of Casper was fairly heavy for six o'clock at night, and Noah resisted the urge to turn on the flashers and pass everyone. Soon as they realized that an undercover police cruiser was behind them, almost everyone hit the brakes and slowed to well below the speed limit. The easy sixty-minute drive took over an hour and a half. Frustrating at times, but it was something he had grown used to over the years.

Following the directions from the GPS unit, they arrived at the small farming community. A large equipment vendor who sold everything from tractors to trailers, dominated the main road. Various small stores and a lumber yard were across the street next to an all-day breakfast diner. Noah had not been here in over twenty-five years, and to the best of his recall ability, it had not changed unless you counted the new tractors for sale.

After they turned left on the county road, they came to a small neighborhood. The cruiser pulled into the last driveway and parked beside an old gray Ford truck.

Noah immediately took off his seatbelt and rested a hand inside his jacket. The polymer grip of the Glock reassured him. He wasn't sure if he wanted to draw it or stay in the car.

"Jesus Christ. That dog's huge."

Lying on the front porch was a dog the size of a pony. It was dark brown except for the massive head, which was black. It appeared to be sleeping, stretched out across most of the porch. Its head almost hung off the edge over the steps, and the tail touched the door.

Angie chuckled. "I think we'll be fine."

She opened the door and stepped outside. The dog opened its eyes, and the tail started to wag. It sounded like a baseball bat hitting the wooden porch each time, stirring the dust.

By the time Noah stood beside the vehicle, Angie had sat on the porch step rubbing the dog's ears, and the tail picked up speed. It sounded like the turn signal in a car. Tap, tap, thump.

"See? He's a good boy."

Noah had never seen a dog like this up close, and he could not help wondering how much it would eat. When the dog rolled over for Angie to rub his belly, he was fairly sure that the dog weighed more than him.

The front door opened, and a man wearing jeans and a green T-shirt smiled at them. He looked to be in good shape and appeared much younger than his forty-nine years. There weren't any signs of gray in his short dark beard.

"Dreyfuss will lay there all day if you keep scratching him."

"He is *so* cute."

Noah had never seen this side of Dickinson, and he was amazed. The dog outweighed her by a hundred pounds, and she showed no fear but leaned down to give the dog kisses instead. Noah had always been nervous around dogs, and this one was big enough to eat a whole turkey for a snack.

"I was expecting someone to show up. Come on in."

Angie gave the dog another kiss before she stood. As Noah moved toward the porch, Dreyfuss stood and shook his head back and forth. Noah was unable to avoid the drool that landed on his suit pants. The top of the dog's head came to the middle of his chest.

He was pushed aside as it followed Angie into the house. Noah got a sense this would be a waste of time, but hopefully, he would learn something that may point him in the right direction.

Chapter 17

The black Chevy Tahoe pulled over on the shoulder of the Interstate and reversed into the dirt laneway. There was nothing but trees, fields, and the occasional billboard advertising for miles in either direction. The vehicle was invisible from anyone driving past unless you happened to look due west at a specific moment. With the sun going down, that wasn't too likely.

The mobile data terminal (MDT) beeped, and the information was quickly typed on the small keyboard once again. After a few minutes, the lid was slammed closed in frustration. A strong fist punched the steering wheel a few times before the Tahoe eased forward onto the Interstate.

Once the traffic cleared, the rear wheels spun on the gravel as the vehicle accelerated south. The syringe kit fell off the passenger seat and rested on the floor mat open after hitting the passenger door. Two syringes and an empty glass vial were held in place with black elastics.

*****

"Dreyfuss is an English mastiff, and if you keep that up, you're going to have to take him home with you. I think he's in love."

Angie sat on the couch, and the large dog lay on the floor at her feet. Dreyfuss could still rest his head on her lap as his ears were being rubbed.

"He's a little too big for my apartment, or I would in a heartbeat."

The older home had a veterinary clinic set up in the large main room toward the front in what used to be a dining room. Noah could see a small kitchen through an arched doorway down the hall. The sitting room was across the lobby, and the dog took up most of the floor space.

"We are here to talk about the fire at the clinic on Saturday night." Noah pulled out his notebook and pen while trying to ignore the tail wagging across his shoes.

Gary sat in a chair he brought in from the kitchen. "Donna and I left the clinic at five o'clock. We locked up as normal and set the alarm."

"Did you come straight home?"

He nodded and pointed a thumb at the dog. "Dreyfuss needed dinner and to head outside. He was alone all day."

Angie absently rubbed the dog's head and asked, "Did anything strange happen during the day?"

"Just the usual, I would say. I had two surgeries scheduled, and the rest were routine check-ups."

Noah tapped his pen on the notepad and avoided taking notes. He would fill in the details once back in the car. "Do you live alone?"

Gary shrugged. "Hard to keep a relationship going after being in jail for over a year. My girlfriend didn't stick around."

"Do you mind telling us what happened?"

"Without my truck, I can't get to work or the farms to check in on the animals. I brought it in to get fixed, and it cost a fortune. The mechanic kept adding fees to the bill, and he fixed things unrelated to the transmission. So, he held my truck until I could pay. I tried to get the police involved, but we were told to work it out ourselves." Gary sighed. "I paid my original bill, and once the shop was closed, I went and got my truck. Evan came back here, and he accused me of stealing. Things got physical."

Noah knew Evan Peddle at the garage outside Arrow Point, but he never dealt with him for repairs. He just filled up at the station occasionally. A young man, and he seemed fairly quiet.

"I lost my temper, and I paid for it over twelve months and eighteen days. However, I know Evan to be a thief and a swindler, but I should have handled things differently."

Noah knew enough not to comment on if it was fair or not. The law was the law. But it seemed the sentence was rather harsh. "What can you tell us about etorphine?"

Angie stopped scratching the dog and looked intently at the vet to gauge his reaction.

"Usually used for sedation of larger animals like horses or cattle. It is closely monitored and available for vets only. Due to its potency, it is considered a *schedule one* narcotic."

Constable Dickinson had pulled out her notebook and flipped back a few pages. "How much etorphine do you believe the clinic had?"

"In town, there isn't much need for it. So, we only kept a small amount. I would say one container of fifteen milligrams. That alone is enough to knock out a full-grown elephant."

Noah leaned forward. "How much would be required to knock out a human?"

At this, Gary's eyes opened wide, "Does this have to do with the garage? I've not been near Evan in years!"

"No, nothing to do with that. It's not related to your incident."

The vet took a deep breath and leaned back in the kitchen chair, relieved. "Okay, well, depending on the size, I would say point-seven-five milligrams for an average adult male of approximately one-hundred and seventy pounds."

"How long does it last? What's the shelf life for etorphine?"

Gary frowned as he tried to recall. "I believe if it is unopened, it can last for two years. Once the seal is broken, it wouldn't last a month."

Angie wrote everything down, but he didn't have any other questions. "Thank you for taking the time to talk with us. I'm glad Constable Dickinson has made a new friend."

He stood and reached over the dog to shake Gary's hand. Dreyfuss must have known they were leaving because he started to whine when Angie stood.

As they made their way to the front door, Dickinson paused for a moment. "Do you have any etorphine on hand here at your home office?"

Gary nodded. "Yes. I mainly work with the farms and cattle in this area, a few horses as well."

"Can you show us?"

They were led into a small office off the kitchen with a small desk against one wall and a large bookshelf behind it. There were several dozen folders on each shelf. Noah thought it resembled his doctor's office. A six-foot-tall metal cabinet was next to a small table with a coffee maker and a few water bottles on the opposite wall.

Gary pulled out a set of keys from his pocket and unlocked the tall cabinet. Inside were shelves with various medicines and medical equipment. A larger stand had suture kits, syringes, and multi-colored bandages neatly arranged next to several large bottles of pills.

Gary pulled down a small cardboard box from the top shelf. Handwritten on the front was M99 in black marker. Gary opened the lid and passed them each a vial.

Each container was half the size of his thumb, and it had a white label around the outside with the medical designation and a small dosage chart. The fluid inside was clear, resembling water.

Handing it back, Noah found it hard to believe that such a small amount of the drug was so potent. "There have been veterinary clinic break-ins across the county and this is what they have been after."

"Jesus."

Noah paused for a moment as an idea formulated. "Do you have a place you could go? Just for the night, maybe two."

Gary nodded. "I have a friend not too far away where I could stay. What's going on?"

Detective Hunter filled him in briefly, then added, "With the clinic downtown Arrow Point destroyed, it may paint a target on your back. I know that the etorphine is a limited resource now."

"It wouldn't hurt then. Let me go lock this up and make some phone calls. Do you want keys to my house?"

"No thanks, I have a place to stay nearby. We'll be back later. If there are any problems, I'll give you a call."

Chapter 18

Constable Dickinson couldn't believe Noah had a place within five minutes of Gary's. The questions started almost immediately, but he asked her to hold off. They drove south on the Interstate then headed west on a long winding dirt road before stopping at a large gate.

Noah got out of the cruiser and walked over to the long metal barrier. Without any streetlights or ambient light from the city, it was pitch black. The headlights from the cruiser were the only source of light around for miles. It was in the middle of nowhere, surrounded by nothing but forest. That is why he loved it here.

He unlocked the gate, and with a squeal, it swung open wide enough to drive through. He jumped back into the vehicle, and pulled it forward enough that the gate could close behind him.

After he locked the gate, Noah stepped to the side of a large tree and flicked a switch on a small hidden black box. There was a similar box at the same height across the driveway where a small LED green light flashed twice, and then it turned off.

"All set. As much fun as it is to sit in the cruiser for five or six hours, this will be better, and there should be something for dinner as well."

Dickinson was not sure what to make of it and kept giving Noah side looks. Once inside the gate, they drove along a winding dirt road wide enough for one vehicle at a time. Weeds and grass grew in the middle, brushing against the underside of the cruiser.

"This place is yours? When did you get it?"

They pulled into a clearing and with a large green A-frame cottage in the middle. A deck was out front, and a few cords of wood were stacked on the left-hand side, between two trees. The southern roof slope had six large solar panels mounted near the top.

"All mine. No one else knows about it, and if you can keep it that way, it would be appreciated."

Angie nodded. "Not a problem. It looks amazing."

"I got it last year, and I've made a few changes. Come on in."

As he walked across the small deck, a sensor light turned on above the door. Noah opened a stainless-steel panel to the right of the front door and punched in a security code. Before using his key to unlock the deadbolt, he turned on the lights inside.

On the left was a small set of stairs to the loft and a small living room on the right with a few chairs and a long couch facing the windows. Between the sofa and the open kitchen was a wood-burning stove with a flat top for cooking. The kitchen table could seat two.

Noah walked through to the kitchen and unlocked the rear door. "If you walk thirty feet along the path, there's an outhouse. No indoor toilets here."

Angie gazed at the small cabin and immediately fell in love with it. "I could easily live here! It's amazing."

"Having solar energy helps." Noah walked over to the fridge. The top half had a freezer. He pulled out some frozen hamburgers and buns. "I'll get the barbeque going. Make yourself at home. There's some beer in the fridge or bottled water."

"Do you have coffee?" Angie took off her vest and hung it over the back of the kitchen chair.

"Sounds good to me as well. Give me a second."

Noah stepped outside and turned on the propane tank for the barbeque. The break-ins at the clinics happened at approximately two o'clock in the morning, and he wanted to keep a set of eyes on Gary's home for the next few nights. Since they were out of Arrow Point's jurisdiction, they were limited to what they could do. Surveillance was permitted, and Noah would have to send a report to the sheriff stating actions taken. Reports kept the machine going.

When the security systems were installed at his home, Noah had a few items placed at the cabin. With the lack of cell phone reception in the area, he wasn't able to tie the system into his phone application, but with the solar power hooked up, there were some alert systems installed. A signal booster was set up, and on the rare occasion, he could get one bar of service. Being off-grid was the main goal, and not being in touch with the internet was not horrible.

If the gate were opened and the switch not flipped, the advanced warning would activate an alarm within the cabin. With over fifty acres surrounding the cottage, it wasn't possible to blanket the area with protection. The gate alarm and the system should be enough to discourage anyone and give some advanced notice. There wasn't anything in the place worth stealing, but the shed in the woods was another matter. The panel at the front door was mostly for show. Hopefully, anyone that found such measures would be discouraged.

"Do you need any help?"

Angie handed Noah a bottle of water and kept one for herself.

"Thanks, all good. I meant to ask, how are you doing with studying for the sergeant's exam?"

She had a sip and leaned back on the railing. "It's all pretty straightforward. The 'what-if' legal questions are tricky, but not too bad."

Noah chuckled. "I remember them rather well. Mary was being assaulted by two men but struggled and managed to free herself. As she ran away, Mary tripped on the sidewalk and fell. She broke her neck and died as a result. What are the two men charged with?"

"Those are the ones. So far, no problems."

"If you have any questions, let me know."

"I just need to go over the exam one more time, but I think I'm good."

Shocked, Noah asked, "You've gone through the whole test in a day and a half?"

Angie smiled. "I'm a fast reader. Plus, I pulled an all-nighter and finished it off."

Noah shook his head and grinned. He remembered those days all too well. Soon the burgers were ready, and they sat at the kitchen table while they finished dinner. The smell of perk coffee filled the cabin.

"I want to spend a couple of nights out here while we watch the house. With the clinic gone in town, this may be the next closest."

"Sounds good. Some of our next steps will depend on the identification of the other bodies. Find out what they had in common, and hopefully, we can identify a person in common."

Noah cleaned up by burning the paper plates inside the woodstove. "We have time to crash for a few hours if that's good?"

Angie looked awkward and blushed. "I—"

Noah realized what she thought he was saying, and his eyes opened wide as embarrassment washed through him and made his cheeks burn. "No! Not like that." He laughed. "Not that there isn't anything wrong with you, but—"

"Stop!" Angie laughed. "I have something to tell you, but it's just between you and me. Okay?"

Noah hoped this wasn't leading to where he thought it would. He could never be with someone he worked with, and it was too soon from the events last fall and losing his fiancée. Regardless, he braced himself. "Yes. Go ahead."

Angie took a deep breath and put her hand on top of his. "You know Sarah, who works at the Tavern?"

Confused, Noah nodded.

"Well … we've been seeing each other since their New Year's Eve party."

Relieved and surprised, Noah grinned. "Congratulations!"

"Thank you. However, if you were a woman, I'd be all over you, but I'm not ready to switch teams."

Noah felt like an ass, but he gave her a wink. "In that case, you can sleep upstairs, and I'll crash on the couch."

Chapter 19

Noah and Angie were exhausted as the sun rose across the eastern sky, and to say nothing happened was an understatement. They had watched the house but were disappointed. The brief rest at the cabin certainly helped, and it wasn't their first time on a stake-out. Now they looked forward to home and proper sleep. The sun shone in their eyes as they headed east on Interstate 26 toward Arrow Point. Depending on developments, they would ask the sheriff to watch the clinic or get a change of clothing and return the next night.

Both officers were startled when an alarm sounded. Noah pulled out his cell phone. *Alert Three* flashed on the screen, and he hit a button to stop the warning.

"Everything okay?" Angie looked concerned when Noah stepped on the accelerator. He pushed the police cruiser to its top speed. With the early hour, the road was empty, and he took advantage of it.

"Someone just broke into my house. Call the station and have them send a cruiser over."

Noah chose not to have it tied into automatically calling the police station when the security system was installed. He could change the settings any time, but he preferred to deal with anything himself. If the sensors were to go off for fire and smoke, the fire department would be notified.

He handed his phone to Angie, and Noah concentrated on the drive. He tried not to get anxious over the code. Alert three meant the man-trap for the front door was activated. Someone was locked in the false entryway.

Angie called dispatch directly and notified them they were less than five minutes out. After the request for assistance, she handed the phone back to Noah. Four minutes after the alarm sounded, they pulled off the Interstate into town. Noah slowed as they entered the neighborhood. The seatbelt was already released, and he made sure his suit jacket was open so he could easily draw from the shoulder harness.

Angie's knee bounced up and down as they drew closer in nervous energy. However, her voice was calm. "Where do you want me?"

"I'll park out front. I want you to circle the house on the west side. Ready?"

"Ready."

Noah drove up his driveway and turned the cruiser sideways in a blocking position as they both exited the vehicle. He drew his Glock and kept it aimed low as he scanned the area. Dickinson held her right hand on the holstered weapon as she sprinted along the driveway.

Noah used the large Douglas fir as cover and crossed the front lawn for the front door. At the bottom of the wooden steps, he brought the pistol up to shoulder height and paused to listen.

Nothing.

He jumped up the three steps, crossed the wooden porch and stood to the side, with his back to the wall. At first look, he didn't see anything, except that the interior light was on and the far door was closed. He stepped closer to the window and saw a figure sprawled on the floor wearing a gray overall, just inside the door—face down.

Jesus Christ.

Heart racing, Noah holstered the Glock and pulled out his cell phone. A few seconds later, the security system was deactivated, and he pulled out a set of latex gloves.

"Detective Hunter, is everything okay?"

Dickinson finished her circuit of the exterior and joined him on the porch. "Body on the floor just inside, don't touch anything."

Angie stepped aside while Noah opened the storm door and swung open the heavy wooden door. A fetid odor hit them as they leaned in to look. It was the work boots that gave away the identity. He'd seen them before, but he had to make sure.

Rolling him over, Noah saw Henry, the caretaker from the cemetery. His eyes were partially open, and he looked as if he was asleep. He placed fingers on the carotid artery, then waited a full minute before shaking his head. "Nothing."

"Does the camera work?"

Angie pointed to the security camera mounted on the underside of the porch ceiling. Noah swore under his breath as he got to his feet. The glass dome of the camera was shattered, and pieces lay on the wooden porch. The aluminum flashing behind it looked torn.

"Normally, it works."

An APPD cruiser arrived and parked at the end of the driveway. Looking down at Henry, Noah shook his head.

Sorry, this happened to you. You were a good man.

The best way to help Henry would be to catch the killer. Noah knew he wouldn't be sleeping for a while. "Let's get to work."

Two hours later, Noah walked behind his house with Lieutenant Piekenbrock and Constable Dickinson toward the barn. Noah had secured the scene, and he found out that two other security cameras had been shot out. No reports of gunfire had been called in, but Noah sent a few uniformed officers to the neighbors to knock on doors.

Noah opened the barn doors with his phone before they arrived. Piekenbrock whistled in appreciation as he checked out the bunker. "Pretty slick."

Noah shrugged. "The security system didn't seem to stop anyone. Maybe I should get a dog."

Angie smiled. "Thought you hated dogs?"

"It wouldn't live inside, more of a guard dog."

As they entered the barn, Dickinson stopped to look around at the concrete structure in the middle of the barn floor. "That shelter is bigger than my whole apartment."

Turning on the interior lights, Noah led them to the third room with the command center. There was a smaller control system built into the house. However, it was mainly run off a tablet, and Noah wanted to see everything off a larger monitor.

At the desk, Noah logged in and scrolled through the timestamp footage. The first alarm came through at five forty-five in the morning as they headed home from their stakeout. Camera one had a panoramic view from the front porch, and the footage was normal. The sun had yet crested the horizon, and everything was in stark detailed black and white relief, but it was a clear recording.

Noah had almost missed it before the camera feed suddenly stopped. There was movement at the base of the large fir tree on the front lawn, then a brief flash of light before the camera stopped recording.

"Can you play that again and zoom in?" The LT leaned in closer to the monitor as Noah adjusted and played the footage, a few frames at a time. "That tree must be eight or nine feet thick at the bottom. Someone used that to block their approach."

"There." Angie pointed at the monitor while Noah froze the playback. A figure leaned out from the tree, a profile image of a baseball cap and the barrel of a long gun. Unfortunately, it was too dark to make out any details and identify the shooter. Also, unlike the movies, enhancing digital recordings caused it to pixelate and distort the more you zoomed in, especially with low light.

"I'll try the other angles."

The other two cameras had views from the side door and the north side of the house. After a brief flash of light, they had stopped working, which was the end of the video footage.

Noah sat back in the chair and rubbed his eyes. "Someone had to have known where the cameras were. Three shots, and they were taken out."

The LT stood and shook his head. "That would have to be a twenty-two rifle with a suppressor, or the sound would have carried easily to the neighbors."

Noah opened the desk drawer and removed a small USB stick, then copied all the footage. "I'll give this to the tech guys. Ideally, there will be something they can get off the recordings."

Piekenbrock nodded. "Someone is sending you a message. Hopefully, the coroner will be able to tell you what it says."

Chapter 20

The Natrona County Coroner's Office was a fifteen-minute drive east of Casper, almost an hour from Arrow Point. The large gravel parking lot led to a large building with three large garage doors and a separate fourth door that could accommodate a fire truck. The offices on the south side of the building were on the second floor, and the examination and refrigerator storage occupied the central area immediately off the receiving bays. The south end of the building had a crematorium installed a few years ago, and it still looked new.

As Noah pulled up in the unmarked police car, he noticed a new structure on the north end of the parking lot. It looked like a small green soccer dome with a stainless-steel block on the outside. The block was half the size of a car, and it appeared to be blowing air inside from the three fans mounted on the upper portion.

Noah parked near the offices and got out of the cruiser. Dickinson had taken the time to go home and have a quick shower and change. She still wore her patrol uniform with a baseball cap. Her long dark hair was still damp, and it was pulled out the back of the hat in a ponytail.

Noah wore the same dark blue suit, but he managed to clean and change his dress shirt and tie. Everything at the new crime scene was processed, and it had left them only more questions. The bullet recovered from the ceiling of the front porch was a .22LR. That type of round was usually good for small game or target practice. Whoever had made those shots had some skill with the rifle. Three cameras were disabled with three attempts at fifty yards from the front of the house.

They entered the front office and Noah signed them both in from APPD. They rang the buzzer and waited until the receptionist came over from the back offices. An older black woman wearing a white button-up sweater and glasses came out. "How can I help you?"

"We're here to see Doctor George Hall."

"Have a seat, and I'll get him, dear."

She had a quick look at the sign-in book before heading back through the door behind the desk. Noah stood off to the side while Angie looked through some of the information posted on the wall. After a few minutes, the receptionist opened the door and leaned through slightly. "He'll see you now. Follow me."

Soon as they entered the hallway, the disinfectant smell hit them rather hard, and the deeper they walked into the building, the more it became prevalent.

After going through a long hallway and a set of double doors, they stood at the end of the large receiving bay, where George supervised an ambulance unloading a stretcher. A small man stood at his side with a clipboard, directing the paramedics to move the body. The coroner and his assistant both wore long white lab coats and blue latex gloves. The whole receiving bay was recently hosed down, and clearly, a vat of disinfectant was used.

Noah didn't want to know what happened to cause a thirty by forty-foot area to be so thoroughly scrubbed. The receptionist told them to wait off to the side, and then she headed back into the building.

Soon as the paramedics left following the smaller man, George turned and smiled at the waiting police officers. "Detective Hunter, you seem to be keeping me as busy. I feel like I was back in New York City once again."

"Sorry, George. I would prefer otherwise."

He smiled and nodded toward Dickinson before he turned back to Noah. "I have barely started on the bodies. Which one are you here about?"

Despite assistance from the county sheriff, they all had to use the same coroner. The coroner acted as the medical examiner for Natrona County, and he had been extremely busy lately with the unusual findings.

"Henry was just brought in a few hours ago. We were hoping something stood out to give us some new information or help to direct the case."

George slowly shook his head back and forth. "I've known Henry for almost twenty years. This one hit close to home. Let's have a quick look. I'll try and move him up on the schedule."

With that, he led them back outside into the gravel parking lot, and headed north toward the green-domed tent. "This is the field refrigeration unit. We don't have room inside, and I had to get this operational."

The door into the dome led into an airlock, and once the outside door closed, it unlocked the interior door. The first thing Noah noticed was the cold air as it hit him, then the three rows of stretchers with bodies on them. Some were lying inside a black zipped body bag, while others lay under a plastic blue thermal sheet. There were fifteen stretchers laid out in three rows of five. The last stretcher was on an angle near the front with a dark blue body bag on top.

"It's been over ten years since the field unit was used."

George pulled out gloves from his coat pocket and put them on before opening the bag.

Henry's eyes and mouth were wide open as if in shock or about to speak. Angie stepped back. Noah heard her swearing slightly under her breath.

"It's okay, perfectly normal." He reached over and used the palm of his left hand to close the eyelids. "I don't have time for a full exam, but let's see if anything jumps out at us."

He pulled down the zipper and the gray overalls that Henry usually wore while working. It had the usual patches of dirt from the cemetery on the knees. George pulled out a penlight from his upper pocket, started at the head, and quickly worked his way down to the feet.

Once he put the flashlight away, he returned to the head and used two hands to feel around the major bone structures. George stepped around to the end of the stretcher and placed both hands under Henry's skull and rocked it back and forth.

The coroner frowned and readjusted his left hand. "No visible wounds, but I suspect he died from a cervical fracture."

He removed the gloves and placed them inside the body bag. "Usually, a great amount of force is needed to break a neck, like a car accident or diving into a shallow pool. This can also happen with a sharp blow to the back of the neck or a sudden twisting motion. I'll check back later. Sometimes contusions will show up."

"Thank you. Not sure how this information will help us. Yet."

George closed the body bag and looked up into his eyes. "Make sure you get the bastard. Henry was a good man, and he deserved better."

"I'll do my best." Noah nodded to George and turned to leave but stopped as an idea came to mind. "Henry wouldn't have been wearing his work clothes at home. I think it is time to pay a visit back at the cemetery."

Chapter 21

After dropping Angie at the station, Noah returned home in his truck to assess the scene. The yellow barricade tape around his front porch flicked back and forth in the late afternoon breeze. Someone had screwed a board across the broken front door and fixed it into the frame. Forensics had long since left, and if it weren't for the tape, everything would have appeared normal.

Despite the current security system, Noah looked around at the property and tried to think of an idea to make it more secure. He could erect a wall and get a guard dog, but that would be too much.

Lately, trouble seemed to find him, and even if he were to build a wall around the property, he figured it wouldn't make a difference. Noah opened the security application on his phone and placed a repair order before he headed inside.

After a shower, he changed into a worn pair of khaki pants and a long-sleeved blue shirt. It didn't take him long to find a small backpack, and he added a few bottles of water, protein bars, and a few other essential items. Once he laced up his hiking boots and placed an APPD blue ballcap on his head, Noah headed out the door and locked up.

Fifteen minutes later, he pulled into the cemetery's parking lot and parked near the wooden barricade that blocked access to the pathway. There weren't any officers on the scene. However, all entrances to the cemetery were blocked off, and a *temporarily closed* sign was fixed to each location.

Arrow Point Cemetery was over one hundred and fifty years old and had served the community well. The older north section had tombstones worn from the passage of time and were no longer readable. Some roads and pathways filled the area like arteries, and the grounds were kept immaculate. The cemetery was divided into three sections: the original north graveyard, the central location nearest the parking lot, and the eastern field. The six acres of the southern property were maintained for future expansion, and it wasn't currently in use.

Noah figured he had three hours to do a full walk about before it became too dark. He pulled on a blue windbreaker, then slid the holster through his belt. The backpack didn't weigh much, but there were a few items he wished to bring, just in case.

A four-foot fence surrounded the land, and there were many open places into the woods. The northern path led into a subdivision. While the main and north areas were searched several times, that left only one portion. Noah headed on the path system that would lead him to the southern portion. Several officers searched the area; however, the cemetery boundaries were blurred with the surrounding forest, making the six acres easily seem like twenty.

A few minutes into his walk, Noah received a text from Lieutenant Piekenbrock. *The mayor and the press are clamoring for updates. Be prepared for a press release for tomorrow morning.*

Noah gave a quick reply before he slid the phone back into his pocket and reassessed the time he had. Two hours would have to be enough to search the area he had in mind before going back to the station. Then, he would come back out tomorrow morning with a few other officers and conduct an extended sweep of the whole property.

By that time, he hoped the full forensic reports would be completed. They were crucial and would help guide the next steps in the investigation.

Fifteen minutes later, Noah approached the southern property of the cemetery. The path system ended, and a field of long grass took over. There were a few trees scattered across the acreage and large brush. The field blended into the forest on the far edge of the property.

Waist-high grass was trampled down in paths from where the officers had searched. Noah could see the areas where it had already started to grow straight after being bent.

He slid off his backpack and pulled out a collapsed walking stick that was strapped to the side. With a series of twists and snaps, he had an extended telescoping pole.

Noah had used it several times over the years, not for hiking but for detailed search parties. The pole was used to move brush, grass, or litter to the side while he looked for anything out of the ordinary.

Birds circled overhead in the warm afternoon breeze, and he was far enough away from the main road that he couldn't hear any street noise. Three hundred feet into the field, Noah knelt to look closer at a crushed pathway.

It was a fairly narrow trampled path, but as he moved on a few feet, he could identify hoofprints from a deer. His brother had taught him much while they hunted and hiked and Noah, for the most part, tended to forget much of what he imparted. However, the heart-shaped prints in the dirt were common enough that they stuck in his memory. He laid his palm beside the track, and they were almost the same size. It could be a large buck.

Noah followed the game trail at a slower pace toward the woods. The walking stick was in constant motion as he wacked and moved tufts of grass. He tried to make sure he didn't miss anything.

When the police searched across a field or area, an extended line formed, and they proceeded at the same pace—taking the speed set by the person in the middle. At times they could have over twenty officers involved in a search. APPD would have to make special arrangements to have that many personnel on scene for such a search. With the high-profile case, he hoped the staffing would be available.

Noah would submit the paperwork for an extended search for the cemetery grounds when he arrived back at the station tonight. For now, he wanted to get an idea of the extent of the property and the area to cover. Afterward, he would call the director and see about gaining entry into Henry's maintenance shed. Then he would confirm they had permission to enter the caretaker's home. There was too much to do, and he would have to bring more in on the case. A team of six would be ideal.

As Noah walked through the field, he didn't see any markings or a fence line to separate the cemetery property and the public lands. When Noah entered the woods, he was certain this property had not seen many people in a while. There were mostly pine and spruce with an occasional cluster of aspens that grew fairly close together. The ground was littered with layers of mulch and needles which made it feel like walking across a living room carpet. It was soft and quiet underfoot.

As he scouted, Noah circled the forest edge where the trees met the field and made his way north while staying in the tree line.

When he stepped around a thick cluster of aspens, the only warning he had was a grunt. Noah turned his head and brought up a shoulder instinctively at the sound.

That subtle movement saved his life.

Instead of the tree limb striking him at the base of his skull, it smashed into the side of his head, just behind his left ear. His eyes rolled back in his head as he fell onto his right side. Noah was barely aware of the sharp prick of a syringe as it was stabbed into the side of his left leg, just above the knee—before the darkness took over.

Chapter 22

Constable Dickinson knocked on the office door and waited until Lieutenant Piekenbrock hung up the phone.

"Sir, do you have a moment?"

Angie wore her patrol uniform and appeared to be rested after working a double shift the day before. Her hair was in a thick braid that hung a few inches below the collar.

"Of course, how can I help you?"

"I'm unable to locate Detective Hunter. He isn't answering his phone. On a normal case, I wouldn't be too worried, but this isn't standard for him."

LT frowned and tapped his fingers on the desk a few times while he thought about it. He wore a light brown suit and green tie and clutched a large mug of coffee in one hand. If the dark circles under his eyes were any indication, he hadn't been getting much sleep either. The case was making everyone work extended hours.

"Agreed. This isn't normal. Head out to his house, then the cemetery, and see if you can find him. I'm sure everything is fine, but just in case, I'll have dispatch make the 10-19 call."

Any vehicles out on the road would be on the watch for Noah, and they would ensure he called in, or they would call it in when he was sighted. It was an informal BOLO if communications were disrupted and for the officer to report to the station.

A few minutes later, while Angie drove east on Main Street, the call was broadcasted for call-sign 4417 to report. After arriving at Noah's home and a quick drive to the barn, she realized that his black Dodge Ram wasn't on the property.

She stepped out of the cruiser and conducted a quick perimeter check of the home. The front door appeared to be secured with a board, and there were no other signs of a break-in.

Following the LT's suggestion, she drove across town and was relieved as she pulled into the cemetery parking lot. Noah's truck was parked near the barricade that blocked access to the grounds. Once she pulled in beside the vehicle, Angie frowned and stepped out of the cruiser. Unfortunately, the feeling of relief was short-lived.

Against the windshield, in the middle of the hood sat Noah's backpack and a four-foot walking stick. A Glock 17 still in the holster was on top. As Angie fought down the sick feeling of dread in her stomach, she called it in.

*****

The peaceful sensation of floating down a lazy river was gradually replaced by the hard-uncomfortable ground digging into his back and an insect biting his neck. The discomforts caused him to rise through various layers of consciousness, albeit grudgingly. The chorus of bird calls sounded above him and competed with the sound of a wrapper being rumpled nearby.

Noah flicked the bug away and tried to lick his lips, but there was no moisture in his mouth. Instead, his tongue felt like sandpaper as it scraped across his cracked lips. The headache rushed in, and he couldn't help but moan as the pain level rose. He gingerly felt the side of his head. His fingers came away with sticky and dried blood.

When his eyes squinted open, Noah quickly realized he was not in the woodlot by the cemetery. The distant sounds of the city were replaced by nature, and even the air smelled different. The top of the trees swayed with the warm light breeze. The rumbling noise resumed, and Noah turned his head to the side. A small tan field mouse, six or seven feet away, tried to chew through the wrapper of a protein bar. Its small black eyes never left his. Beside the bar was a bottle of water, and Noah recognized the brands. They were in his backpack before he was ambushed.

As he fought the thunder in his head, his feet shifted, and a great weight on his right ankle held him back. A length of metal clanked, and the mouse darted twelve inches away and froze.

A primal fear quickly replaced the shroud of confusion and pain as he focused on his right ankle.

A five-inch band of metal was clamped around his right lower leg with a thick heavy chain secured through the eyelets with a lock. The chain was then wrapped around the wide base of a white pine tree and secured with a large matching padlock. He had four feet of loose chain between his leg and the tree. Despite the age of the links and the rust that had formed, it looked solid enough to tow an eighteen-wheeler with ease.

The chain was fairly tight as it wrapped around the tree trunk, and Noah noticed a grooved circular wear mark around the base. Someone had been in this situation previously and spun the chain multiple times around the tree—enough to strip the bark in a band. The bare circle of earth about the trunk was devoid of any plant life, all within reach of the tether.

Noah gave a little tug to confirm his suspicion. He wasn't strong enough to break the inch-thick metal links.

The movement and noise from the chain were too much for the small rodent, and it scampered into the woods as he struggled to his feet.

With the density of the forest, Noah had no idea where he could be. As far as he could see, there was nothing but trees and brush. With the medicinal after-taste in his mouth and with the stiffness in his body, he realized he could have been unconscious for many hours as he rubbed a hand over his cheeks. The stubble let him know it was easily the next morning. He had been out for over twelve hours, and he could be anywhere within Wyoming or even a neighboring state.

Noah took stock of the situation. He still wore his hiking boots and khaki pants and a long-sleeved blue T-shirt. There was no sign of his backpack or windbreaker. A quick check of his pockets showed them to be empty, but he still wore his belt. He glanced at the protein bar and bottle of water and realized he faced his first challenge. The four feet of the chain from the tree to his ankle, plus the length of his body, placed the items over four feet away.

Fuck.

This would have been the situation where many had found themselves before they had ended up buried underneath a coffin. The coroner had stated that the last body of Steve Misevski had been severely dehydrated and had starved to death. There was no doubt who had captured him, but he was surprised he was still alive.

Noah walked to the tree, held the large link, and forced it to spin around the trunk. He needed to have a full view of the area, not just one angle.

The wear mark in the wood helped ease the movement, and Noah wasn't surprised to discover more of the same view on the opposite side. The ground appeared to be slightly different, with a slight depression caused by the roots of the pine. It was difficult to tell with the cloud cover, but he believed that to be the north side of the white pine.

"Hello? Is anyone there?"

Noah felt compelled to call out, despite the situation. He couldn't hear any traffic from a road, or any other noise associated with living in a built-up area. Nothing but the sounds of nature.

After he spun the chain around the trunk once more, he looked at the protein bar and the lone bottle of water. It was time to get to work.

Chapter 23

Noah removed his left hiking boot and belt. Once he tied the laces on the buckle, he had a tool with a six-foot reach. He held onto one end of the belt, swung the boot out beyond the water bottle, and slowly pulled it in. The protein bar quickly followed suit.

This would be his only supply of water and he had to fight the temptation to drink. Noah had to make this last. The foil of the protein bar had a corner chewed open by the mouse, and a little nibble was removed. Once he got dressed again, he sat down with his back against the tree and went over his options.

Unless he were to gnaw his right foot off, there didn't seem to be any way out of the situation.

Yet.

One item in his favor was the weather. Despite the cloud cover, it was unusually warm for the early spring season. Without a jacket, he was fairly comfortable. That may change once the sun goes down and he had to survive the night.

Noah had a small sip and enjoyed the moisture as it trickled down his throat. Being drugged had left him parched, and he had to fight his instinct to drink the whole bottle. Unless it started to rain, he had to make the fourteen-ounce bottle last.

He brought his right leg in closer and examined the lock. He knew the theory of lock-picking, but he didn't have the equipment for the job or any practical experience. The only tools available were easy to take stock: his hiking boots with laces, belt, socks, pants, T-shirt, and underwear, as well as the protein bar and water bottle.

After looking up at the tree, he realized that this area was prepped to keep a prisoner beside the chain and shackle. Any branches low enough to be used as leverage were trimmed with a saw close to the trunk. The nearest branch was ten feet off the ground, and the closest tree was twenty feet away.

Noah closed his eyes and crossed his arms over his chest as he rested. He needed to conserve his energy and not waste calories needlessly until the situation changed or an idea came to mind.

*****

Lieutenant Piekenbrock led the officers as they conducted an extensive sweep of the cemetery. The Wyoming Highway Patrol and the Sherriff's Office had been alerted, and officers from all over the state were on the lookout for Detective Hunter.

"Left turn," the LT waited until they shifted direction toward the southern cemetery grounds. "Forward."

The extended line stretched over a hundred yards, with ten to fifteen feet between the searchers. Some used their collapsible batons to help beat the bush, while others used sticks or smaller branches. Zane kept a hockey stick in his car with the blade broken off for this purpose. Thankfully, he hadn't had to use it much over the last twenty years.

As they made their way across the waist-tall grass field, searchers would occasionally call out when they spotted an irregularity. At that point, the whole line would halt while it was investigated.

"Deer tracks."

The message was passed up and down the line. Again, communication was a key element.

"Forward," Piekenbrock called out once again. The hockey stick moved large tufts of grass aside and, at times, helped him regain his balance. Unfortunately, there wasn't any traction in his dress shoes, and he found it difficult to work in the suit. Nevertheless, he didn't want to head back to the station and change. Time was of the essence, and he didn't want to waste a single minute.

Once Constable Dickinson had called in, he rushed out to the cemetery and confirmed that it was Noah's weapon. At that point, word went out that Detective Hunter was missing. Arrow Point, the county, and the state were placed on alert. Offers of assistance began to pour in.

Noah's pistol and other items were handed over to forensics, and they were currently being processed. They were considered a priority, and they jumped the queue, with all hands assisting.

At the edge of the field, the LT paused before he decided to carry on. Constable Dickinson stood to his immediate left and pointed off to the woods. "This goes on for many miles and is no longer on the cemetery property. Detective Hunter had wanted to check the forest where it surrounded the cemetery."

The LT nodded. "Agreed. We'll do an external sweep of the woods." He had everyone form up and proceeded north within the wood line at a slower pace. The trees and brush caused the officers to cluster, but it couldn't be helped.

It was getting late, and they only had a few hours of daylight left. But, once they moved through the woods, Zane realized that their time here would be much shorter. The taller spruce and pines blocked out the setting sun. Darkness would arrive sooner in the dense forest.

The call to halt came from the left end of the extended line, and Lieutenant Piekenbrock was called over a moment later. Behind a large aspen tree, a stout branch lay on the ground, and a large area had been disturbed on the forest floor. The layers of pine needles and decayed leaves were scraped away, and the dirt lay exposed.

The end of the branch had a dull rust-brown patch with a few hairs sticking to the end. "Clear back." The LT looked up at the people surrounding him. "It appears Detective Hunter was taken by force. Try and find a trail from here."

Once he stood up straight, Piekenbrock looked down once again at the branch. He had a feeling that things were about to get worse. With a shake of his head, the search resumed.

Chapter 24

Noah knew that a person could live up to three days without water before their body began to shut down and they would die. They could survive longer without food, but the water was essential.

The bottle sat on the ground before him, and he figured there were over seven ounces left. Throughout the day, he had sipped sparingly. Just barely enough to wet his tongue. He had eaten only two bites of the protein bar, and he had to control himself not to finish it as the hunger set in.

The first night chained to the tree wasn't as bad as he thought it would be. A few times throughout the night, he had woken when he heard a noise within the forest. Noah wasn't worried about too many things when he tried to sleep. However, black bears or even a grizzly were high on the list. Although grizzlies were more aggressive, black bears could be equally dangerous. Especially when they were out with their cubs at this time of year, searching for food.

The lump behind his ear had shrunk in size, but it was still tender, and the headache remained as a dull throb throughout the day.

It was hard to estimate the time, but Noah figured it was late afternoon when he heard scratching and a clicking noise. It only took a few minutes before he found a large beetle as it crawled up the tree trunk. It was almost the size of his thumb, and it was a deep reddish-brown color.

It had been over eighteen years since Noah had taken a survival course with the 15th Infantry Regiment at Fort Benning. However, one piece of advice had stayed with him after all these years. *Do what you have to do to survive. Others will depend on you.*

With that in mind, Noah grabbed the beetle with two fingers, and with the other hand, he twisted the head off. Before he could think about it, he popped the body in his mouth and started to chew. He could feel the legs move in his mouth as his teeth crunched down. A bitter fluid squirted across his tongue, which he disregarded. He needed the protein and any juices the insect would impart. Noah ignored the mental image of the beetle crawling up his throat after swallowing.

A scan of the tree and his immediate area didn't reveal any other edible insects, but he did find a weed that grew on the northern side of the tree, barely within reach. It was only a few inches tall and looked like a dandelion sprout. It did not have any taste, but Noah could feel the moisture from the stem and the few leaves as he chewed.

I will survive and do whatever it takes.

*****

Lieutenant Piekenbrock printed the report and logged off the computer before heading into the cube, where several people waited. The police chief stood at the back, near the conference room, with his arms crossed on his chest. Chief Birch nodded for the LT to begin, and once he started to talk, the room became silent.

"The branch was analyzed by forensics, and two DNA samples were found. The blood and hair follicles matched Detective Hunter and no match for the second set of DNA from the skin samples."

The chief cleared his throat before talking. "However, we now have a profile that we can build from. We're one step closer."

Piekenbrock nodded in agreement. "I have set a schedule for a constant patrol for the cemetery. Check your assignments with the duty sergeant before you head out."

The chief had authorized an extra shift that would assist and help track down any leads. Constable Angie Dickinson waited until everyone had left before she walked over to the lieutenant. "Sir, would you like me back on patrol? I had a look, and I'm not on the roster for today's rotation."

The LT nodded. "I had you taken off. We had something already scheduled. I see no reason why we can't go ahead with it."

Angie frowned as she failed to understand. "I'm not too sure what …."

"Come with me." Piekenbrock crossed the cube and opened the door to the conference room. Sergeant Bydal sat at one end of the table, and at the opposite end was a stack of paper and a pencil and a bottle of water.

"Constable Dickinson, have a seat, please." Stan Bydal gestured to the other end while Angie looked more confused.

"Detective Hunter had scheduled your sergeant's exam for today, and we saw no reason to cancel it. You have ninety minutes for the written portion, and Sergeant Bydal will ask you a series of questions once you're done. Any questions?"

Angie sat and asked the obvious question. "Shouldn't I be out there helping find Detective Hunter?"

Stan leaned forward, the worry and concern on his face evident. "We're doing all we can. Either we will be successful, or we won't. Noah will have to do his share and let us know where he is or escape. Unfortunately, he also may be dead. Right now, I need you to put all that aside and help him as best you can by doing *your* best on this exam. After you're done, you can go out and drive around town all night."

Angie nodded. "I'm ready then."

Lieutenant Piekenbrock smiled. "Good luck. Come and see me when you are done."

Before he closed the door, a *beep* sounded from a watch, and Sergeant Bydal spoke. "The exam has begun. Turn to the first page."

Chapter 25

The second day was spent trying to escape. The belt prong was too big to pick the lock, but it did help as a tool for digging in the soil. Noah had searched the base of the tree for earthworms or grubs, but he got dizzy fairly quickly, and he had to rest. Not that he could get far or found anything, but it gave him something to do.

The next night chained to the pine, was beyond uncomfortable. When the temperature dropped, he couldn't stay warm and found himself shivering against the tree for warmth. Only a few brief moments were spent sleeping scattered throughout the night. The slightest noise would jar him from a dreamless sleep.

The morning of the third day of his imprisonment began the hottest day of the season. The toll from lack of food and water, even proper sleep, was evident. Noah became lethargic, and an inability to focus was a major concern.

He tilted the bottle and drained the last of the water onto his parched tongue. The liquid was hot, stale, and tasted like plastic. It was also barely more than a mouthful, but there wasn't much sense in hoarding it further. He had eaten various insects over the last two days, but they did little to sustain him.

"Maybe another day or two until I fall unconscious." He was not sure.

With the day's heat and humidity, he wouldn't last another twenty-four hours. To make matters worse, the hot sun was directly overhead, beaming down through the trees. He felt like a baked potato. Unfortunately, there wasn't anywhere to hide, so he pulled off the dirty blue T-shirt and wrapped it around his head to try and protect him a little longer.

At midday, he must have dozed, for when his arm fell from his knees, it landed on a length of chain. The sun had heated the metal enough that nearly burned the back of his hand. Startled, Noah jerked his arm back and looked at the red mark.

He reached out and felt along the length of chain and the band of metal that circled his lower leg. The heat of the sun had warmed it up quite a bit. There would only be one chance. He had to take it.

Noah stood, and it took a few seconds for him to maintain his balance. He kept his left leg close to the tree and then side-stepped outward until the chain was stretched out at the four-foot distance. He stepped over the chain with a turn, then brought his shackled foot over, causing the chain to twist and tighten.

He repeated the maneuver six more times until the end was only a foot away from the tree trunk. The links of metal had turned into a ball. The band around his leg prevented any injury from the chain as it was tightened. The padlock clanked and slapped against the housing as the tension increased. Noah turned around yet again, and the chain balled up further and was snug to the side of the tree.

With the next turn, all slack was taken out the length and he was pinned in tight. He slowly lowered himself down the side of the tree while keeping his left leg straight. The chain links tightened to the maximum, leaving him hanging off the ground from the tension. Noah rocked up and down as he placed his entire body weight on the ball of chain.

Over the last two days, he had inspected each link he could reach, and he discovered that they were not continuous. Each oval loop was bent and welded to close the circle, and the next link in the chain was added. He couldn't tell how many seasons the chain had been wrapped around the tree and exposed to the elements. Some of the thick links were separated from the wielding. It was the barest gap, but it was there.

As hard as he tried, there wasn't any physical way for him to twist the links. However, the hot sun had warmed the chain enough that Noah hoped the tension from torquing them would enable one link to bend just enough.

He laid his back on the ground and brought his left leg up and rested it on the ball of links, and then he straightened out his right leg, which raised his torso off the ground.

Noah was suspended off the ground at the shackle. The tension of the wrapped chain tightened even further against the tree. Now and then, a link would skip and pull farther, causing his body to fall back.

Already, his vision darkened around the edges as the effort cost him. Noah raised himself a few more inches, then dropped his whole weight down on the extended leg. The length of chain ground against each other, and a small chunk of the tree fell from being gouged.

Noah pushed himself up off the ground with his hands as his full body weight rested on his extended legs. He took a few deep breaths and screamed with effort. At first, nothing happened except a few black spots appeared in his vision. Then inch by inch, Noah was slowly lowered to the ground as the tension was eased. The chain did not clank or shift—it just had slowly lowered him.

That was different, and difference was good.

Noah wasn't sure if he had blacked out for a brief moment or not. But when he sat up, he smiled at the burning sun as his lips bled from the deep cracks.

The combination of heat on the metal and torque caused a damaged link near the tree to twist slightly.

An adrenaline surge gave him the energy he needed. Noah stepped over the chain several times in the opposite direction before examining his handiwork.

He took the twisted link and turned it to the side. The three-foot length of chain fell into the dirt at his feet. Noah could not help but laugh. Despite the metal band secured tight to his leg with the padlock and a chain length, he was free.

He picked up the empty water bottle and the wrapper from the protein bar in one hand and the end of the chain in the other. He had thought of this moment for days, and he already had a game plan. First, clear the area. He was in no condition to deal with anyone checking on him. The second order of business was to get water.

He headed downhill into the forest with one last look at the tree that kept him company for the last three days.

I hope you get hit by lightning.

Chapter 26

The total size of Wyoming is 98,000 square miles, and over eighteen percent of the state is forested. It's divided into conservation areas, national parks, native lands, and a few public ownerships. Vast tracts of acreage are not managed and are considered wild. The predominant species of trees are lodgepole pine and spruce, and the wildlife consists of everything from wild bison, mountain lions to deer and elk and bears. If he came across a grizzly, he would feed it eight pounds of chain at high speed. There were not too many other options.

Noah had camped and hiked with his brother dozens of times, and they had never encountered anything dangerous on their expeditions. With all the noise he made while carrying the chain in his left hand, he doubted he would run into anything. The constant metallic clank sounded like a bell throughout the forest as he stumbled through the trees. Long as it did not sound like a dinner bell to the wildlife, he should be fine.

The three-foot length of chain grew heavier the longer he walked. Noah had used up most of his energy reserves to break free, and there wasn't much gas left in the tank. As he stumbled across the forest, he constantly headed downhill. Noah paused for breaks and leaned against a tree or sat on a fallen log to catch his breath before moving on. If he stopped to sleep, he might not have the energy to get up and carry on.

After a thirty-minute walk, he found a small spring that trickled out of a mossy outcrop of rock. It pooled at the bottom before it was absorbed into the forest floor. He dropped the chain and knelt in the damp soil and drank a few mouthfuls, and then sat back and waited. He knew better than to gorge himself on water after he had so little over the last few days. There would be no point in being sick.

It was easily the best water ever. Even with the mineral taste of the natural spring. After a five-minute wait, Noah drank some more and filled up the plastic water bottle. The water source seemed to be a gathering place for the deer and the other forest animals. The damp soil had several dozen hoofprints embedded into the ground, and he saw the one print he had hoped to avoid—that of a large cat.

Even if there was a disease he picked up, there was no choice. God only knew what an animal had done in the water.

Near the spring, the trees grew close together, and he couldn't see far into the forest, maybe fifty feet at the farthest point between the tree trunks. At times the woods were fairly dense, or there were open fields with waist-tall grasses. He needed to rest and let the water hydrate his body. He didn't want to travel too far from the spring for now.

On the side slope twenty feet away, Noah spotted a large Douglas fir, similar to the tree that grew on his property. The low-hanging branches formed a natural cave, and after Noah crawled inside, he felt safe for the first time in days. It was naturally cooler under the boughs, and within seconds, he fell asleep.

*****

Angie held the keys in her hand and tried to figure out which one would work. By nature, she was organized, but there didn't seem to be any order to the mess.

Even though she was sure she had tried that same key previously, it opened the lock, and the gate swung open. It took a while to find the hidden switch behind the tree, but the system was disarmed. Not that Noah could respond, but she wanted to be respectful. After she jumped in the cruiser and drove it through, Angie locked the gate behind her.

After four days of zero progress, she signed Detective Hunter's keys out of evidence and drove north to his cabin. She had taken a few wrong turns, but determination paid off. Noah didn't want others to know about the property, so she kept that information to herself. It had been a week since she had been there last, and it had not changed since.

After she walked around the A-frame cabin, Angie unlocked the front door and stepped inside. The alarm system beeped for two minutes then shut down. The heat from yesterday's weather had kept the interior extremely warm. She left the front door open and began her search.

It only took a few seconds to determine no one else was present. There just wasn't anywhere to hide. However, Dickinson was also there to see if she could find any clues that may lead to Noah.

She started her search in the kitchen and slowly made her way through the building. There was little to be found that were personal effects. In fact, there was nothing—no pictures or knick-knacks. Angie did see a small note underneath a plastic plant that read, *Do not water.* It was written in a feminine handwriting, and she guessed it was from his former fiancée.

The only item that seemed out of place was a single key inside a small pottery cup high on a shelf above the kitchen sink. There were no marks or anything written to identify it. She replaced it and had a final look around before she gave up. There wasn't any indication or clues as to why he was taken here.

Angie stepped out the back door and headed over to the outhouse for a quick look inside, but it too was empty. However, when she was about to leave, she spotted an old trail that headed into the woods.

With one hand on her pistol, she kept her head on a swivel and walked along the trail. Eighty yards into the trees, it opened up into a small clearing revealing a shed in the middle. The structure looked like it had been fortified with steel on each side and angle iron for the corners. The reinforced door would withstand an assault from the Marines, with the bands of riveted steel. A single large padlock blocked the bolt from sliding out of the frame.

Despite the many keys on the ring, none of them opened the lock. Angie pounded on the door. "Detective Hunter, are you in there?"

She put her ear to the door and listened. Nothing.

Dickinson remembered the key from the cabin and ran back. She prayed that he wasn't trapped inside. With the heat from the last few days, he would be cooked alive. Once inside the cabin, she grabbed a bottle of water and the key before heading back to the forest shed. Despite not being religious, she prayed as she ran the whole way back.

Chapter 27

Noah had enjoyed the sleep under the fir tree, and his body needed it. The boughs formed a natural cave, and he burrowed into the mulch to stay warm. Then, before the sun came up, he drank his fill many times over before continuing cross country.

With the rising sun at his back, he turned to head downhill. Now that he was fully hydrated, Noah made better time, but the rumble from his stomach reminded him food was his next issue to tackle. It was too early in the season for berries, and the mushrooms were not appealing. Besides, he wasn't exactly sure which were edible and which ones were poisonous.

The only food that he could identify with any certainty was wild onions. Finally, he found a small patch at the base of a hill, and after he cleaned the dirt away, he found himself staring straight into the eyes of a black bear cub.

Noah stifled a scream and quickly made up his mind.

He stood and tucked the onions into the front pocket of his pants and slid the water bottle in the other. A quick look around showed that he was alone with the cub. However, he knew that its mother would be nearby.

The attached chain wasn't long enough to swing as a weapon, so he held the end tight in his left and slowly backed away. The cub followed and sat at the base of a birch and watched as Noah climbed the nearest pine. The bear didn't look alarmed or afraid. Instead, it appeared to be curious, but that could change in the blink of an eye. Even small bears had teeth and claws.

Noah wasn't interested in finding out if he wanted to play or not. He climbed several feet until the branches would no longer support his weight. The three-foot length of chain dangled from the leg iron and swayed back and forth while his knuckles turned white.

The cub walked over, looked up at Noah and gave a little bark. Then, it stood on its hind legs and gripped the tree. The black claws easily found grip as it climbed a few feet.

Noah couldn't move any higher, but he lifted his left leg and took up the chain's slack. He stared down into the dark brown eyes. His face remained pressed tight against the rough bark while he waited.

The tree was barely a foot across, and it swayed back and forth with his weight alone. With the added weight of the black bear, Noah thought it might topple. The cub cocked its head to the side, and it shuffled up the tree another foot.

Once it was in range, Noah pointed his left leg and dropped the end of the chain. It swung in a slight arc and clipped the bear's nose before it bounced off the tree trunk.

The cub let out a sharp bark and dropped five feet to rest on the forest floor. It sat still for a moment in disbelief before giving out a few high-pitched barks. Oh my God, it was crying.

"Move along!" Noah made a gesture with his free hand to wave the bear away. Fifty feet on the side slope of the hill, Noah spotted the mother bear and another cub as they sauntered along.

The cub let out a noise between a bark and a squawk before lumbering off to join the family. Noah tried not to move as the mother bear turned to look directly at him. She held his gaze for a moment then strolled away. The cubs stayed close to her side.

Not willing to chance it, Noah stayed in the tree for an hour. He popped an onion in his mouth and took a sip of water. He could wait it out, no problem.

*****

Angie turned the key in the lock, then moved her right hand to her pistol grip while she opened the door. The shed was six-by-eight feet, and three shelving units mostly took up the interior on the left side. Opposite the shelves were long green wooden boxes with thick rope handles on the ends. The boxes were of a uniform size, just over three-feet long and eight-inches tall. At a quick count, there were twenty boxes stacked up.

On the shelves were stacked several small stainless-steel boxes, the size of a briefcase, along with thirty metal ammunition canisters.

Her first emotion was relief. Detective Hunter wasn't inside. She didn't think Noah was a doomsday prepper or a collector, but she was wrong.

The first wooden crate had an AR-15 semi-automatic rifle and it looked like it had never been fired. The second crate held a new Remington tactical shotgun, with a flash-suppressor and adjustable stock, nestled in the molded foam.

Angie didn't want to waste any more time in the shed. She wanted to talk with the vet since she was in the area. Maybe he had seen Detective Hunter or had further information on the fire.

She spotted a green duffel bag on the top shelf by the door as she turned to leave. It resembled the bag Noah used for the gym, but she wasn't sure if it was the same one. Angie slid it off the top shelf and was surprised at the weight and more surprised at what was inside.

Stacks of hundred-dollar bills, still wrapped in the paper band from the bank. Angie was stunned at the amount of money in front of her, stored in a shed hidden in the woods. Millions?

What's going on?

The only possible answer made her feel sick.

Chapter 28

Throughout the night, Noah remained comfortable, and when the temperature dropped, he buried deeper into the dry pine needles. When the false dawn arrived, the chorus birds woke him along with a rumble from his empty stomach. He could not count on stumbling across another water source but drinking a third of his bottle was essential. It helped quell the hunger pains and held back the headache. Barely.

Once the sun had cleared the tree line, he kept his left shoulder in line as he walked south. Noah found another small patch of onions, but they had barely grown, and the bulbs were just forming. He took them regardless.

Throughout the morning, the chain began to slow him down as he grew weaker. The weight in his left hand felt like twenty pounds, and it grew heavier as the day went on.

It was late Friday afternoon when Noah turned and headed west following the contour of the land. He simply didn't have the strength to climb another hill, and the rocky outcropping before him looked too dangerous.

The breaks Noah allowed himself grew longer each time he sat. The last full meal he had was on the Sunday afternoon before he was taken, and five full days later, he'd only had one protein bar and half a dozen insects, along with a handful of immature wild onions. There have been enough small creeks that crisscrossed the forest and open fields that Noah no longer was in danger of dying from thirst. He filled up the plastic water bottle at every chance, as well as made sure to drink his fill before he moved on.

Noah had thought he was about to enter another small clearing when he paused, and the water bottle fell from lifeless fingers. His strength and will-power fled, and his knees buckled as he sat with head bowed.

Stretched out before him was a one-hundred-foot drop down a rock-strewn slope. At the bottom and as far as he could see were nothing but trees and open fields. The forest stretched for many miles, and he could not see one sign of habitation.

He shuffled forward and looked over the side. Noah closed his eyes and hung his head low, chin resting on his chest while he struggled to regain hope. Even if he were healthy and in prime physical shape, it would have been doubtful he would have been able to climb down the escarpment.

Noah would have to circle back and try to go a different way. It would be a dozen miles added to his journey, one he was not sure he could endure. The afternoon heat and exhaustion caught up with him, and he laid back on the rock and dozed off.

An hour later, a distant noise grew louder, and Noah's heart leaped in his chest as he struggled to his feet. A Cessna flew due north, a thousand feet above the trees, and would soon pass straight over his position.

Even if he were to stand and wave, he wouldn't be noticed. So, he dug in his pocket and pulled out the wrapper for the protein bar, then turned it inside out. The interior was shiny foil, the most reflective material he had.

He held his left hand out, palm pointed toward the plane, and made a V with his first two fingers. He held the foil wrapper with his right hand and tried to reflect the sunlight through his two fingers toward the plane. He had watched a British survivalist television host use this same method to signal for help. If this worked, Noah would find that man and hire him to run his survival course.

Noah flicked the wrapper back and forth several times, with his fingers aimed toward the plane as it flew directly overhead and continued north. Finally, the sound of the engine disappeared, and after the excitement was over, Noah collapsed.

"Fuck."

He picked up a rock, threw it out over the edge, then watched it bounce down the slope until it was lost from sight. Noah was about to climb to his feet and begin the journey to retrace his steps when he heard the engine noise from the small plane once again.

The plane had circled west, and now it flew along its original path. However, this time it was five-hundred feet above the ground.

Tears rolled down his cheeks and were lost into his growing beard as he cheered. He pulled out the wrapper and once again pointed the reflective foil at the pilot and flicked the light back and forth across his fingers. It was hard to make out the specific details, but Noah was sure the pilot waved.

When the plane flew overhead a third time, Noah waited. Within five minutes, the white Cessna flew barely sixty-five feet above the ground. Noah could see the passenger in a red shirt holding up a sign written with a black marker on a piece of cardboard pressed to the window.

Stay right there!

At that moment, the men smiled, and Noah gave him the thumbs-up sign. A few minutes after the plane passed overhead, Noah sat on the rock to watch the sunset and decided to feast on the three remaining onions and finish the water. He never noticed the tears that fell from his beard, nor the clean streak left behind. He recognized the red shirt. It was the uniform shirt of the Wyoming game warden.

Help was coming.

An hour after the sun came up, Noah expected to hear the sound of an ATV as it crossed the country to his position. Instead, branches being snapped and the sound of hooves as a large chestnut mare forced her way through the brush and walked into the clearing.

The man wore jeans and a long-sleeved red shirt, with the game warden patch on the upper shoulder. A leather vest matched his Stetson hat and Sam Brown. He appeared to be in his early fifties, and he wore gold-rimmed glasses and had a white goatee. Noah noticed the Glock .40 holstered at his hip and a shotgun in a special holster near the pommel. A bedroll and a pack hung down to either side behind him.

"I think you're the man I was sent to find."

Noah smiled as he gained his feet. "Noah Hunter. Am I ever glad to see you."

When he heard the name, the warden's eyes widened, and he slid off his horse. "Detective Hunter?" When Noah nodded, the game warden chuckled. "Most of the state is looking for you."

"Long story, but I'm okay. Mostly."

The game warden examined the length of chain and shackled leg and frowned. "I don't have anything to get that off you for the moment. Let's get out of here while I call this in. Molly will carry you while I walk. I would love to hear more about your story."

With help, Noah mounted and grinned. "You wouldn't happen to have a hamburger by chance?"

Chapter 29

The Weston County Hospital was a modern two-story building in Newcastle, Wyoming. Noah was found forty miles west of Newcastle, and it was the closest medical facility. The forested area where he was held was the second largest in the state. However, Noah was only a dozen miles from the open plains and grass meadows.

Once an IV was inserted and after being thoroughly examined, a hearty beef broth was brought in under the supervision of the nurse. After being given the all-clear for a short visit, Noah worked with the game warden. Using maps, they tried to retrace his steps to find where he was held.

In a cloth bag under the hospital bed was the chain and lock, with the leg iron. They had to step outside to the rear parking lot, where a grinder was used to remove the lock.

"Anyone traveling to this area would have to carry you in for over a mile across rugged terrain from the logging road." Logan Allen pointed a thick finger along the contours of the ridgeline.

In Wyoming, there were only sixty-two zones for the game wardens to patrol and manage. Each zone had one person dedicated to that area, and Logan was the senior game warden for the Newcastle district.

"I didn't know which direction to go, so I headed downhill to search for water. If I just headed east, I would have come across the road …."

The game warden shook his head. "You did good. With the elevation change, there wouldn't have been any water until you hit this area." He tapped his finger on the map, east and south from where they estimated he was held.

"I'm just glad you saw me from the plane." Noah leaned back on the bed and had another sip of water. "Doubt I would have lasted much longer."

"We had word of poachers in the area. Sometimes you get lucky and can spot their trucks from the air." Logan folded the map and tucked it into the back pocket of his jeans. "I'll head up to that section and look around for the tree you described. Molly will be glad for the exercise."

Noah shook his hand before Logan headed out. He was about to close his eyes for another rest when the phone beside his bed rang. It had not stopped since word had gone out that he had been found safe. The nurse threatened to remove the phone from his room if he didn't rest.

"How are you doing?" Lieutenant Piekenbrock must have been in a vehicle. Noah could hear the wind noise in the background.

"Better now. I'm ready to head home, but they wanted to keep me for one more night."

"Rest up. I'm just headed to the forensics lab. Results have come in from trace material found from your house."

"Keep me informed if you can. I should be good to go back to work tomorrow."

"Monday at the earliest," a woman said.

Noah looked up at the nurse in the doorway. Miss Woodhill had her arms crossed, and she shook her head back and forth.

"Okay, Monday at the earliest," Noah repeated her statement to the LT, then she nodded and held up one finger before she closed the door.

"Sounds good. Don't rush back. Constable Dickinson will pick you up in the morning. She volunteered."

"I'm not going anywhere. I'll be ready."

Noah pushed the cart with his food tray off to the side. They had given him an order of toast and Jell-O for breakfast, with orange juice and coffee. He was about to get ready to leave when he realized he had a problem.

He had no clothes. The T-shirt and khaki pants he'd worn were too dirty, and they were thrown in the garbage. All he had left to put on were his hiking boots.

It would look a little strange with the blue hospital gown. He was ready to head home regardless. Thirty minutes later, the nurse ran through his vitals and had the doctor sign him off, with many warnings to take it easy.

Soon as she left the room, Angie knocked on the open door.

"Did someone call for an Uber?"

"You didn't have to come all this way, but thanks!"

Angie stepped in, shouldering his backpack. "I picked up a few things from your house. Hope you didn't mind."

"Much better than wearing this home. Thank you."

A quick look in the pack showed much the same thing she wore, jeans and a white T-shirt. His Glock and keys and wallet rested on top.

She stepped outside while Noah got dressed, and he immediately felt better. However, he must have lost more weight than he thought. Without a belt, the jeans hung loose.

Noah shouldered the pack and joined Dickinson out in the hall after one last look around the hospital room.

"Ready."

He kept one hand at the waistband to hold them up, and the other held the backpack and the cloth bag while they walked to her car. As they left the hospital and made their way through the parking lot, Noah could tell something was wrong. She kept her head down and seemed quiet.

Soon as he buckled up, Noah turned to her. "Okay, what's wrong?"

Angie turned her head quickly and saw him staring. She took a deep breath and lowered her gaze. "I'm not sure what to do."

Confused, he asked, "What do you mean?"

"I'm not sure whether to arrest you or not."

"Okay … can you explain, please? I'm listening."

Soon as she started talking about his cabin, Noah knew where this was going. He held up a hand and looked at the clock on the dashboard. "We have a two-and-a-half-hour drive home. More than enough time for me to tell you about my ex-fiancée and what happened."

Noah knew he should have taken care of the cash in the shed but never got around to it. Time for some explaining.

Chapter 30

During the long drive, Noah explained what had happened last fall. However, he left some of the details out. That was between Megan and himself. Angie had seen the cache of weapons and money in the forest shed behind the cabin and had thought he was a dirty cop. The life insurance policy and his fiancée's investments listed him as the sole beneficiary, and he explained the money that way. Angie didn't need to know it was found in a mafia hit-man's home after he attempted to kill Noah. And he certainly didn't want to explain the millions of dollars in secret bank accounts hidden in the Caribbean islands. Besides donating money throughout the community, Noah wasn't too sure what to do with the funds.

Angie had remained silent for a while after Noah finished, digesting the information. "I would suggest possibly a savings account."

He gave a little chuckle. "I'll look into it. Sorry it alarmed you. However, feel free to ask me anything. Okay?"

He could tell Angie felt better when her dimples appeared. Noah talked of his capture and what he had to endure over the last week, and before he knew it, they pulled into his crowded property.

Four cruisers lined the street by his house and several cars were parked along the length of his driveway.

Angie grinned. "Welcome home."

Noah laughed at the large gathering of friends that waited. The chief opened the door for him and helped him out of the car.

"Hope you were surprised!"

As Noah stepped out of the vehicle, the smell of barbeque hit him, and his mouth watered. He had enough of the hospital food. Zane Piekenbrock and Steve Hutchings flipped burgers near the side door while they waved. Noah noticed the cooler beside them. No doubt it held some cold beers.

"You guys are the best trespassers ever." Noah laughed as he shook hands with the crowd. "I'm still tired, but I won't kick you out for an hour at least."

The story had circulated at what happened like wildfire, and Noah had to retell it several times as he made his way through the crowd. Soon he found himself standing beside the LT and staff sergeant as they cooked on his barbeque.

"Looks like you could use a burger." Steve handed him a plate and a can of beer.

"Light beer?" Noah chuckled.

Piekenbrock brought his can up in a silent toast while he winked. "Not until you have fully recovered. No need for a fancy craft beer with flavor." After he took a sip, he let out a sigh of satisfaction. "Too bad, you would have really enjoyed this."

Soon enough, Noah found himself yawning, and the guys took that as a sign to clear everyone out. Those on duty headed back to work, and Hutchings handed him a plate of burgers. "Heat these later and enjoy. Put some meat back on your bones, rookie."

Steve had completed Noah's on-the-job training when he started at APPD, and after all these years, he still called him a rookie. At this point, it just made Noah smile.

Almost everyone had cleared out within a few minutes, and Steve loaded the cooler into the car and drove off. Piekenbrock opened the side door and jerked his thumb inside. "Get to bed and recover for the rest of the day. If you're up to it, pop by work tomorrow. If not, I'll see you Tuesday."

Noah picked up the cloth bag next to the door and handed it to the LT. "I doubt there is any trace left, but here's the lock and shackle. Maybe forensics can find something."

"Thanks, I'll let you know. Now go rest."

"Yes, sir." Noah chuckled and headed inside.

Everything was neatly placed back where it belonged in the kitchen, and Noah put the burgers away in the fridge. Angie had brought in his backpack and left it on the kitchen chair.

He pulled out the Glock and ensured a round was chambered, then brought it with him into the bathroom. It was time for a hot shower. The shower at the hospital, while welcome, didn't have the three jet sprays and rain shower. Not that he was getting soft, but it did feel good.

By the time he climbed in bed, Noah knew he had pushed himself too hard. He may have to take Monday off as well to recover. As he drifted off, his phone chimed with an incoming text message.

He automatically reached over to turn off the volume so he could sleep when his hand paused. The cell phone was not in the bag when Angie picked him up. The last he saw it was seven days ago before he was abducted.

Even if she did have the phone with his belongings, she wouldn't have plugged it in to charge in his bedroom. *Would she?*

Noah picked up the phone from his nightstand and saw he had several text messages from friends, emails, and missed phone calls. He sent Angie a quick text message and leaned back on the pillow while he waited for her reply. Within a minute, the phone vibrated and chimed.

It wasn't with your things we found. Maybe it was in your truck, and someone brought it in for you.

Noah stared at the ceiling above his bed and ran through the scenarios. There wasn't a chance he had left his cell phone in the truck. He scrolled through the text messages from a week ago. Noah definitely had it with him. He would ask around, but he knew what the answer would be.

However, he knew someone that could help—time to call in favors.

Chapter 31

Bob Murphy stood just under six feet, and after thirty-plus years of work for the US Marshals, he appeared to be worn down. Deep lines on his face and a receding hairline made him appear to be older. However, the sparkle in his eyes was from the fact that he was due to retire in September. During his career, he had placed so many in covered protection (witness protection) and helped set up a new life for them that had lost track of the numbers.

After he caught up with Detective Hunter over the phone and knew the reasons behind the request, the Marshal was glad to help out. He leaned back in his desk chair and reread the report from the NSA. At times they could take a few days or weeks to respond to a request for information, but he had an answer within a few hours. Apparently, Noah Hunter was becoming known in certain circles.

The phone was traced from various towers within Arrow Point to Casper, then north to Newcastle, Wyoming, for the time period in question. The return trip was at four o'clock in the morning as it followed the same route back to Arrow Point.

Bob tapped his finger on the desk while he looked at the technical data. The US Marshals have tracked many fugitives as their primary task. While Bob was in charge of the Chicago field office, he did mostly administrative work for the last ten years and had not been out in the field. It was those days he missed the most.

The operation last fall to bring down a mafia family with Noah was the most action he'd had in a long time. Bob made sure that the whole office was in on the takedown, and they had received a blanket commendation for the work.

He knew Hunter was lucky to be alive, and he would gladly help him out, even if it were just information. With a quick look at the small office, Bob's eyes settled on the wall with several mug shots lined up across the corkboard. Bringing in a wanted man and serial killer would be a great way to finish off his career.

Years ago, when hunting with his hound dog, Bob would send him out in the brush to flush out the birds. At sixty-four years old, the marshal knew he wasn't much for the physical work, but he certainly could play the part of the hound dog—anything to help.

With that in mind, he called Noah back with the information and to propose an idea. The sparkle was back in his eyes, and he could not help but grin at the prospect.

"Detective Hunter, Trish MacLean, CNN." In a light green pantsuit, the young woman stood and tucked her clipboard under her left arm while she raised her other hand in the air.

Noah took a sip of water and replaced the cap before he nodded to her. "Go ahead, Mrs. MacLean."

The reporter pulled out her paperwork. "Two questions, Detective. First, how close are you to identifying the victims found? And, what leads are currently being pursued to help identify the killer?"

Noah leaned forward on the podium and spoke into the microphone. "At this time, six of the bodies have been identified. Unfortunately, we have been unable to reach the next of kin for two of them, so their names are being withheld." He glanced down at his notes before he continued. "The names and information of the other four are currently being handed out. As of this moment, we have no ties that link each of the victims."

Noah paused while Constable Dickinson handed out the printed pages. "There will be a conference tomorrow as well, to go over the four bodies that we have identified. As to what leads we have and are pursuing, there are three partial prints from different scenes that we're working with the FBI to hopefully, soon, come up with an identity."

With this revelation, the six reporters shouted more questions, but Noah held up his hand. "This is all the time that we have for now. There will be another update in a few days, hopefully with the murderer behind bars. Thank you."

Noah picked up his notes and water bottle and walked back into the station. A couple of reporters darted off to the side with their cameraman to broadcast the results of the press briefing. After he tucked the notes back into the inner pocket of his suit, Noah strode over to Bob Murphy. The marshal wore jeans and a tan golf shirt, and he kept his badge in his wallet. His visit to Arrow Point was unofficial.

"That was good. Always keep it short and sweet. When they ask the same question with different variations, it's to trip you up. That's when I call it."

Noah chuckled. "It went as planned. I'll take it."

He was surprised to find the US Marshal knock on his side door at his house early Tuesday morning. He flew out that morning, and after landing in Casper, he rented a car for the forty-minute drive to Arrow Point. Bob sat down with him over coffee and went over his idea. It didn't take Noah more than a few seconds to think about it before he grinned and shook his hand.

"Okay, now for the real briefing. This will be hard."

Noah gave a slight nod. "Ready."

Bob stepped forward and squeezed his shoulder before they walked to the station's second floor. The cube was packed full of officers on duty and off, and when the chief saw them enter the room, he yelled for everyone to listen up.

"Thank you, sir." Noah stood in front of the conference room so that everyone could see him. The desks were all full, and the others stood around the outside walls of the cube. Murphy stood off to the side while Noah began.

"If you caught the news briefing, we're moving in on the killer for the cemetery bodies. The partial prints are being matched up. The reporters don't know there was some DNA trace left on the padlock that had me secured. Game Warden Allen was able to find that location, and the evidence was collected."

At this news, a murmur of hope rippled through the room of police officers. Chief Birch stood at the back and smiled while he crossed his arms over his chest.

"Our next step will be to—"

Noah was cut off as a cell phone let out a series of beeps. Bob Murphy grimaced and mumbled an apology while he pulled out his phone. He was never introduced, and everyone in the room wondered who he was. They could tell he was law enforcement. The older man carried himself in a certain manner that they recognized.

"You're going to want to read this, Detective Hunter." Bob handed over his phone.

Noah frowned while he read the message before he looked up. "They have a hit on the prints. The FBI wishes to see me first. Looks like I am off to Cheyenne. That's everything. Thank you."

A buzz of excitement swept through the station as everyone realized that the information would hopefully soon lead to an arrest.

Noah handed the phone back to Bob, and they quietly headed out of the station and drove off in his truck. Several cars and news production vehicles were parked on Main Street. Noah tried not to meet the eyes of the reporters that hung around out front of the station. Noah pulled the visor down and headed west, driving through town.

"How long do you think?"

The marshal looked at his watch, then shrugged. "Two hours, maximum."

"Let's grab some lunch, then start the show."

A set of eyes watched them leave from a second-floor window before the blinds were closed.

Chapter 32

Arrow Point Police Chief Jason Birch sat at his desk on the third floor of the station and read the budget reports. Regardless of what was going on in the real world, they needed to be submitted to the town. When they had to justify and fight for every penny that they needed to do their job, it made him want to throw his hands up in disgust.

With the current case listed as ongoing, their budget was being eaten up at a rate that alarmed him. Everyone wanted results, but they didn't want to pay for them.

The chief's personal cell phone rang, and he recognized the number. "Detective Hunter, how can I help you?"

"Chief, I have a request to make. I need you to conduct a fan-out and Emergency to Report drill."

All officers and civilians employed by APPD had to arrive at the station or contact the station to explain why they could not attend. In addition, should a person be away on holiday or out of state, they had to contact their superior officer and be prepared for their vacation to end. Once every two years, the chief conducted the drill as procedure.

"We're not due for another nine months. What's going on?"

"Sir, I'm not at liberty to fully state the reasons. However, it is relevant to my current case."

When he heard this, the implication of what the detective stated shocked him. "Noah, how sure are you?"

"I have narrowed it down. I'm ninety-nine percent certain."

Jesus Christ.

"If this goes down, you better be one-hundred percent. There can be zero room for error. It must be textbook perfect. Understood?"

"Yes, sir."

Chief Birch took a deep breath and made a decision. "I'll conduct the drill. Be prepared."

"I'll fill you in on everything within the hour, Chief."

"I look forward to it."

Jason pushed himself away from the desk and stared out the window. Closure would be good, and to catch the bastard responsible. Hunter was solid enough that he took the request seriously. The chief picked up the phone. "Doreen, begin the fan-out and Emergency to Report drill."

Birch removed his pistol and holster from the bottom right drawer before he straightened his suit and tie. He trusted Detective Hunter's ability and instinct. However, in this situation, he prayed he was wrong.

*****

It didn't take long for Noah's cell phone to ring, and he acknowledged the order to head to the station. Noah handed his truck keys to Bob. "Call me if you see anything."

"No problem. Good luck."

Noah looked both ways across Main Street before he crossed the road and walked in the station's front door. After a brief lunch, they had parked at the café across the street to wait. It also gave them a view of the station and the many vehicles that came and went. Noah recognized a few cars and cruisers while they had a coffee, but nothing seemed out of place.

As he walked to the second floor, Sergeant Bydal handed him a stack of papers. "We're several months early for this drill. Start at the third page."

Noah looked down to find updated phone numbers and contact information arranged alphabetically. "Got it."

Soon as he sat down at a desk, he began to make calls. No one seemed to notice that he should have been in Cheyenne and not back at headquarters. Soon the station filled up with officers and civilian employees that were called. Most lived nearby. Noah had a small list of those on holidays that were unable to make it in. He reassured them it was a drill and to enjoy their vacation.

Noah had gone through his list within an hour, and he moved to the conference room where the chief sat with human resources and Sergeant Bydal going through the lists.

Noah handed in the sheets, and they checked off the names from the master list and kept it updated as more people were accounted for.

It didn't take long for the chief to pull Noah to the side, and he showed him the master list. There were only nine names on the page that they had not been able to contact. Three names were civilian employees absent and four constables away on vacation, but he had left a message for them to report in.

Only two names stood out.

Lieutenant Zane Piekenbrock and Staff Sergeant Steve Hutchings.

Chapter 33

Detective Hunter closed the chief's office door and sat in the leather chair across from the desk.

Chief Birch called up the report on his monitor, and with a flick of his hand, it spun around to face Noah. He had never seen the chief angry before, and he pointed a thick finger at Noah then tapped the screen.

"Explain."

"The shooter had to have been at my home previously to know the exact location of the security cameras and where to take the shots. They also left me a present taped to my side door."

Noah went over the story of the handcuff key and the path used to avoid facial recognition. "They knew too much."

Detective Hunter pulled out his cell and showed it to the chief. "This phone was on me when I was taken. It was tracked from Arrow Point to west of Newcastle, and it was then kept in Arrow Point for a week. It bounced the signals off of various towers in the area. However, the day of my return, it stopped. When I went to bed after I was home, it was plugged in beside my bed as it charged."

The chief collapsed in his chair, and it was dangerously close to tipping. His fingers drummed on the desktop to a slow beat.

"Constable Dickinson used your keys to open your house so we could set up the barbeque and welcome home party. I'm fairly certain you wouldn't mind, or I wouldn't have asked her to do so."

Noah shook his head. "Of course, I don't mind. However, there were thirty people there that would have had access to my house. They are all cops or employed with us."

"What about the DNA evidence and prints? Who does that point to?"

Noah winced. "It doesn't exist. I haven't heard back from the game warden yet."

The chief let out a sigh once he understood. "What did you hope to accomplish today?"

Noah pointed at the monitor with the fan-out results. "I believed the suspect would run. However, I can't see either Piekenbrock or Hutchings being the killer. So, I hope we can clear them and move on. Right now, I just find it strange that both of those men were in attendance at my homecoming, and now they have not responded to the ETR drill."

Chief Birch called up all the evidence logs, and they went over it together for the next hour. "Sorry, sir. Everything seems to point toward someone that works here. Now, today was a test, but …."

The chief stood abruptly. "First, let's find the LT and staff sergeant before we move to that next step. I'm sure something has just come up."

Noah called Bob and mentioned there were two possibilities, and they were going to check them out. He would call back with updates in a few hours. Everyone was dismissed as they found out it was just a drill. However, the LT and staff sergeant were still to be found, and those on duty were to look for them.

Detective Hunter headed back to the cube and found Constable Dickinson wearing jeans and a nice blouse at a desk. Her hair was curled with a light touch of makeup.

"I was on a lunch date with Sarah and had to run out on her."

Noah had a quick look around at the cube. There were too many nearby that could overhear. "Come with me for a minute."

He led her into the conference room, locked the door behind them, and explained what was happening. It didn't take long for Angie to understand the possibilities and the implications of what the results of the fan-out could be.

"You are off today. Did you want to go back to your lunch or go for a ride and see if we can find them?"

"Sarah's shift starts in an hour. I'll go with you. Let me grab a gun, and I'll meet you out back in a few minutes."

He started the cruiser, and within five minutes, they were headed across town to Piekenbrock's home when the call came over the radio. The LT's Jeep was spotted at Hutchings's home, still running in the driveway. No sign of either man.

Noah flicked on the flashers and turned the cruiser around to head north. He instructed the constable to remain at the end of the driveway and not to approach.

Constable Warren Wright stood next to his vehicle and waited for Detective Hunter. "I looked in the Jeep. It's empty."

The young police officer stood a few inches taller than Dickinson. Noah couldn't help but wonder what was in the town's water when he had to look up at him.

"Wright, I want you to search the perimeter with Dickinson. I'll try the door."

They both nodded and darted around the right side of the old bungalow. The home was at the end of a quiet dead-end court, and there wasn't any foot traffic in the area. Noah had been here many times over the years.

When he reached the running Jeep, Noah tried the driver's door, but it was unlocked. Once he turned off the vehicle, he left the keys on the floormat before going to the front door. Hutchings's old Ford pickup truck wasn't in the driveway. It could be parked in the double car garage near the back.

Noah made sure the button on the suit jacket was open to draw his Glock without any issue. He tried the front door only to find it locked. He knocked a few times and called out, "Steve? Are you home?"

White curtains hung in the window, and he couldn't see inside. By the time he moved to the side door, the two constables had joined him.

Angie kept one hand on her pistol as they circled the home, while Wright was confused at their actions. Noah moved to the side door but found that locked as well. "Garage next."

The double garage took over most of the backyard, with a large barn-style roof and two doors that were opened by remote. Noah had helped build it over twelve years ago, and he knew of the side door that led into the backyard.

The two main doors were locked, and so was the side door. He shone a light inside the window built into the door, and his blood instantly chilled.

A pair of dress shoes and pants were visible on the floor, but the workbench blocked the rest of the view. Noah did notice the unnatural angle and the lack of movement. "Oh my God."

Noah's forehead rested against the glass as he fought down the desire to be sick. "Hutchings … what's going on?"

Chapter 34

"Warren, call an ambulance."

Noah turned his back to the door, brought up his left knee, and bent over at the same time the heel of his dress shoe connected solidly beneath the handle of the door. The maneuver cracked the frame. A second blow blew pieces of wood inside, and the door flung back into the wall.

He turned on the light and momentarily froze. Lieutenant Piekenbrock lay face down on the concrete floor. His left arm was underneath his torso, and his right arm stretched out above him. Noah knelt down and slowly rolled him over onto his back. He placed his ear down to the LT's nose and confirmed he was still breathing.

His chest rose and fell in a steady rhythm.

Noah loosened Zane's tie and top button and rolled him into the recovery position. "Wright, stay here with the LT. Dickinson, you are with me."

As they moved to the rear door, Noah heard Wright on the radio calling for an ambulance. Hunter held open the screen door, and Angie stepped forward. Her heel connected below the handle. The door exploded inward. The short hallway opened to the large kitchen. Straight ahead was the living room, and to the left, the opening led to the hallway, two bedrooms and a bathroom.

"Steve? Are you here? It's Noah."

The detective drew his Glock. He braced his grip with his left hand and gave Dickinson a nod. "Going in."

She drew her pistol and covered the corners as they entered the empty kitchen. There was nothing in the living room either. They worked well as a team. The first bedroom down the hall was set up as an office, and it looked ransacked. Drawers were open on the desk, and it appeared items were missing. The laptop and the few pictures on the wall were no longer there, just a bare nail and a dust ring on the desk.

Noah stepped out into the hallway and felt Angie's touch on his left shoulder. He glided forward, and they stepped through the doorway into the bedroom. Gun barrels led the way as they cleared the room.

"Begin secondary sweep."

They checked the closets and all possible hiding spots but came up empty. The bedroom dresser drawers were open, and the closet had mostly empty hangers.

Noah holstered his pistol, and with a last look around, he grimaced. "It looks like someone packed in a hurry."

Angie nodded and placed her gun away as well. "I hear the ambulance."

Within a minute, two paramedics started work on Piekenbrock while Noah moved off to the side to call the chief. He didn't want to jump to any conclusions, but this didn't look good. The only person with answers just received a dose of naloxone to help stabilize him as he was lifted onto their cart and loaded into the ambulance.

"Mr. Hunter?"

A hand touched his shoulder, and Noah opened his eyes to see a nurse beside his chair.

"He's awake?"

She nodded and gestured for him to enter the room.

"Thank you."

A glance at his watch showed he had been asleep for over an hour. Before he entered, Noah sent a text message off to the chief to let him know the LT was conscious. As far as Noah could recall, Piekenbrock didn't have any family nearby, maybe a few cousins in Florida, but he was not sure.

Zane sat in the hospital bed wearing a pale green gown. An IV was taped to the back of his wrist, and he was connected to various machines besides the bed as his vitals were monitored.

When he saw Noah, he groaned. "Now I know what you went through. I feel like crap."

"Pounding headache, dry mouth?" Noah sat on the only chair and passed over a cup of water.

"Thanks." Piekenbrock drank most of it. "The doctor said I would be kept for a few hours, and if the blood test is fine, I can go home."

Noah nodded and pulled out a notepad and pen. "It's time for your statement if you're up for it."

The LT took a deep breath before he started. "After your briefing, I headed home, and, on the way, Hutchings's truck drove past. He was easily forty miles an hour over the limit across Main Street. I followed him to see if everything was okay."

He paused to have another sip of water. "When I got to his place, he was in the garage and had grabbed a cardboard box and started to tape it up. I asked what was wrong, and he said, 'family emergency' and he had to go."

Constable Dickinson knocked on the door and poked her head in. "Is it okay to join you? Are you okay, sir?"

"I'm better by the minute. Come on in."

She gave a slight smile and stood just inside the room.

Piekenbrock had another sip of water, then frowned as he recalled the events. "I asked if he wanted me to lock up his service pistol at the station while he was gone. He handed it to me, and as I walked away, I felt a sting on my ass. Next thing I know, I woke up here."

Angie took a deep breath.

Noah's mouth dropped open. "I've known him my whole career …."

The LT held up his hand. "I've known him longer, and this doesn't look good at all. Follow procedure above all else. I hope there's a logical solution because I don't see this will end well."

Noah finished his notes, then told Zane everything he found within the house. "It looks like he packed in a hurry, and we've been unable to locate him."

The LT's hands clenched with controlled anger, and his blood pressure spiked on the display. "Follow procedure. Inform the chief. I'll check myself out of here. We have work to do."

Chapter 35

To say the chief didn't take it well would have been an understatement. Birch went from one end of the spectrum to the other with his emotions. Denial and disbelief turned to shock and horror as the facts aligned. Within a minute, rage and retaliation came out on top as he went to work. Twenty minutes later, pictures of Staff Sergeant Steve Hutchings were sent to every law enforcement agency across the country.

Every airport and rail depot, and bus station would have his picture shown to every worker. "I want your focus to shift. Assemble anyone you need. I'll have the proper paperwork drawn up soon to tear his house apart. Start there. Move." The police chief had leaned forward on the desk. He never blinked as he stared at Hunter, but he could see his teeth grind as his jaw clenched.

"Yes, sir." Noah slowly closed the office door and took a minute to stand in the hall and collect his thoughts. One thing he did know was to never get on the chief's bad side. He had never seen him like this, and to be quite frank, it scared him.

Noah took over a desk on the second floor and typed in the notes from Piekenbrock's statement. While he thought of it, he sent an email to IT and told them to suspend Hutchings's login for the system and to grant his information to himself. He would start the search there.

Waves of disbelief still washed over him as he closed his eyes to think back over his career. After Noah completed his courses and training at Douglas Law Enforcement Center, he paired up with (then) Sergeant Hutchings. When you spend forty to sixty hours per week in a cruiser with someone, you end up knowing them quite well.

They ended up being together for over two years before Hutchings's hip had bothered him too much. When Staff Sergeant Don Andersen retired, Steve had moved to work inside the station. Despite being called rookie, they had always gotten along, and Noah considered him a brother. At this point, it was almost a sign of affection. Not that Hutch would admit it.

The fact that Hutchings had a secret serial killer life, Noah found hard to believe. However, every interview from a neighbor he had ever done ended with, "he was so quiet and nice, I had no idea he could have killed his wife," or something to that effect. In the end, almost everything can be hidden from others—a hard lesson to learn about the dark side of humanity.

Noah opened his eyes, ran his hand through his hair, then sent off the warrant requests to obtain cell phone records, internet and finances. He was about to head back to see the chief when the front desk had him paged.

As he walked behind the desk, Noah smiled. Bob Murphy, dressed in his marshal's uniform, stood among six other large men, similarly dressed.

"Detective Hunter, nice to run into you again. I just happened to be in Arrow Point on vacation when the call for a fugitive came in. As the senior marshal in the state, I asked for assistance to apprehend."

The six other men looked like they played for the NFL in their spare time. All were large, and they packed the small lobby, almost shoulder to shoulder.

Noah could not help but chuckle. "Glad APPD accepted my application. I doubt I would have made your height requirement. Come on in, and I'll brief everyone in the conference room."

Noah was glad for the help, and he knew he would learn a lot from the US Marshals. He did not know too much about tracking a fugitive, but he was a fast learner.

*****

The log cabin had seen better days. The crack in the southern window on the second floor had expanded last winter and allowed a family of squirrels to explore and build a nest inside. Thirty years ago, the cabin was a beautiful place, filled with laughter from a family that visited on the weekends and holidays, and a group of men used it in the fall and spring as a hunting camp.

The open-timbered ceiling was twelve feet tall over a large room with a fieldstone fireplace on the west wall. The opposite end had a kitchen with a wood-burning stove and cupboards. The long pine table with two benches that filled up the other corner could have easily sat twelve.

A set of steep stairs went up to the loft in the living room, and around the fireplace were three couches that had seen better days. The fabric was gold and brown plaid color that was popular several decades previous. The small coffee table had a stack of outdoor fishing and hunting magazines. Mixed in were a few National Geographics from the seventies.

Everything was covered in a layer of dust, and the ceiling above the kitchen looked like it had water damage. The cabin had not been used in a long time.

Until recently.

The low rumble of snoring filled the main floor as he shifted on the couch and attempted to get comfortable.

He gave up, grabbed a magazine off the table and threw it at the ceiling. "Shut the hell up. Fucking squirrels!"

Steve Hutchings couldn't wait to take his revenge on the rodents. He had definite plans to shoot each one in the head. He grumbled about squirrel stew as he lay back down and drifted off to sleep.

Chapter 36

"I always start at one end and work my way to the other. If you work with a partner, each takes a room. That way, nothing will be missed."

Despite being on the APPD for over eighteen years, Noah took mental notes when he worked with the marshal. Bob's experience and ten years as a beat cop in Detroit were evident. The majority of his career was spent mainly in the pursuit of fugitives, and he was excellent at his job.

"I have one officer upstairs and another outside. So, let's get started."

The warrants had come through, and Noah had begun to go through every aspect of the staff sergeant's life. One of the marshals specialized in forensic accounting, and he remained at the station while the rest of the team started at the house. Constable Dickinson began in the garage while Noah watched for a moment as Bob started. He checked for false panels and lifted the carpet.

Noah was uncomfortable with someone over his shoulder while he worked, and he figured the marshal felt the same, so he moved to the kitchen. He had been in Steve's home several dozen times over the year, but he had never looked around, and it made him feel awkward. Noah pushed those feelings aside and began to work.

He took out all the contents of the freezer and examined each before he placed them back. Same for the refrigerator, then each cupboard. The latex gloves made his hands sweat, and he grew warm enough that his hair grew damp. In the third drawer, down under the cutlery, Noah found alcohol swabs individually wrapped, like the type found in a first-aid kit. Unsure if they could be related, he used a camera to photograph and record the finding, then bagged them as evidence and noted where they were found.

Under the sink, he grabbed a large black garbage bag and laid it out on the floor before he took the trash and upended it over the makeshift tarp. The small piece of orange plastic was mixed in with the coffee grounds, and he almost missed it. Noah held it up to confirm what he found. It resembled the cap that went over the end of a syringe.

Each piece of evidence hit Noah like another nail in the coffin, and it almost felt like a physical blow. He took a few more photographs and filled out another evidence bag and dropped the cap inside as he took a deep breath and slowly let it out.

"Detective Hunter? You'll want to see this." Angie leaned in the door off the kitchen to the backyard.

Noah could feel the hammer ready to drive the final nail home as he followed her out to the garage. Angie had been busy, and it looked like she had found a few items worthy of note. Her camera was set up to take a picture. However, it was under the workbench. Once he knelt, Noah could see a syringe up against the wall. It was fully depressed and empty.

"I also found this wrapped inside the canvas tarp."

It was a small black cloth case with a zipper around three sides. It was open and inside were two empty syringes held in place by the elastic retainer and a small empty glass container with a stainless-steel lid.

The plastic cap he found in the garbage matched the two that were still on the unused syringes. "Document it fully and log it in as evidence."

Noah had noticed the printed label on the glass container. It was the exact match to those used at the veterinary clinic. He left Dickinson to her work, stepped outside the garage into the backyard and sat down at the small patio set. He had sat in this same chair many times over the years.

As a rookie, one of the harder lessons had been to partition his mind and not bring it home with him when he left work. Noah had lost a couple of girlfriends in the past because he was unable to flick the switch in his brain and turn the cop part off. Right now, he found himself in the opposite situation. He had to turn off the personal feelings and emotional side of his brain and keep the switch jammed into the professional police position.

Noah pulled out his cell phone and called the station. He wanted to be updated and kept in touch with any financial actions taken. The taller US Marshal, Daryl Sedore, took up the same amount of space as a refrigerator. Once he sat at a desk and wore his dark-rimmed glasses, his large fingers flew over the keyboard.

"Go ahead."

Noah heard the click-clack as he typed. "Any updates?"

There was a pause before the deep baritone voice grunted, "Yes, and no. New information is coming in every minute, but no leads as of yet. I'm now going through income tax statements from 2001 onward and soon will move credit card transactions."

"I'll let you go then. Call me if needed."

Noah hung up, and he was about to return to the kitchen when Bob opened the back door. He carried a photo album in his latex-covered hands, placing it on the table so Noah could see where he pointed.

The first picture had two little boys walking along a creek, and each had a fishing rod over one shoulder. The next image had a large family gathering, with almost two dozen people as they sat down to eat at several picnic tables. In the background, against a forest backdrop, was a large log cabin.

"Do you know anything about this place?"

Noah stared at the pictures before he identified the one boy. "That looks like Hutchings, but I can't be positive."

The marshal flipped to the last few pages of the album. "There are a few more pictures, taken several years later. I believe it's him."

The picture was of a young man with long hair as he sat with his arm around the shoulder of an older woman (more than likely his grandmother) as they sat in front of a large stone fireplace inside the cabin.

Noah nodded in agreement. "That's him, I believe."

Bob closed the album. "Do you know anything about the cabin? Location?"

"Nothing. I do know that he doesn't have much family left. A few distant cousins, possibly. His wife died over twenty-five years ago, and he has no children."

Bob sat down across from him. "How did his wife die?"

"Heart attack. She was only thirty-years old."

The marshal let out a sigh, then shook his head. "Once you dig into his past, you may find more people who have died around him. Their deaths will be questioned. It may not have been just a heart attack."

Noah looked down at the closed photo album and he felt the world tilt under him. Everything would be suspect if it had to deal with his old partner. Every case he worked on as well.

"I need to get back to work. It helps to take my mind off things."

He headed back to the kitchen, but he couldn't help wonder what he had gotten himself into. *Hutch, you better have some answers ready.*

Chapter 37

By the time Noah finished, he was tired, physically and emotionally. They didn't find anything else inside or out. There had not been any reports from the Wyoming Highway Patrol or anything on his credit cards or bank account activity.

When they were back at the station, Bob took him aside. "This isn't technically our case, and I have heard that our help is limited. So, we have to pull the plug tomorrow, and fly home."

"I can't thank you enough for what you've done. It's appreciated." Noah shook his hand and shrugged. "We have a great head start on the search, thanks to you."

"Any time. If, at any time, you're up for a career change, let me know. You're a good man."

"Will do."

After they said their goodbyes, Noah headed into the station to log the evidence and finish the reports.

When he arrived on the second floor, he saw Marshal Sedore bent over the keyboard. Noah figured he was six-foot-three and must weigh close to three-hundred pounds of muscle. He seemed to know his way around a computer. Thick fingers flew across the keyboard with accuracy, then a brief rest while reading the screen before starting again.

Noah had a glance at the stacks of paper on the desk. They were all financial statements from the bank. They went back over two decades.

"Everything okay?" Noah sat down beside the marshal at an empty desk.

Sedore was jarred from his world of numbers and facts before he turned to Noah. "After I talked to Murphy, I went through the bank records once again." His large hand tapped the second pile of paperwork beside him. "Last fall, it appears that Hutchings wrote two separate checks for property taxes."

Noah raised his eyebrows as the implication sunk in. "He had a second property?"

The marshal nodded. "I believe this cheque was for his home, written to the town." He showed Noah the printout, and he recognized Steve's writing on the paperwork. In the memo section on the cheque, *Property Taxes* was filled out.

The date in the upper right corner was mid-November last year. At that time, Noah was in the hospital in Chicago as he recovered from a few injuries.

The marshal pulled out a second photocopy, and it showed him a similar cheque. "This one is made out to the Natrona County Tax Office for a lesser amount."

Property Taxes was once again written in the memo section.

"My LT has the contacts with the county offices, and we can locate the property when they open in the morning. Good job."

Daryl smiled. "Thank you, however, this was fairly easy. Just follow the money."

Noah couldn't help himself, so he added, "If you're ever looking for a job, let me know. We'd be glad to have you."

A range of emotions danced across the large man's face when he smiled. "You never know. Thanks, Detective."

"I'll see you in the morning. I hope we can wrap this up and get some answers."

As they packed up, Noah couldn't help but wonder if some answers were better left hidden.

*****

Hutchings sat upon the old but comfortable couch. The squirrels' antics had calmed down last night, and he had a good sleep. Several magazines lay in front of the fireplace after he'd thrown them at the ceiling. The stack on the coffee table remained several inches tall. He had plenty of ammunition to keep them quiet for their next party.

Unable to stand the mess, he shuffled over to the fireplace, picked up the lot, and stacked them on the table. The cabin contained many happy memories from when he was younger with his family. However, a mess was never tolerated. He had hoped to fix it up and retire here. He gave a sharp bark of laughter at this absurdity.

That isn't likely to happen now.

The former staff sergeant sat down, planted his elbows on his knees, and held his head. No doubt his days were numbered. For the tenth time, Steve went over the steps that led him here and tried to find the mistakes made.

Alone, with his memories in the old cabin, he vowed not to go down without a fight. It was time to find out what this old dog had in his bag of tricks.

Chapter 38

Noah awoke before his alarm sounded. The night sky had just begun to lighten into shades of red with the sun well below the horizon.

With all the stress of the past week, he felt the need to burn off some energy and get back into his routine. Wearing running shoes, shorts, and a T-shirt, he stepped outside and started some stretches before he went for a light run.

In his mind, Noah went through all the countless hours that he had spent with Hutchings—when they trained together, worked cases, to beers and barbeques. He had no warning indication of what went on in the man's mind. He was certainly rough around the edges on some points, and most considered him old school. If there was a problem, Steve had no issues with a few smacks to the head to drive the point home. *Take your lumps, learn from them, and move on. Don't make the same mistake again.* Those were some of his first words of advice when he was a rookie.

Soon the rhythm and pace carried him along while he tried to let his mind drift. Finally, after fifteen minutes, he stumbled and nearly fell as one thought leaped to mind. An inconsistency in one of his reports. It would be something he would have to clarify later. *This* is why he used to love running in the morning. It gave him time to reflect, as well as it kept him in shape.

Back at his house, he showered and shaved. Instead of the normal suit, he dressed in his blue tactical uniform and placed the large duffel bag of knee and elbow pads, vest, and helmet into the backseat of the truck. Noah figured today would call for something other than a suit and tie, and he wanted to be prepared. He pulled the Glock from his shoulder holster and slid it into the right leg harness. Even though he was now used to a suit at work, he preferred the uniform.

Noah ran a finger across the old rank on the shoulders—three chevrons of a sergeant. *Was there an insignia for a detective?* Another question for another time. He grabbed a bottle of water and a protein bar as he headed out the door. The morning sun gave the promise of a nice day in a cloudless sky, and Noah took that as a good omen.

Once he arrived at the station, Noah looked over a few reports and the marshal's findings. He was impressed with how Sedore navigated the financial background. A look at the large clock on the wall showed the day shift wouldn't start for another hour, and the county offices wouldn't be open for three hours.

Soon Noah was lost in the paperwork as he went back to the first report and worked methodically through the whole case. He started a page of handwritten notes, items to follow-up. Now that Hutchings was a suspect, all the facts seemed to make more sense. He had access to the new carbon handcuffs when they were issued.

When Lieutenant Piekenbrock arrived, Noah gave him a quick wave while he tried to hide his amusement. Of a similar mind, the LT had forgone his usual suit and wore his tactical gear as well. His Browning Hi-power 9mm was in the drop-leg holster, too. He always preferred the Browning, while Noah was fine with the Glock 17.

"Just in case we have to kick in some doors."

Noah agreed. "Unfortunately, you may be correct."

Piekenbrock pulled up a chair and sat. "I wanted to talk to you for a minute." When Noah nodded, he continued. "Hutchings could have killed us both if he wanted. I don't know what's going on in his head, but he is sick. He needs help. I want it to be us that brings him in. Keep this in house, so to speak, as much as we can."

That had been one item that had bothered Noah. They could have been dead, but they were fine. "I understand. I would rather it be just us as well."

Noah filled him in on the financial statements, and Piekenbrock added, "That's good work. I'll call Caroline at the county offices when they open."

"What would you like for the press brief today?"

The LT paused. "I'll get Sergeant Bydal to handle it. There are no new developments, as far as the press needs to know. I don't want him tipped off that we may be closing in."

They went over a few logistical items, and then the lieutenant went into the corner office. A phone call from Bob Murphy confirmed that they would be unable to assist further but to keep him informed. He would be on the eight o'clock morning flight back to Chicago.

Noah made a mental note to send him a nice bottle of single-malt for his help once this was all over.

Constable Dickinson arrived, and they went through the new developments. Angie wanted to continue the search for Hutchings's truck and go through the state-wide reports. In Wyoming, it seemed that every other household had a pickup truck, but Angie seemed determined.

As Sergeant Bydal headed out to the press brief, Noah emailed the chief to keep him in the loop. The early morning hours passed without event until the office door opened and Lieutenant Piekenbrock stepped into the cube.

He held a piece of paper up and gave Noah the thumbs-up sign. "I have the location. Ready?"

"I'll meet you out back in a few minutes. I'll sign out a few things from the arsenal."

The LT nodded. "Hope we don't need them, but I better join you. I don't know what state of mind he's in or what weapons he has by now. A cornered animal is more dangerous."

Noah knew what to do with a trapped animal, and he hoped it wouldn't come to that. Right now, he wasn't sure if he could pull the trigger.

Chapter 39

The countryside didn't change on their drive south of Casper along the 220 West. The plains of Wyoming stretched before them, with the prominent low mountain ranges and large outcrops of rock that filled the landscape. There were small patches of pine clustered, and they became more common as they approached the town of Alcova.

As they passed a large trailer park, Noah pointed out the driver's window. "I used to camp there when I was a kid with my family in an old pop-up trailer. I don't think that lake ever warmed up."

Alcova Lake had a reservoir, and it was a popular place for tourists and families to camp. The town only had a few dozen people that lived there full time, and they depended on the travelers and tourists for their livelihood.

On the southern side of the lake, off an old road, was the cottage, nestled midway down a canyon. The satellite imagery showed an area partially forested with a creek that would eventually empty into the lake.

Noah pulled the unmarked cruiser to the side and picked up the map. "What would you figure is the best approach?"

The LT pointed to an area outside the property. "I couldn't get the map to show any better detail, but it looks as if there's a long driveway. I would say to park down the road, and we advance on foot. He may have surveillance on the main approach."

Noah was about to comment when both their cell phones chimed with a text message:

We have located Sergeant Hutchings's vehicle. It was in the police impound lot behind AJ's! I'll keep you informed of any new information. Cst D.

"How could it have been in the impound lot?" Noah thought out loud. AJs was the mechanic APPD used, and he had an acre lot behind the store. Against the western fence, a few dozen wrecked vehicles were constantly being salvaged for parts, and the town paid for the police to use the east side as an impound area.

The LT put his phone away and shrugged. "If his truck is still in Arrow Point, there's no way he could make it out here. Maybe we should head back. It's your call. You are lead."

Noah drummed his fingers on the steering wheel while he thought about it. Hutchings had been missing for three days, and they didn't have any leads besides the newly found truck. If they could cross the cabin off the list as a potential hideout, they could focus elsewhere. Besides, he didn't want to waste the trip, and the property was only another fifteen minutes. "I would rather carry on and confirm the cabin is vacant. We're almost here, but if you want, we can head back."

Piekenbrock shook his head. "I'm good. Let's go."

The road from town stretched around the western edge of the lake, and it soon became a gravel road. The dust plume rose behind the unmarked cruiser as Noah slowed and swerved to avoid the potholes.

There was only one other driveway along the way, but it looked as if the cabin was fairly remote with no close neighbors.

"Here." Piekenbrock pointed to the side. One hundred yards ahead, they could see a four-foot pyramid of rocks that marked the turn. The area was mostly covered in a scrub bush and small clusters of pine. The hillside sloped toward the lake, and the cabin was built in a small flat canyon that leveled out before it continued.

Noah turned off the cruiser and stepped outside. As he looked toward the property, he realized how much lower it was than the road, and he could see the tops of the trees. "The area around the cabin seems to have a lot more vegetation. It'll provide us cover on the approach."

The LT went over to the side. "No tracks. Nothing has gone farther than us in a while. It hasn't rained in a week, so no tracks have been washed out."

"We should be out of here within fifteen minutes then."

Noah opened the truck and rifled through the duffel bag. He slipped on his elbow, knee pads, and vest while Piekenbrock did the same. Noah needed a haircut when the tactical helmet felt snug. Once the chin strap was in place, he picked up the yellow Taser and slid it into the utility belt holster. He confirmed the Glock was loaded and ready to draw from the leg harness. Noah opened the weapons case and pulled out a black 12-gauge Remington shotgun, while the LT removed his own 300 Winchester magnum. With the terrain, it made sense to have a ranged weapon. Noah was a horrible shot with a long gun. While Zane grew up with one in his hand, he loved to hunt and had fired rifles all his life.

Noah fed the communication earpiece up through his vest, and after he inserted the plug, they did a quick comms check.

Within a few minutes, both men were ready.

"I'll take the high ground to the north of the cabin and approach. Will radio once I'm in position." Lieutenant Piekenbrock strode down the road and headed into a thicket of pine trees, past the driveway. Noah double-checked his gear a final time, followed the LT's prints down the road but headed into the property fifty yards before the driveway.

The ground was rugged, and he had to slow the pace or easily turn an ankle on the loose rock. He held the first position inside a large cluster of trees while he waited for the LT to let him know he was ready. Pine needles littered the ground, allowing him to walk through the area in silence.

Noah was surprised when his cell phone chimed with another text message. He didn't want that noise to alert anyone of his presence and pulled it out of his vest pocket and switched it to vibrate. After he read the message, he couldn't help but grin. Dickinson was hard at work:

I thought AJ didn't have any security cameras for the rear compound, but some were installed last week. We are going over the footage now, will update. Cst D.

With one bar of reception, Noah was surprised he had a signal at all. He hoped the LT also turned his volume down.

Through his earpiece, Noah heard a low whisper, but the static was fairly bad. They were only a few hundred yards apart, and the signal should have been fine. Nevertheless, he recognized Piekenbrock's voice.

"Moving in," Noah replied before continuing down the rocky slope toward the cabin. The shotgun stock butt-plate tight into his shoulder. Soon the peaked roof came into view as he drew closer.

Hopefully, this will be resolved soon.

Chapter 40

Angie sent the updates and headed toward the building. The forensics team would be at the compound shortly to tow the Ford truck back to the lab.

AJ's Garage had three large work bays and an office off the lobby. Two mechanics worked on vehicles on the hoists while she walked through the lobby and knocked on the office door. AJ was a large black man with hands that could wrap around a football. His short hair had started to turn white around the temples and in his mustache and beard. Despite that, he looked much younger than his fifty years. He wore a dark blue set of overalls, like the other mechanics, that were stained from hard work.

He pushed his glasses back up on his nose as he stood when Angie knocked on the office door. She could tell he was surprised to see that she was taller than him by a few inches.

"Constable Angie Dickinson, just need to ask you a few questions about the Ford pickup truck on the police side of your yard." She ignored his dirty hands and gave him a firm handshake.

"Sit down, please." There was one chair on the other side of the metal desk. The small office had a bookshelf against the long wall and a calendar next to a window that overlooked the rear of the building. The faint smell of grease and oil fought with the air freshener. "I don't know anything about the truck. It was just there a few days ago."

AJ pulled down a large blue binder and opened it to the midway point. "This is the police log for vehicles that enter or leave." He spun it around and showed Angie. "There's no record of it being dropped off."

Disappointed, she nodded. "Okay, thank you. We're trying to locate the driver."

"I may be able to help you with that. With the insurance changes, we got a break on our rates if we had cameras installed. They have been here for only a week now."

"That would be great! Thank you." Angie pulled out her cell phone and sent a text message off to Lieutenant Piekenbrock and Detective Hunter. She wanted to keep them informed of any developments.

"We had three cameras installed. Give me a second. This is all new to me." AJ pulled out a small notebook and used his hand-written notes to log into the computer and navigate the security program. "How far back do you want to go?"

"Last Sunday, after one o'clock in the afternoon."

He pushed his glasses back up his nose once again and leaned forward, closer to the monitor. His large hand turned the monitor to the side so they could both watch.

"After seven days, the system would start to record over old footage. However, we're good. Here you go."

The camera angle was from the corner of the building on the roof, and it had a good view of anyone entering or leaving the compound.

"There it is." His voice was calm as he pointed at the monitor.

Angie looked at the timestamp: 1:17 p.m.

The white truck drove straight through the open gate, and it disappeared into the yard. Angie couldn't control herself when the driver got out. She stood so fast she knocked the chair over backward.

"Holy fuck! You have to be kidding me."

Her hands shook as she reached for her phone.

*****

The thick pine provided Noah cover as he went downhill toward the cabin. A few old trees had fallen, but he easily walked around or stepped over them. Fifty feet away from the tree line, the cabin sat within a large clearing.

The building was over eighty feet long, and it appeared to have a loft second floor. Noah could see the covered porch, and the front door was closed. He searched but could not spot the LT. He would have an angle and good coverage of the front door and the north side.

He kept the cabin in view as he stayed within the pine trees, making his way to the rear. The building had seen better days. Saplings and tall weeds grew up next to the stone foundation. A second-floor window looked broken, and a large piece of glass was missing.

The rear of the building had a small set of wooden stairs that led down from the back door. A rusted stove pipe came out of the side, and it rose above the roof. Noah guessed it was the kitchen with a wood stove. He had much the same arrangement at his cabin. The larger stone chimney on the far side would have been from a fireplace.

Noah toggled the comms switch. "Moving to the rear of the cabin. Maintain coverage on the front."

He kept his index finger across the trigger guard, and the barrel pointed down as he stepped out from behind a large white pine. Then, with tentative steps, he crossed the clearing to the back door.

The breeze picked up, which made the treetops dance back and forth. Besides the occasional bird call, Noah couldn't hear a thing. They could easily have been a hundred miles from civilization.

He stepped forward, lowered his weight onto the first step, and reached up with his left hand to try the door. It easily turned, and with a slight click, it opened.

Noah expected the door to creak and make a lot of noise, but it was silent. He could smell the age of the cabin, and a faint hint of mildew and dust hit him as he stepped up to the kitchen door.

Just inside was an old kitchen table. In the middle of the table was an issued police utility belt and holstered sidearm.

Jesus Christ!

Noah brought the shotgun into his shoulder and started to sweep the area inside. He almost fired into the kitchen cupboards when a voice croaked out. "About fucking time you got here, rookie."

Chapter 41

Noah blinked for his eyes to adjust to the inside. Across the kitchen into the living room, a figure sat on a couch near the fireplace. The window on the far side had him in a silhouette, but Noah recognized him right away.

The shotgun barrel came up smoothly. "Hands in the air, stand and turn around." He was surprised that his voice sounded firm, and there weren't any tremors in his hand. This was the moment he dreaded.

"I can put my hands up, but you're going to have to help me stand."

Noah moved farther into the kitchen, past the table. Steve Hutchings sat on one of three couches, with both hands in the air.

He was in uniform and appeared to have problems. His hands shook, and he couldn't raise them too far. Then Noah heard a noise that sounded familiar.

He took one more step and looked down. A feeling of dread washed over him like a tidal wave.

An iron shackle attached to Steve's ankle was held in place with a large black padlock and chain. The chain was seven feet long, and the other end was attached to an eye-bolt drilled into the base of the stone fireplace.

"What the hell?"

Steve's arms dropped, and he had trouble keeping his head upright. Noah stepped back and placed the shotgun on the kitchen table before rushing forward to his friend.

"Can you stand?"

"Think so. Could you help me? I don't have much energy."

"Do you know what happened? How did you get here?"

Noah grabbed his hands and helped him to his feet, then turned his attention to the chain. As he was about to kneel, his cell phone vibrated. He could feel it through the Kevlar vest.

"Just a second."

Noah read another text from Dickinson, and he couldn't believe what he saw. It was a picture of Lieutenant Piekenbrock as he walked out of the police compound. Angie wrote:

I'm confirming that LT Piekenbrock dropped Sgt's truck off at the impound lot. I don't think it was Hutchings! Be careful!!

Noah tilted the cell phone and showed his former partner what the text read. He had a little trouble, but eventually, his eyes focused. "After I left the briefing at the station, I was in the garage when Piekenbrock showed up. I had brought him out to this cabin a few weeks ago, and he said he was interested in buying it. I thought he wanted to talk more about it. I don't remember what happened. One minute I was in my garage, the next I woke up here on the couch."

The gears operated at full speed in his mind, and Noah put it all together as the glass window behind them exploded and he was sprayed with blood. A round went through Hutchings's shoulder, exited just under the collarbone, and passed Noah on his left side.

Noah caught his friend as he fell and lowered him down to the ground. A second round came through the window, and he scrambled to place them out of any line of sight.

He flipped Hutchings over onto his back, and he realized he was unconscious. Three days without food or water had proved too much, and he had no energy reserves left. Noah pulled out his pocketknife and cut the bottom off Hutchings's uniform, then pressed the make-shift bandage tight under the uniform against the exit wound.

A third round was fired through the broken window, and it went through the back of the couch, right where Hutchings had sat. Noah rolled him into the recovery position with the wounded side up against the fireplace. The chain scraped along the wooden floor as he kicked it to the side.

He stayed low on his belly, moved back to the couch, and picked up his cell phone. After he wiped away the blood spray off the screen, he sent a text to Angie:

Hutchings found, and he isn't the killer. It's Piekenbrock. Send backup ASAP and medical, under fire. Code 30.

He pressed send, and he saw that there was no reception. Zero bars. "Seriously?"

As he kept low, Noah made his way to the kitchen table and grabbed the shotgun. It wouldn't be close to the range of the rifle, but he knew it would be needed.

When he reached the back door, there was no doubt in his mind that he was the target when another round passed just above his head and into the wall. Splinters of wood fell on his helmet just before he crawled out the backdoor. With the cabin between him and Piekenbrock, Noah sprinted for the wood line and the coverage.

After running thirty yards into the trees and up the slope, Noah stood with his back to a large pine and tried to get his breath. Then, he reached down on his belt and hit the comms switch.

"What the fuck is going on, Piekenbrock!"

He didn't expect a reply. However, through the earpiece, he could hear the LT crystal clear. "It seems that your current partner spoiled my fun. She's next."

The LT's last words sent a chill through him as he figured out what he meant. Noah sprinted up the hill as fast as he could manage. After five minutes, he stumbled on a few rocks, and he had to steady himself before he ran out onto the gravel road. He turned to look at the cruiser, but he could just see a large plume of dust as it drove away.

Chapter 42

Noah rummaged around in the kitchen, and he found a stack of hand towels in a small Rubbermaid container. The others had been left on the counter and were chewed and covered in mouse droppings.

He had just come back from the walk down to the creek. Noah had no way to tell if the water was pure or not, but after he smelled it and had a sip, he found it to be fine. The old plastic container looked like it had been used for juice, cleaned up fine after he scoured it with sand. But, at the moment, his options were limited.

Back in front of the fireplace, Hutchings hadn't moved. The makeshift bandage had become saturated and needed to be replaced. The entry wound on the back of the shoulder seemed much better. The shirt had acted as a plug and stopped the bleeding. Exit wounds were always worse.

He poured water over the wound and carefully pulled the bandage off before replacing it with a folded hand towel and applying direct pressure.

Noah used his knife to tear a long towel in two, then used that to keep the bandage on tight. It had been a long time since he had done his emergency first-aid course, but the lessons were drilled into him.

He tried to get water over Steve's dry and cracked lips, but there was no response. However, his pulse was steady, and most importantly, he continued to breathe without issues.

The phone chimed with another text message from Dickinson:

Highway Patrol en route. Game Warden in area and should arrive soon.

Noah sent a message back with an update and confirmed that Piekenbrock is now a wanted man and a few other details they would need to start the hunt. He wasn't sure if the signal had gone through or if the message had been received. With Hutchings unconscious and in his weakened condition, Noah couldn't leave him.

There had been enough death surrounding him. He would hold off the Grim Reaper from taking his friend.

*****

John Mason headed east along 220 toward Casper to pick up a few items and get his wife's gift. They were celebrating their fiftieth wedding anniversary next week, and the gold necklace he ordered had come in. With the gas price being so high, John drove his Chevy truck only a few miles over the speed limit before setting the cruise control. It saved him on the mileage, and he never had to worry about a speeding ticket.

However, when he looked in the rearview mirror and saw the flashing lights, he was surprised. Even as he pulled over to the shoulder, he couldn't believe the cruiser followed him. He thought it would drive past once he gave it room. It'd been decades since he'd been pulled over.

John lowered his window and turned off the truck while he waited. He had never wasted gas, and he wasn't about to now. Soon the officer stepped out of the cruiser and approached. He was a tall man, putting them at the same height despite John being in a truck. The cop looked like an army officer, tall and ramrod straight, with a short crewcut, even if his hair was white.

"License and registration, proof of insurance."

After seventy years, John knew when to joke and keep his mouth shut. He handed over the documents and waited. The cop headed back to his vehicle and looked busy. Two minutes later, the officer returned. However, his hands were empty.

He stood back and on an angle from the driver's door. "Step out of the truck, keep your hands where I can see them."

John had done nothing wrong. "What's the problem? I wasn't speeding, of that, I am sure."

The officer opened his truck door, and his right hand drifted down to his holstered weapon. "Last warning, step out of your vehicle. Now."

The tone of his voice sent a chill through him, and it didn't take much thought to comply. He unbuckled his seat belt and got out of the seat. Once his feet hit the ground, the officer spun him around, so his chest was pressed hard against the side of the truck. A strong hand grabbed his wrist and wrenched it to the small of his back.

"What's going on? What did I do?"

John winced as the handcuffs tightened on his wrist, and soon both arms were secured. The cop was strong, and he almost carried John back to the police cruiser and opened the rear door. One hand pressed on the back of his head as he was shoved inside.

"Hey! What is going—"

The car door was slammed in his face. The police officer then opened the cruiser's trunk, pulled out a large duffel bag, walked over, and threw it in the back of John's truck.

John struggled, but there was no room between his shins and the seat in front of him. He couldn't get his hands free in any case. The cop was about to get into the cab of the truck when he paused and turned back to the cruiser.

There was a total lack of emotion in the officer's eyes, and as the man walked back, John prayed. Then, as the rear door opened, John said goodbye to his wife, daughter, and his grandchildren.

When the officer drew the pistol from the leg holster, John wasn't surprised. He closed his eyes. He never saw the shot that killed him and sprayed blood and gray matter over the windows and interior.

Chapter 43

The paramedics monitored Steve Hutchings as they flew straight to the medical center in Casper while Noah tried to stay out of their way. He continued to look out the window of the helicopter as they adjusted their angle of approach. He figured the pilot had countless hours of experience as he didn't feel the slightest bump when they landed.

Thirty minutes after the last text message, Noah heard a helicopter circling the cabin and landing on the gravel road. The trees were far enough back to give the pilot more than enough room. Noah had checked on Steve one more time before he headed outside and met them as they came down the driveway.

They worked on Hutchings right away, but after one look at the chain, the younger EMT left the cabin and sprinted back to the helicopter. He returned with a cordless grinder and within a minute the lock was separated from the shackle, and the chain lay on the cabin floor.

It took the three of them to carry Hutchings up the long driveway on a spine board and load him into the helicopter. An IV was inserted, and they lifted off and flew directly to Casper.

Noah wasn't sure who lit the fire to mobilize the rescue, but it happened rather quickly. After they landed at the hospital, Noah stayed on the phone with the chief and gave him the full details. Zane Piekenbrock was now the county's most wanted man, and all law enforcement agencies were directly involved.

Noah turned down the offer to be picked up in Casper by an APPD officer. The Wyoming Highway Patrol would drive him and have him at the station within thirty minutes if he stepped on it. He wanted to stay until he heard the update on Hutchings's condition.

The nurses and doctors were comfortable with Noah as he stood around to wait, but he could tell that some patients were uneasy. He still wore the tactical uniform with pads and helmet, vest and shotgun that he carried unloaded at his side. What disturbed them most was the spray of dried blood across the front of the uniform, face, and helmet.

"Mr. Hunter?"

A young blonde nurse stood by his side. She wore a set of green pastel scrubs, and the red lanyard around her neck carried her photo ID; Ariel McCarthy.

"Do you have an update? Is everything okay?"

"The man you brought in is stable and is currently in surgery. How about you come with me for a minute?"

Noah thought she would lead him to the surgical waiting area, but instead, she guided him into a small cubical and drew the curtain around them for privacy.

"Sit on the bed, please."

Confused, he followed her instructions. "What's going on?"

She smiled, moved a tray over and tore open the packaging for the alcohol disinfectant cloths.

"I'm going to clean you up just a wee bit."

Noah detected a faint Scottish accent. "Thank you. It's appreciated."

She gently cleaned his face and made a few passes across the Kevlar helmet and smiled. "That's a lot better."

It took Noah a moment to realize he had been lost in her brown eyes, and he cleared his throat as he noticed his cheeks grew warm. Soon they were back in the waiting room, and Noah saw the police cruiser outside through the large windows.

"I have to head out. If there are any changes, have them call me."

"Number?" Ariel grinned. "I can't call you if I don't have your number."

It had been a long time, but he was *fairly* sure that Ariel was flirting with him. He pulled out his wallet and found a business card with the APPD logo. He wrote his cell phone number on the back and handed it over.

She may have noticed that he glanced at her bare ring finger as she tucked the card away in her breast pocket. Then, it was her turn to blush.

"Thanks again."

As Noah headed outside, he hated to do it, but he forced those dimples out of his mind. He had a job to do, and he couldn't let any distractions get in the way.

With all the agencies now involved, the Arrow Point Police Department was too small to hold the number of personnel arriving on scene. It took the police chief three phone calls, and the community center conference room became the new headquarters.

The FBI was the first to arrive in a large mobile truck which resembled a Greyhound bus. The US Marshals from Cheyenne arrived in a Chevy Tahoe right after the county sheriffs in their cruisers. The Wyoming Highway Patrol was the last to arrive.

Noah had time to head home, and after a two-minute shower, he dressed in a dark charcoal suit. Then, he drove his truck straight to the community center.

The large room outside the lobby was usually rented out for parties, but it was now a command center. Four rows of tables were set up, with cables and wires that ran to various outlets. A dozen people worked on computers with each agency at their stations.

Noah walked to the front of the room, and after a brief talk with the police chief, he worked his way around the room and introduced himself to everyone.

"Nice to see you again, Daryl." The marshal was back and could now work in his official capacity. The large man was behind a keyboard and had two monitors set up.

"Murphy suggested I hang around in case things change. We are ready to go as soon as the warrants are approved. It should be any minute."

"Perfect. Thank you."

Noah headed over to the FBI liaison officer when a highway patrol trooper ran into the room. "Detective Hunter, we found the cruiser. There was a body inside. It isn't Piekenbrock."

Chief Birch swore as he opened a briefcase and pulled out a large map of the area. Within a minute, they had the cruiser position marked and had drawn a large circle for the potential search area. It covered half of Wyoming and three other states.

Any remorse Noah had over the eighteen plus years he'd worked with Piekenbrock and their friendship—was gone. The thought of what he had done, to himself, Hutchings, and the other victims made him feel sick. One thing he could not figure out was *why*? What sent him over the edge and compelled the killings?

Regardless, it was time to live up to his last name and go after the prey.

Chapter 44

This would be the first time Noah had worked with air support. The FBI had the budget and resources, and he would make use of it for as long as he could.

Once the warrants had been approved, everything started to happen at once. Marshal Sedore and the FBI began to delve into Zane Piekenbrock's life and tore it apart. All accounts and assets were now frozen, and they looked for his cell phone. It was either turned off or destroyed.

After almost two and a half decades with the APPD, the former LT knew how to cover his tracks and avoid detection. Noah had no idea how long his sociopathic rampage had gone on, but they would find out.

"Go now. Greenlight."

Four teams converged on a small bungalow from all four directions. The helicopter circled overhead, and thermal imagery cameras monitored the house. They were ready to track anyone who may flee the area. The sun had set an hour ago, and the helicopter was hard to see. However, they could all hear the engine as it circled overhead.

The front door was breached with a fifty-pound Enforcer. After the flashbangs went through the door and windows, two four-person teams entered the home and began to clear each room.

Noah stayed at the end of the street with Dickinson and a dozen other officers. Over the radio, he heard the teams report the area clear.

"The house is cleared and empty. It is *totally* empty."

Noah frowned and joined the rest of the team as they crossed the lawn and stepped through the broken door into the small home. They pulled out their flashlights and he scanned back and forth until he found the light switches. The kitchen and living room were illuminated.

When they mentioned the home was empty, the teams had underestimated the word. There wasn't any furniture or even appliances in the kitchen. The fine layer of dust over the hardwood floors only showed prints from the assault teams' recent disturbance.

Jesus Christ.

As Noah went from room to room, he tried to recall how many times he had been inside the home, but he couldn't. Over the years, he had been in the driveway countless times as he picked up or dropped off Piekenbrock. However, he had never stepped one foot inside.

He turned to the teams. "Gloves on. Tear it apart. Look for false doors, anywhere large enough that could hide a mouse."

Angie had followed him inside, her mouth agape. "How could he live here like this?"

Noah stepped outside the front door to give the guys room.

"He couldn't. My guess is he knew things were getting tight and he started to prepare. Either that or this home was a prop. Right now, I'm not sure, but we'll find out."

He smiled when the sound of drywall being torn down sounded throughout the home. An act of petty revenge, but apparently, it was one he was okay with.

"I'll start with a neighborhood canvas. Someone must have seen something like a moving truck." The usual glimmer of light in her eyes was gone, replaced by steel. Dickinson was more than up to the task.

The bungalow was in an older area of Arrow Point, and there were only a few homes on the street. "Sounds good. Keep me informed."

Two things seemed to happen at once. The Wyoming Highway Patrol called on his cell while someone shouted for Noah to come to the backyard.

"Detective Hunter, this Trooper Gaston. I'm currently twenty miles south of Casper, and I've just finished the preliminary inspection of the police cruiser."

"Go ahead." Noah started toward the backyard.

"The onboard dash camera had been disabled, and there is no ID on the body. We do have a claim receipt for jewelry on the victim. But it was covered in too much blood, and we can't make it out."

Noah tried not to groan. "Thanks, John. Collect the evidence and log it properly. Could you drive it straight to the forensic lab? I'll call ahead and have them ready for you. Thanks."

As Noah hung up, he looked around the backyard. Three officers were with an FBI agent as they stood just inside the small metal shed. He was waved inside, and one person had to leave so there would be room.

The FBI agent pointed to the peaked roof then at the interior wall. A small camera was installed just under the eaves, and it was connected to a panel on the wall. "I don't think it can broadcast audio, but it certainly will transmit video."

The unit was plugged into an extension cord that disappeared under the shed. The box on the wall had a small flexible, black antenna and the LED lights were all green along its length.

Noah looked at the unit, then looked at the feed. "Do you know how far this could broadcast?"

The younger officer looked closer at the system. "If it's just going to send out video, it may be a close range of a few hundred feet. Unless it's tied into the cell network, then it could transmit to anywhere in the world."

Fuck.

Not what he wanted to hear. "Thanks."

Noah looked at the other homes over the fence. A few people stood in their windows, silhouetted by their interior lights as they watched the drama unfold. He went to stand under the camera, and it pointed at the corner of the house. It was a perfect view of the rear and side of the home. There was no doubt the assault was captured.

Why would he only have one security camera for half of the perimeter coverage?

Noah moved to the front of the bungalow and began to search. It didn't take him long to find the second camera. Near the fence was a small garden with a few tacky lawn decorations and a large three-foot lighthouse. In the housing unit, on the top of the ornament was the second camera, and it pointed to the front of the home and the right side. Between the two cameras, there was full exterior coverage.

Noah resisted the urge to fire a few rounds into the garden decoration. They were being played, and Piekenbrock appeared to be several steps ahead of them, but that made him grin on reflection. If Piekenbrock had placed the cameras out of fear of being captured, they would get him. Fearful men make mistakes, especially in a moment of panic.

Chapter 45

Noah sat in the conference room and flipped his notebook open to a blank page. The FBI profiler stood at the end of the table, and once Chief Birch entered the room and took a seat, she began.

Special Agent Carol Saunders had a soft voice, and with her dark-rimmed glasses and her brown hair up, she resembled a librarian in a smart dress suit. "This is the preliminary report, and it may change at a later date when more information is available."

"Zane Piekenbrock, born August 1962, to Edward and Anne Marie Piekenbrock. Both his parents died of natural causes in Mercer, Ohio. Edward was a dairy farmer."

Noah continued to write, and with a quick look around the table, he realized that he was the only person to do so.

Saunders continued, "In 1980, Zane Piekenbrock signed up for the combat arms branch of the US Army, more specifically, the 1st Cavalry Regiment in Fort Bliss, Texas. He achieved the rank of captain before he was honorably discharged after nine-and-a-half years of service."

Noah had worked with Piekenbrock for over eighteen years, and he had no idea that he was in the army.

What else was he hiding?

"First, you must understand, there is no generic profile for a serial killer. Each one is different, and the events that led to their first kill may or may not be logical. From his previous career choices, I can tell you about Zane Piekenbrock that he gravitates toward rules, law and order, and discipline. The myth is that serial killers are dysfunctional loners, but we have found this to be extremely rare."

"Most of them go about their everyday life blending in so well that it's difficult to locate them. Even more so when they are law enforcement officers. I believe the thrill of breaking the law and having stepped outside the normal boundary was his motivation. The first kill for serial killers tends to be an accident or an impulse. One that they got away with. Their next thought tends to go along the lines of, 'If I got away with it once, I could do it again. I will never get caught.'"

Noah wrote down—*check accidental deaths over last ten years.* He had no idea if that first motivated Piekenbrock, but he had to investigate the possibility.

"There is a misconception that serial killers wish to be caught. However, in this case, I can say that is the opposite. It appeared that the person responsible had attempted, on multiple occasions, to eradicate evidence and mislead his fellow law enforcement officers. Right now, I'm not sure of the code that he operates. However, I can say with certainty that Zane Piekenbrock is intelligent and disregards the value of human life. I also firmly believe that he had a plan for the execution of his victims, they were disposed of meticulously. A plan for not being captured, and a contingency plan if he was discovered or captured."

Noah continued to make notes while a few others asked questions. By the time he finished, the FBI profiler had packed her notes away, and they were alone in the conference room.

"Thank you." Noah glanced at his notes, then back up. "I had to get a few thoughts down now while they were fresh."

"Do you have any questions?"

Noah flipped through the pages. "Right now, I must have over a hundred questions, but nothing you would be able to answer."

Agent Saunders smiled and pulled out a card from her briefcase. She handed it to him. "Feel free to call, especially if you have new information. It would be another brick in the wall and help overall with the big picture."

He slipped the card into his breast pocket. "Will do. Thanks again."

It didn't take long for Noah to get another call, and he drove to the community center to find Marshal Sedore outside waiting.

"Detective Hunter, not sure if it's a lead or not, but it's certainly interesting."

They entered the command center, and Noah was surprised to see only a few people inside. "Where's everyone?"

"The feds are securing a warrant for a records search at Sentinel Storage. However, it may be a fishing expedition."

Sentinel Storage had a two-acre lot on the west side of Arrow Point, with several storage units. Some units were the size of a closet, and you could park a pickup truck inside the largest.

"What information led us there?"

Daryl sat at his makeshift desk and logged into his system. "Basically, nothing. The FBI figured he had to have an area nearby since his house was empty, they guessed."

Noah shook his head at this information. "We can't blind search without just cause. So, if we *did* find anything there, it wouldn't be admissible in court."

The marshal shrugged. "That isn't why I called you here. The APPD switched to direct deposit twenty-two years ago after Piekenbrock had already been on the force for eighteen months. Here was his original mailing address on record."

4032 Somerset Circle, Casper WY

"That was before I started at the department. It's definitely worth checking out. Can you start with Arrow Points' financial records on his current home and any details on his previous home in Casper? Who it was sold to and when would help."

Sedore wrote the information on a notepad and nodded. "I should have thought of that. I'll get right on it."

"In the meantime, I'll place surveillance on the house. Hopefully, it'll pay off."

The further they dug into his past, the more questions he had. Noah figured he was long overdue for answers.

Chapter 46

Noah hefted the charred piece of wood and threw it over the yellow barricade tape in the pit. The home on Somerset had caught fire a day and a half previous. Despite the best efforts of the Casper Fire Department, they were not able to save it, and they focused their efforts on containment. The smell lingered in the air, and despite the light breeze, it did nothing to disperse the odor of burned wood.

"This can't be a coincidence." Angie shone her flashlight through what was left of the home. "When can we see the fire marshal's report?"

"They read it out over the phone. It didn't say much, just that a neighbor called in the blaze. Suspected electrical fire from the kitchen, no casualties." Noah kicked another charred piece with his dress shoe.

He shone his flashlight through the timbers and the foundation of the home. The floor had burned through, and the house had collapsed into the basement. The spruce trees that divided the property from the neighbors were singed from the intense heat, and the grass and plants had browned twelve feet from the building.

Angie turned and pointed to the neighbors' homes. "I'll start knocking on doors, try and find out who lived here."

Noah shook his head. "Leave the door knocking to the Casper police, but they are going to need a reason to do so. If this appears to be an accident and the marshal confirms it, they won't ask around."

As they walked to their cruiser, Noah could see the lights turn on in the home across the street. The silhouette of an older man standing in the living room window watched them as they walked away from the destroyed house.

"Maybe we can knock on one home."

The figure in the window moved, and by the time they arrived at the front door, an older man, white hair and glasses with a blue golf shirt and khaki pants waited. He looked between the two officers before he shrugged. "Just a little late. I called yesterday."

Noah frowned. "Who'd you call?"

"The fire department, I haven't heard from anyone since."

"I'm Detective Hunter, and this is Constable Dickinson from Arrow Point Police Department. Did you see anything suspicious before you called it in?"

He stared at the shoulder flash on Angie's uniform, and then he seemed to nod to himself. "The house has been vacant for a few years, but a maintenance company comes by once a week to check on the property and cut the lawn."

Noah pulled out a notebook and pen from inside his suit jacket and took a few notes. "Do you remember the name of the company?"

"Cranston something or other."

Noah wrote it down and tapped his pen against the paper a few times. "Did you know the people that used to live there?"

"Over the years, people and families have come and gone too many times."

Angie pulled out her cell phone and showed him a picture of Piekenbrock. "Have you seen this man previously, living there or visiting?"

The man adjusted his glasses and leaned forward. "Not too sure, but that could have been the maintenance guy that was here a few days ago."

Noah felt good with this information. A spark of hope. "Do you happen to have any security cameras?"

"None. I have this, though, not too sure about it. My grandson set it up." He stepped to the side and pointed to a doorbell with a small video screen behind him.

Angie turned to confirm where it was aimed. "It would have a view of the home. Is there any way we could look at the footage?"

"I don't know how it works, but you're welcome to try."

He stepped inside the front door and returned with a tablet, handing it to Angie. With both men over her shoulder, she went through the menus and found the recorded video for the previous day.

They could see the action of the fire and the trucks as they battled the blaze, and the only recorded movement previous was a black Chevy truck. It pulled to the end of the driveway, and a taller man walked toward the home. He wore a long tan set of coveralls with a blue baseball cap and carried a large green duffel bag in his left hand.

They were unable to see his face or zoom in enough to make out any details, but Noah nodded. "I think that's him. Same build."

A few minutes later, they could see the man as he walked back to the truck. The duffel bag appeared to be heavy, and he had to carry it with both hands. He lowered the tailgate and placed the bag in the back. Once he closed the gate, the man drove off. They couldn't see the plates from the side angle, but it appeared to be a 2010 Chevy Silverado.

"Just give me a second ..." Angie navigated her way through the various sub-menus before she handed it back. "I just sent a copy of the video to my email at the station. Thank you."

Once they sat in the cruiser, Noah called US Marshal Sedore and kept him informed of new information.

"Hold on a minute ...."

Noah had placed him on speaker as they drove off. They could hear him typing on a keyboard.

"I have a missing persons report for a John Mason, filed from his wife, Betty. A seventy-year-old man has been missing for two days. He drove a black Chevy Silverado. Physical description matches the John Doe found shot in the cruiser."

Noah punched the steering wheel in excitement. "Get the plate number and description out to all forces. I want cruisers at the Interstate ramps and County Road 44 into town. Good work."

Angie could barely contain her energy, and her left leg bounced up and down at a rapid pace. "We now have a chance."

"Only if he's still in town or coming back." Noah paused. "I have an idea, but I'm going to need some help."

Angie's knee stopped moving. "What do you have in mind?"

He just smiled and headed back to Arrow Point.

Chapter 47

Noah made the last connection and stepped to the side of the lighthouse in the front garden. The technical team from the FBI looked at an open laptop and nodded.

"There's no audio, but the video feed is now being broadcasted."

Six men stood on the front lawn of Piekenbrock's home out of sight of the camera. The house was taped off with yellow barricade tape, and the sticker seals were across the doors and windows. The early morning sun had crested the roof, and a light breeze blew through the residential neighborhood.

Sedore held a construct the size of a football with six-disc sensors embedded in a white plastic frame, and all pointed in a different direction. The flat blue top had a digital display with a myriad of buttons under a flexible plastic dome.

"The CRFS RF Eye Array will be able to find any spectrum monitoring and tracking signals. It can track multiple bandwidths and display them on the map. It works best at short range, but we can mount this in the vehicle and conduct a spiral pattern search until it gathers the signal once again. The only problem is when there are multiple signals on the same bandwidth."

The marshal synced the signal from the array and overlaid it on the street map for Arrow Point. The man looked at Noah and nodded. Twenty different vehicles waited throughout Arrow Point and a dozen more on the highways.

Detective Hunter lifted his radio. "Prepare to move. We'll be live in five, four, three, two … one."

Sedore pressed a large black button, held it in for three seconds, then lifted the pressure when he heard a *beep.*

"Signal acquired. Standby."

All eyes shifted to the open laptop as concentric rings flashed on the screen before they condensed into a tight red circle.

Noah stood for a few seconds before he picked up the radio. "Forty Water Street, apartment building. I say again, four-zero Water Street. Go! Lock it down."

As they raced to the cruiser, he couldn't believe the coincidence. That was the same building his former fiancée, Megan, lived in and where he also stayed for a while. He hadn't been back since he bought the farmhouse property last fall.

The marshals followed, and they did their best to keep the police cruiser in view. Noah used his knowledge of the town and side streets to arrive at the destination within three minutes while avoiding the high traffic roads and lights. He wasn't light on the accelerator. The tires hugged the road and squealed at the abuse.

He wasn't too surprised to see Constable Dickinson parked sideways on the street, jump out of her cruiser, and run over as he approached. She was near the station at a central point. Within the next minute, several cruisers from the sheriff's office and the FBI's Crown Vics had the building surrounded.

Marshal Sedore and his partner ran toward him with the laptop and the Array open. "I'm confirming that this building is receiving the signal. I can't pinpoint which unit. It isn't that precise."

"I have an idea," Noah muttered as he ran through the front door and turned left in the hallway. He knocked on the first apartment and waited.

Claude was the superintendent of the three-story building. His job was to ensure all the units were operational. He also cleaned and maintained the grounds. There wasn't an elevator, but there was underground parking and facilities for the tenants. Noah had a good relationship with him previously.

When Claude opened the door, he was surprised to see Noah with several other officers behind him in the hallway. "How can I help you?"

"My old apartment, number 302. Who did you rent it out to?"

Claude ran a hand through his short dark hair and looked at the large officers filling the hall. "Are you kidding me?"

Noah shook his head. "Tell me."

"It's rented to you and the APPD."

At this information, the officers in the hallway grew silent.

"Give me a key to the unit. Quick. I also want the building evacuated. Now!"

Fears of an explosion or another fire to cover his tracks leaped to mind. With ten apartments per floor, it would be a nightmare.

Claude opened a steel cabinet secured to the wall. He handed Noah a key with an orange fob. "This is the master key."

He grabbed it and ran up the stairs to the third floor. As he passed the second-floor landing, the fire alarm for the building went off. The klaxon drowned out the sound of boots behind him.

Seconds later, Noah stood outside his old apartment. He was about to place the key in the lock when the FBI agent spoke. "Stop. Let me."

The slim man pulled out a flashlight and stepped in front of the door. He shone the light into the lock and around the frame, then underneath. "Step to the side."

Once everyone was against the wall beside the door, he reached over and turned the deadbolt, then opened the door an inch. The agent repeated the same scan with the flashlight around the opening.

"Okay, looks good."

As residents began to exit their units, Sedore bumped Noah to the side and called out, "Breaching."

All of the men were professionals and had cleared homes and rooms on hundreds of occasions. Within seconds, the one-bedroom apartment was checked.

As Noah holstered his Glock, he looked around and was surprised to see some of his former fiancée's furniture still present. Claude had mentioned that he would see to it being emptied and donated.

The living room had dozens of boxes stacked against the long wall and in front of the window was a table. Two computer monitors were on, and they watched the live feed from the lighthouse camera.

"Bingo."

Sedore turned off the Array and cleared his throat. "There may be an issue. We entered without a warrant. None of this may be admissible."

Noah swore under his breath, along with a few others. The FBI agent, Kennedy, let out a chuckle. "I'd say you're normally correct, but the superintendent mentioned the unit was in *your* name. We just entered your own apartment."

He pointed at Noah, and a few of the other guys paused, then they were relieved. There would be zero issues with legalities on this entry or evidence collected.

"Piekenbrock has been known to cover his tracks. Conduct a primary search for explosives or incendiary devices." Noah turned to the stacked boxes and started to go through them along with Kennedy. They found only clothing and household items.

The bedroom didn't produce any results, but Marshal Sedore called him over to the dining room. On the table was a large green canvas duffel bag, and he had opened the zipper.

"Jesus Christ …"

Inside were the remains of a body. Dirt was caked on the skeleton, and it appeared to be quite old. There was no doubt that it was real. The lower third of the bag was filled with dirt, and it was caked on the bones. Noah could see a fresh gash across a leg bone from a shovel blade.

"Don't touch anything else. I have to call the medical examiner and forensics. We have another body."

Chapter 48

The Chevy truck was parked on a side street, and the man behind the wheel clenched his fists and swore. White knucks cracked with the intensity. The Browning Hi-Power pistol sat on the passenger seat behind him. Next to the wallet and identification of the previous owner of the vehicle. Three full replacement magazines rested in the cup holders instead of a cup of coffee.

He had a clear view of the cruisers from the parking spot as they surrounded the apartment building, and the officers rushed in.

A few minutes later, the fire alarm sounded as people began to exit the building and walk across the street. More officers arrived on scene.

They'd be focused on the objective, so he wasn't worried about being spotted.

"Fuck!"

His fist pounded the steering wheel again as he made a right turn onto Oak Street. This route would have him drive by the police station, but he still wasn't worried. In the state of Wyoming, it seemed every third vehicle was a pickup truck. He blended right in.

Once he was on the Interstate 26 toward Casper, the knot of tension started to ease. He knew what evidence they would take and where they would take it. But, before that happened, he had a chore to do.

His hand twitched as he turned on the radio and whistled along to a Billy Joel song. *Only the good die young.*

*****

Once the fire alarm was turned off, the residents were allowed back inside. Noah was glad someone had thought to call the fire department for the false alarm. There were enough confusion and people on the ground without them on scene as well.

Then the real work began.

Noah had restricted all access to the apartment, and three officers began a systematic search. They documented the contents from the boxes and the computer link system. The green duffel bag and the morbid contents were handed over to the coroner's office.

The computers were given to the FBI technician, and they were immediately flown to Denver to be processed at their computer forensic laboratory. Noah, Constable Dickinson, and Sergeant Bydal slowly and methodically tore through all the boxes and contents of the unit.

Noah started in the bathroom, and he collected evidence—toothbrush, fingerprints, even hair samples from the sink. When they caught Piekenbrock, he didn't want any loopholes. He wanted the evidence to speak for itself.

Six hours later, Noah's phone rang. The coroner's number flashed on the screen.

"Detective Hunter, go ahead."

"Noah, it's George. I finished the examination of the duffel bag. Male, approximately six-foot-two inches. At the time of death, I would say he was approximately twenty-five to thirty-years old. I've had the sample sent to FSL, and they will hopefully be able to narrow down how long since death has occurred and the cause."

The forensic science laboratory had some of the best technology in the world, and they should be able to help. "Thank you. How old would you say the bones are? Your best guess?"

George hummed as he thought it over. "Anywhere between twenty to forty years. Of course, it depends on where it was found and about a hundred different variables."

"The lab should be able to narrow it down?"

"Definitely. With the new genealogy addition, they could even extract enough DNA to do a family search as well."

"Good, the family should be notified even if it happened decades ago. Thanks for the overtime."

A few minutes later, Noah collected the evidence bags and memory cards with almost eight thousand pictures. Again, everything was documented to the utmost.

Bydal and Dickinson were finished, and Noah sent them home. He called in a few junior officers and set up a twenty-four-hour watch on the apartment.

Back at the station, he logged in the evidence and sat down to file the reports. Despite the long day, the adrenaline still coursed through his body, and he knew it would be futile to head home and pace.

After two hours of paperwork, Noah couldn't stand the inaction. The laboratory would close in an hour.

Noah headed to the evidence room and signed the transfer forms to bring several samples to the laboratory direct. He knew he wouldn't be able to sleep, and maybe they could get a head start on some of the evidence.

The governor's office had pushed this case as a priority, and while the personnel and resources were available, Noah would try to get as much use out of it as possible.

The lab was a few minutes west of Casper, off Interstate 26, and Noah called ahead to let them know he would be there soon. The normal forty-minute drive would be greatly reduced without traffic, and he wouldn't have any problems in a marked cruiser. After parking in front of the offices, he lifted the cardboard box of evidence out of the truck and headed inside.

With his mind on other matters, Noah failed to notice the black pickup truck parked at the end of the building. It had good coverage behind the storage shed.

Chapter 49

Noah set the large cardboard box on the counter and pressed the call button. The receptionist had left hours ago. Within a few minutes, Dr. Singh opened the door behind the desk and smiled when she saw who had waited.

"Detective Hunter, you got here in time. We're about to do a DNA extraction from a sample."

He lifted the box. "I have a little more work for you on the same case, but this isn't as much of a priority as the bones."

He signed in and clipped a visitor pass on the pocket of his suit jacket, then followed her. Their first stop was the receiving office for evidence login. It was a large room filled with steel shelves along the walls with two rows in the middle, and refrigeration units along the back wall.

The doctor asked, "Anything need to be kept cold?"

Noah shook his head. "Nothing like that."

She signed the evidence in and placed it on the middle shelf. A bright yellow sticker went across the cardboard box with a seven-digit code. Once it was stored, she locked up the office, and Noah followed her to the lab.

"We started the extraction. Despite the age, I think there's enough material left in the marrow for sampling."

Within the large warehouse were several laboratories, and she led him to an office door painted light green with a green band along the top of the wall.

"Do you know the age of the body and how long deceased?"

She sat behind her desk, opened a blue folder, and pulled out the first page. "The good news, the soil was dry and void of insects. I would have said it was buried in a container in a cellar or barn. The sagittal fusion wasn't complete on the skull, so definitely under thirty-five years of age. I've sent the dental picture and X-rays to our odontologist, with the wear, and he believes the body was twenty-five to thirty-years old at the time of death."

Noah smiled. "That's the range the medical examiner had mentioned."

Dr. Singh laughed. "We all have worked with George Hall many times. Sometimes we spend weeks to arrive at the same conclusions that he comes up within a few minutes of examining the body." She pulled out a second page. "Carbon dating wouldn't work with this body as it's too new. Three of us agreed that it was buried twenty-five to thirty years ago. However, within the duffel bag, there were two different soil samples. At one point in the past, it was relocated."

Noah pulled out his notepad and wrote a few notes. He would get copies of the full reports, but it was a habit he couldn't break. He was on his third notebook for this case, and the way he was going, many more would be expected.

He noticed a previous memo, and he read it a few times before asking, "Trophy? This may have been his first kill, and he kept it with him when he moved, or it had significant meaning to him."

Dr. Singh shrugged. "Could be." She pulled out a photograph of the femur. "This scrape was recent and free of any dirt. No doubt it happened recently."

Noah recalled the security footage of the neighbor. "Within forty-eight hours possibly."

She placed the paperwork back in the file and stood. "Jessica Ross is our genealogist. She founded MyFamilyTree, and we have access to their technology and resources. The use of DNA has helped us in three cases so far. We followed the family tree, and it led us to the correct person every time."

As they walked along the corridor, Noah asked, "Is it foolproof? The courts allow it as evidence?"

She opened the door to a lab surrounded by large glass windows, with a large office on the far side. A woman stood at what looked like a drill press as she worked the control arm on a large bone. In her mid-fifties, she had long blonde hair tied back, and large circular glasses covered most of her face. When her sleeve slipped back, colorful tattoos decorated her lower arm. A thin trail of smoke rose from the drill where it met the bone.

"So far, the courts have allowed it. It's a new science as far as evidence is considered. Yet, so far we haven't been wrong."

When they entered the lab, Jessica finished with the machine. She inserted a tool into the small hole and scraped it in a circular motion. It looked like a small ice cream scoop, one-sixteenth of an inch.

"Jessica, this is Detective Noah Hunter from Arrow Point. He is working that case."

She pushed the glasses up on her nose and smiled. "Nice to meet you. The marrow is intact, and a sample will be possible."

Noah didn't want to get too near any of the equipment. The stainless-steel countertops were covered in millions of dollars of high tech. He felt more comfortable in the middle of the room. "How long for results?"

She carried the extractor to the counter and held it above a test tube that rested in a large machine. She dropped the sample inside and filled the glass with a clear fluid, then capped it. Once the lid was lowered, she hit a few buttons, and the device activated. With a quiet hum, the tube spun in a tight circle.

"Eighteen hours for the extraction and separation. After that, it's research." She shrugged. "I could get results and matches within minutes, or it could take days."

Noah felt good about where this research was headed. It was important. If for nothing else, closure for the victim's family. He handed her a business card. "Feel free to call me direct once results are in."

"No problem." She tucked the card into the breast pocket of her lab coat.

"Where is the rest of the skeleton?"

Dr. Singh pointed to the large bone. "We don't need the whole skeletal system. That will do. They just sent the sample and the dirt in the bag. We'll do our best to—"

They all were startled when a pistol fired shots deep within the building. Two rounds were fired, then a short pause, followed by one more.

Noah looked at Dr. Singh. "That was a little loud. Ballistics testing?"

She shook her head and frowned. "They are at the other end of the building and in a soundproof lab. If they were testing, we wouldn't be able to hear them."

Fuck!

Noah pulled out his Glock from under his jacket and looked at Jessica. "Turn the lights off in here. Move."

She stood frozen for a split second before rushing to the wall, just inside the door, and except for various equipment, the lab lights went out. There were too many windows on the interior wall that let in the light, but it was better than nothing.

"I want you both to go to the back of the room and hide behind some of the equipment. Then, if you have a chance to leave through the front door safely, take it. Understood?"

Noah did not wait to see if they followed the instruction. He stood at the window and tried to look both ways in the hall. Nothing.

"There are no such things as coincidences." He muttered to himself as he took a deep breath and stepped out into the hall.

Chapter 50

Noah closed the door behind him gently and paused in the long hallway. There had been no other shots fired, and he couldn't tell which direction it had come from. The genealogy lab was midway within the large building.

He pulled out his cell phone and sent a text to the duty sergeant for help. He didn't want to take a chance of being overheard. Casper PD should be the closest to respond.

Noah knew ahead of him were the three receiving bays for an ambulance or a truck. Large enough, they could pull in and unload. As he moved farther into the building, he realized he should have asked how many others were in the building. Too late now, he didn't want to draw attention to those in hiding by backtracking.

Noah looked down at his dress shoes. Wearing a suit in these situations wasn't the best. He'd have to dress more casually or go back into uniform.

He crouched to look around the corner at the end of the hall, giving him an elevated view of the receiving bays; in front of him, the staircase split. A flight of stairs went down to the large open area, or he could continue straight down the hall but be exposed. The open hallway acted as a catwalk over the bay area.

He pulled the slide to confirm there was a round in the chamber. That left him sixteen rounds in the magazine. Another downside to the suit was the lack of places for spare magazines.

Goddammit!

Noah started across the exposed walkway when he heard a series of crashes, and someone screamed from within the building, followed by a single pistol shot, then silence. People were being killed, and Noah was unable to remain cautious. He kept his weapon at the ready and rushed down the hall.

The corridor opened into a large area of the building with several offices and laboratories to either side. Toward the southern end of the building were the indoor storage inventory and ballistics. The storage facility had large refrigeration and freezer units and an open caged area with rows of steel shelving. A guard was face down on the polished concrete floor before the security door to the fenced-off site. A large pool of blood had bloomed and spread on the ground in a circle. From fifty feet away, Noah saw the wound to the back of his skull.

The gate to the inventory room was open. Noah eased around the corpse, brought his Glock forward in a high ready position and stepped inside.

There were over a dozen rows of shelves that stretched eighty feet toward the rear wall. Each shelf section was over twelve feet tall, and almost every space was filled with various objects and boxes. At his shoulder was a stack of tires next to a series of snow globes stored in a large evidence bag. He could see everything from car parts to a mannequin stacked along the open shelves.

The majority of the shelves were filled with large cardboard boxes with a plastic sleeve on the outside with a reference number. A dull thud sounded from the rear. It repeated several times before Noah could hear someone mutter as they swore.

He walked heel-toe along the outside edge of his shoe to try and remain silent down the first aisle. There was an open area in front of the refrigeration units, and the man stood with his back to him, using a long prybar to work on the lock for the central unit.

The left door was open, and Noah could see the mangled mess of the handle and lock. At the man's feet lay a second security guard. He didn't see any blood or obvious wounds on the large man. He did note that the guard's holster on his right hip was empty.

Piekenbrock swung the bar down on the lock mechanism once again. He wore a gray hooded sweatshirt and jeans, and black running shoes. The holster on his right hip held the Browning pistol.

Noah aimed at his former lieutenant and lined up the shot as he stood at the end of the shelf unit. At this point, his moral compass began to spin out of control. Shooting someone in the back when they were unaware would have legal problems down the road. Of that, he was sure.

Then he lowered his shot to the back of Piekenbrock's knee and smiled. He was about to pull the trigger when the door handle popped off, and Zane moved inside the large fridge. An easier opportunity presented itself. Before he could second guess, Noah ran forward to slam the freezer door behind him.

As he passed the guard, two things happened at the same time. Noah's dress shoes slipped on the slick floor, and his right foot shot forward, so he landed on his left knee. From inside the refrigeration unit, a shot was fired. The round passed over his head by inches. Noah immediately rolled to the right and placed the door between them.

"That was close! Are you getting tired, Hunter?"

As he scrambled to regain his feet, Piekenbrock walked around the open door and pointed the Beretta right at his forehead. "Where's the bag with the bones?"

Chapter 51

As the shot echoed in his ears, he stared at Piekenbrock. To all appearances, he remained the same, but the gleam in his eye told Noah a different story. He was off the deep end. He also noticed a tremor in his left hand. The right, however, remained steady as the barrel was rock solid.

"I haven't seen it."

"Nice try. Green duffel bag you removed from the apartment. Where is it?"

Noah saw a movement out of the corner of his eye, but he remained focused. Slowly, he stood and left his Glock on the ground at his feet. "It would be with the coroner. I just dropped off some evidence to be processed. That's it. Do you want to talk, man?"

Piekenbrock grinned, but the gesture never reached his eyes. They remained flat and cold. "We're long past that stage. Turn around."

The guard on the floor exploded into action, swung his feet, and clipped Piekenbrock behind the ankles. As the former LT began to fall back, Noah rushed forward in a tackle. His left hand brushed the Beretta to the side.

They fell across the guard's legs in a tangled heap, and Noah put both hands on the weapon to keep it aimed elsewhere while the guard struggled to grip Zane's shoulders. The guard screamed for Noah to help, but neither man could get a hold of Piekenbrock's left arm. He used Noah's momentum, brought his left arm out, and sent the elbow back in a tight arc. It connected with the guard's head, just behind his left ear. The guard's eyes rolled back. Immediately, the grip on his shoulders loosened, and despite Noah's weight, he began to move.

Noah brought his knee into Piekenbrock's ribs, but there wasn't any strength from the blow with that angle.

Zane arched his back and twisted at the same time. Noah felt a punch to his kidney, and suddenly, he was flipped. He landed hard on his back. Both hands remained above his head, where he retained a grip on the pistol. Despite the awkward angle, he managed to keep the muzzle pointed to the ceiling.

Piekenbrock pivoted and slammed another elbow into the guard before he brought up his left leg and slammed his heel down on Noah's head.

Stars danced across his vision, and his jaw clicked shut. Noah knew he couldn't take another kick like that, and he had to let go of the gun. He spun around on the floor and stomped his heel into the side of Piekenbrock's leg. He had aimed for the knee but connected with the quadriceps.

The gray sweatshirt rode up, and the guard's pistol was tucked into the waistband. Noah dove forward and attempted to grab the second weapon.

Soon as his hand brushed the polymer grip, Piekenbrock brought his Beretta down into the side of his head. The guard's gun skittered across the floor, well out of reach as he brought his arm up to block the second strike. Noah needed time to get his own Glock, and he brought his fist around and connected with a sucker punch to the side of Zane's skull.

As Piekenbrock's head snapped to the side, Noah dove for his pistol. When he turned and aimed toward Piekenbrock, he wasn't surprised to find that he was already on his feet as well. The Beretta, instead of being aimed at him, was pointed down at the guard's head.

"One move and I shoot him."

Fuck.

"Soon as you do that, you are dead."

The former police officer shrugged. "If you kill me now, you will be killing others. Right now, I'm the only one that has certain information. Go for it."

Noah stared into his eyes. He couldn't tell if the man was lying or not. He had to act on what he knew *now*. "Drop your weapon, get on the ground."

Piekenbrock grinned once again and shook his head. "Not a chance, Noah."

The guard let out a groan and raised one hand to his head. Zane held the barrel of the Beretta tight against his temple and yelled, "Stand down, and I don't shoot you."

Noah brought his left hand up to support his right as he aimed, but he couldn't do it. It was one thing to be the target, but this had turned into a hostage situation. He didn't want the innocent man to die.

Piekenbrock lifted the guard to his feet and kept the muzzle tight to the base of his skull. He also used the larger bulk of the guard as a shield as he walked backward, out of the storage area.

"Don't worry. We'll run into each other again one day."

Noah kept his pistol trained on Piekenbrock as he followed at a distance. Once they passed the large shelving units, Piekenbrock slammed the security gate closed, locking Noah inside the cage. A glance showed he would have had a twenty-foot climb.

Piekenbrock grinned and gave Noah a wink as he headed for the rear emergency exit, the large gray steel door with a crash bar across the front.

Noah could only watch as the two men went through the door and the alarm sounded throughout the building.

*****

Zane spun the guard around and threw him to the ground, then kicked the emergency exit door closed. The alarm continued to sound throughout the building.

Frustration levels peaked as he kicked the door once again with the heel of his foot. The noise echoed across the rear parking lot.

The guard started to crawl backward as he kept his eyes on the tall man. Piekenbrock ignored him and walked over to where the truck was parked.

The guard stood and pointed a finger at his back. "You're dead motherfucker!"

He turned to the guard. "Are you serious?" He let out a little chuckle and brought the Beretta up to shoulder height, aimed straight at his head. "I suggest you run."

The security guard knew the man had a screw loose, and he didn't hesitate. He bolted to the corner of the building.

Piekenbrock took a steady aim at his back and gently squeezed the trigger. Instead of a sharp retort and kick of the 9mm pistol, nothing happened. He dropped the empty magazine and pulled the slide. The last round ejected, and he snagged it mid-air. The primer was stuck—faulty round.

Noah would have had him dead to rights.

As he laughed at the universe, Piekenbrock climbed into the cab of the Chevy truck and started the engine. He turned to the woman in the back seat. "You're not going to believe this! I was out of ammo."

He continued to laugh as he drove away. Angie couldn't reply. She was secured with layers of rope, and a cloth that was used as a gag was too tight. Her eyes narrowed in rage as she watched his every move.

Chapter 52

It took the Casper police thirty minutes to clear and make their way through the FSL building. Six bodies were discovered, and a seventh person was shot. However, he was expected to survive.

Police officers surrounded the building with a cruiser across the entrance. It took a while to locate the key, but Noah was released from the inventory cage with help from the same guard Piekenbrock had taken hostage.

It took three hours before Noah could check on Jessica Ross and Doctor Singh. Once he'd left the genealogy lab, they hid in a storeroom down the hall that they could lock from the inside.

Everyone had to give statements to the police several times, Noah included. He would have his own paperwork to complete back in Arrow Point.

Jessica promised to get the DNA results as soon as possible, and it was midnight before he arrived back in Arrow Point. Stan Bydal met him in the cube, and he explained what had gone down.

It took a few minutes for Noah to notice that Sergeant Bydal was dressed in a dark suit and tie, which had to have been custom-made. His arms were the size of most people's legs, and he had a deep chest and thick neck from over twenty years of hard workouts at the gym.

"Did you have a court today?"

Stan smiled. "No. Just work."

Noah reached out and pulled the suit jacket to the side. A wide grin crossed his face when he saw the gold badge on his belt.

"Congratulations!"

Lieutenant Arrow Point Police Department was engraved on the new badge. Stan looked worried. "Thanks. Are you going to be good with this?"

Noah winked. "Damn right. Better you than me." The two men had worked together for nearly two decades, and despite Noah having more time in, the potential for issues was possible. "I do have one official item to bring to your attention. This is my last day wearing a suit. I can't do my job properly with it. Civilian clothes or tactical uniform."

Lieutenant Bydal shrugged. "Surprised you lasted this long, and frankly, the chief is shocked as well. With my knee bothering me more every year, I knew this was coming."

They chatted and talked about the press briefing tomorrow and what direction Stan wanted to move on the case when Noah's phone rang. Calls at one o'clock in the morning were not common, and they both saw *unknown caller* on the display screen.

The sinking feeling returned to his stomach.

Bydal pulled out his phone and hit the voice recorder application, then nodded.

Noah placed the call on speaker. "Hunter, go ahead."

At first, there was silence, then a familiar voice said, "Glad you got out of the cage, Noah."

The signal seemed weak, and they could hear a static *pop* in the background. Stan's fingers tightened on his phone, but he held it steady as it recorded.

"How do you see this ending, Piekenbrock?"

"Either good or bad. There's no middle ground. Now, down to business."

Noah had a feeling of what was coming. "Let me guess."

"You bring me the duffel bag with the bones, and I disappear."

Noah laughed at his former supervisor. "What kind of deal is that? You are going to jail for a long time, and I wouldn't be surprised that they make the death penalty an option for you."

"Normally, I would agree with you. However, now there is another option. You get the bones, and we trade them, and you get Dickinson."

His heart bottomed out at the same time his face grew flush with rage. "What are you talking about?"

"Don't worry. She's fine for the moment. I'll call back later and tell you the details of the exchange."

The call disconnected, and Stan ran into his office to contact dispatch while Noah sprinted down to his truck. Angie lived ten minutes from the station on the second floor of an apartment building on Central Park. Afterward, he couldn't recall the drive, just a vague sense of panic and fear as he pushed the truck to its limits through the side streets. At that early hour, they were deserted.

Noah parked in front of the main doors and ran inside, but the door from the lobby was locked. He had to be buzzed inside. On the panel, he pushed for the superintendent several times, but there was no response.

He had never been inside Dickinson's building, and he wasn't sure which unit was hers. He knew it was on the second floor but that was it. Outside, he scanned the apartments. They were all dark, except for one unit on the second floor—the northeast corner of the building.

The first-floor unit, instead of a balcony, had a small patch of grass and an area for a few chairs. Noah drove his truck over the front lawn and parked under the corner balcony.

He left the door open and used it as a step to stand on the roof. From that height, his fingers were able to grab the bottom edge of the balcony, and he pulled himself up and over the railing.

The small apartment's kitchen and living room lights were on. Any doubt that it was Dickinson's place vanished when he saw her holstered Glock 19 on top of the coffee table and the uniform hanging in the doorway to the bedroom.

The sliding door was unlocked, so Noah stepped inside. The small one-bedroom apartment was neat, with one exception. One kitchen chair was knocked over. Over his shoulder, he could see the blue and red lights on the cruisers as they parked at the front of the building and behind his truck. Noah's shadow flickered in time to the strobe of the lights across the ceiling.

Everything else looked like Angie had just stepped out and was due back at any moment. He knew what would happen next, and he had a plan.

Time to fix the game in his favor.

Chapter 53

After the apartment was secure, Noah headed home for a brief shower and to change. He felt more comfortable in his tactical uniform and vest, and he made sure that he had plenty of loaded magazines stored in his utility belt. Instead of the collapsible baton, he holstered a Taser on his left hip. He packed a few protein bars in his pocket and brought a coffee with him. There would be no time for sleep.

By three o'clock in the morning, he was back at the command office in the community center where he was joined by an FBI hostage rescue team (HRT), Marshal Sedore, and Lieutenant Bydal. Special Agent Brent Madison commanded the rescue team, and they were loaded with gear and weapons, ready to move at a moment's notice. A helicopter waited in the north parking lot of the community center with a pilot on standby.

The row of coffee machines on a long table cycled through pots of black coffee as the twelve men waited for Noah's phone to ring.

Sedore had the cell phone hooked into a StingRay 3 device, which would track, record, and monitor any information as a caller made a connection. The best hope was to locate where the signal came from and what tower they were connected to. At that point, the HRT would deploy to the location and await further details.

By six o'clock in the morning, despite the coffee, everyone dozed in their chairs as they waited. When the cell phone rang, however, everyone was instantly alert.

"Unknown caller." Sedore flicked two large toggle switches on the StingRay unit and then nodded to Noah. "Go ahead."

He cleared his throat, then accepted the call on speaker.

"Speak." Noah wasn't in the mood for chit-chat. He remained focused while the anger simmered deep inside.

"Hope you got some sleep. Did you get what I wanted?"

"It's en route. But, first, I want to talk with Dickinson. Put her on the phone, or there won't be any deal."

They heard a hand go over the mic and some muffled voices as they spoke. Marshal Sedore's fingers flew over the keyboard that was connected to the electronic equipment.

"Before she talks, I want you to hear something."

Everyone sat up straighter when they heard the familiar sound of a magazine as it clicked into the housing and a slide pulled back as a round was fed into the chamber.

"Right now, if she says anything *untoward*, I pull the trigger."

After a moment, Noah spoke, "Angie, are you okay?"

"I'm alive."

At the sound of her voice, the knot of tension relaxed slightly. Proof of life was an important step. She didn't sound in pain or forced. Sedore scribbled on a paper pad and handed it to Madison, who raised his right hand in the air and made a circle gesture. The HRT team quietly and quickly moved out of the command office as they headed for the helicopter.

Noah had to confirm one item. "Angie, what day is it today?"

"Umm, it should be early morning on Thursday."

Agent Madison gave him a thumbs-up. No chance her response was previously recorded. She was alive.

"Can you tell me the details of the exchange?"

They heard a muffled scream. It sounded like she was gagged.

"That's enough. Get a pen and paper, and I'll give you directions. You *will* follow them to the letter, or I disappear, and you'll be left with another corpse. Got it?"

"Let me guess. I'm to come alone to a place you choose for the exchange?"

"Bingo. Ready?"

After he wrote down a few notes, Noah looked at his watch. "That doesn't leave me much time."

Piekenbrock sounded amused. "Not my problem."

Noah was about to answer when the call was disconnected. He turned to Sedore. "Tell me you have a solid lead."

The large Marshal didn't look away from the laptop. "*Very* solid. It seems too good, actually."

He turned the screen and showed the map-overlay.

"West of Arrow Point, near Rock Springs, over two-hundred miles. One cell tower in the area, and there is only one farm in that location. It stinks."

Noah looked down at the instructions. "This tells me to head in the other direction."

The door into the conference room slammed open, and the county medical examiner, George Hall, ran into the room carrying the green duffel bag with both hands. Noah noticed he still wore flannel pajama bottoms and a black Star Wars T-shirt.

Daryl Sedore closed the laptop and ran to get the bag while Noah looked at his watch once again. "I have ten minutes. Let's get to work."

*****

Angie took a slow deep breath through her nose and held it against what was coming. She exploded into movement and wrenched her left wrist sideways, then rotated her forearm another two inches.

The pain shot into her jaw as a large swath of skin peeled back against the ropes before the circulation started to flow once again. The gag helped keep her scream muffled as she increased a steady pull against the binding.

Her hands were tied behind her back, and another rope kept her ankles together. The noose around her neck was tied to a bolt in the back of the pickup truck. Even if she were to gain her feet and jump off the side, she would hang herself. The blue plastic tarp covered her. She was glad for the concealment. It hid her efforts at escape.

The truck bottomed out, and she was temporarily lifted from the truck bed, then slammed hard on her right shoulder.

She swore and redoubled her efforts. The blood had slicked down over her hand and dripped off her fingertips, but despite the pain, it acted as a lubricant against the strong nylon rope.

When she pulled back her wrist, it slipped down the loop, and it moved almost two inches before it stopped at the large knuckle joint of her thumb. Angie tried to fold her thumb tight against her palm and resumed her efforts, but it wouldn't slide through.

The truck slowed, and it seemed to be going across country. The sound of the gravel road disappeared. She heard grass and brush scraping against the undercarriage of the vehicle.

The truck stopped, and the driver's door opened, but the engine didn't stop. She remained still while struggling to hear anything. There was a rattle of chains, and after a few seconds, she felt Piekenbrock climb back behind the wheel. They moved forward, then the vehicle stopped once again, followed by the sound of a chain as it clinked against a metal object.

Was that a gate?

They had to be close to their destination. She knew what she had to do. With a sharp pull against her bonds, her thumb popped. As her eyes rolled back in pain, she continued to struggle.

The skin on her wrist shifted and slid toward her knuckles before she pulled her hand free of the loop. As she ground her teeth together, she started on the knotted rope around her throat. Without the use of her thumb and her blood-slicked fingers, Angie couldn't find purchase until she realized it was tied in a noose. The slipknot slid back along its length, and with a quick movement, she was free.

She knew enough not to sit up under the tarp and let him know what was going on. Angie quickly freed her other hand and slid along the length of the truck bed where she lay flat against the tailgate.

When the truck turned a corner, she quietly slid out of the truck bed and fell to the ground. The young woman rolled a few times on the thick weeds and grass. She struggled to sit and worked at the rope that bound her ankles together while she glanced around. It looked like the edge of a farmer's field with a large track of woods behind her.

Despite the aches and pains and the lack of use of her thumb, she was free within a minute. She picked up the rope and tried to fix the grass where she sat to avoid leaving a sign that she was there.

As the truck drove away, Constable Dickinson gingerly made her way through the long grass and weeds and headed straight for the woods.

She had hunted enough with her father and brothers all her life. She knew how to track and move through the countryside. However, Angie had never been the prey and preferred to be on the other end of the spectrum. Cradling her arm, she limped into the tree line and grinned. *At least this prey fights back.*

Chapter 54

Noah pulled his truck over to the side of the road and waited. In the backseat was the green duffel bag. He kept his Glock in the cup holder on the center console next to a protein bar and bottle of water.

As the sun rose in the eastern sky, it cast a red tinge to the low clouds against the mountain ridges on the horizon.

Red sky morning, soldier's warning.

During basic army training, he had corrected a drill sergeant on that saying. Noah could not help but grin at how bad he was chewed out. "Yes, Drill Sergeant. I know I'm in the army, not the navy, Drill Sergeant." The young private had sweated and been adamant that he didn't want to go and be a sailor. The army was where he wanted to be. Ever since when he recalled the saying, "soldier" was substituted.

He could hear the engine of the truck tick as it cooled, and he drummed his fingers on the steering wheel as he waited. The first instructions were to come alone and remain at the corner of Interstate 25 North and Smokey Gap Road, north of Casper. Noah had arrived at the exact location with over ten minutes to spare. At that time of the morning, he flew north on the Interstate. Besides, the Highway Patrol knew where he was headed and to watch out for his truck.

As the sun began to rise, he had a clear view of the countryside, and it was primarily flat with farmers' fields. When a lone vehicle approached his position, he could see it from over a mile away. A small new Toyota hatchback, two-door Yaris flashed their high beams, pulled a U-turn behind his truck, and stopped.

Noah picked up his pistol and kept it straight behind his right leg as he stepped out and began to walk toward the car.

The window was down, and a young lady sat behind the wheel. She wore a University of Wyoming blue T-shirt with oval glasses on the end of her nose. Her long brown hair was up in a ponytail and freckles were scattered across her cheeks and nose. When she smiled, deep dimples appeared. "Noah Hunter?"

"Yes?"

He kept the pistol hidden and turned to the side. She wasn't part of this.

"Your Uncle Zee called for me to pick you up. Your Uber ride is already paid for."

Noah nodded. "Okay, let me grab a bag and I'll be right back."

As he turned and headed back to the truck, she called out, "He said he would give you a new phone, that you don't need yours. Does that make sense?"

Fuck.

"All good, thanks."

On the way back to the truck, he slid the Glock into the holster and pulled out his cell phone, leaving it on the driver's seat. When he was back at the small car, she had the hatch open. He placed the bag inside and sat in the front seat.

Once he was buckled in, she looked in her mirrors and turned the Toyota around, then headed south on the Interstate, toward Casper.

Back the way he had just traveled.

******

Angie wiped her hand on her jeans while she leaned forward to catch her breath. She had popped her thumb back in the socket, but her hand had started to swell, and she couldn't use it. Better to have that than be dead.

Once she entered the treeline, she tried to head east continually. The rising sun drew her like a beacon, and she knew the hazards of walking in the woods. Those who were lost and didn't know their way tended to walk in a large circle and eventually returned to where they started.

There wasn't too much cover in the trees, but it was better than nothing. Predominately, spruce and pine were in the area. She'd looked for a place to hide, but so far, there hadn't been anything. The spruce trees were too small to get inside the branches.

After ten minutes of travel, she came across a large field at the edge of the tree line. On the far side, a quarter-mile distance was the edge of another tract of woods, it appeared to be denser, and it stretched north and south for as far as she could see.

Angie picked up the twenty-foot length of rope and sprinted across the open space. There wasn't enough cover where she was, and she knew the risk would be worth it. Her running shoes dug into the soil and provided good traction.

At one point, the open field had to have been farmland. It was fairly flat and free of rock. The grass grew in small clumps, however, it was mostly bare hard-packed soil.

A puff of dirt jumped up in front of her—a split second later, the crack of a rifle echoed across the countryside. She couldn't tell which direction the shot was fired from, but she immediately turned to the north and began to zigzag randomly across the field. It would take longer to reach the safety of the woods, but she went on the best guess as to where Piekenbrock was.

The next shot kicked up the dirt twelve feet to her left, and her long legs reacted to the adrenaline boost. She poured all her energy into closing the remaining distance to a cluster of aspens.

As she reached the first tree, the white bark splintered as a round found its way into the bark. Inches beside her head. Her heart leaped in her chest, and then she was among the thick trees. Branches scraped across her arms and face, but she didn't slow. Soon as she got in far enough, she turned north.

"Good luck trying to get me now."

A little tension left while she slowed to make her way through the woods. There wasn't any need to have a path of broken branches that pointed directly to her location. Angie was unsure how much of a lead she had, but he still had to cross over four-hundred yards of field.

Time to disappear.

Chapter 55

As they headed south toward Casper, Noah talked with the Uber driver, Candice, to learn more about the arrangement. It was done through the application on her phone—she hadn't spoken to a person. The request came through prepaid and destination. There was nothing further she could add.

He did not question her on the drop-off location. He would find out soon enough. When they were fifteen minutes north of Casper, Noah felt uneasy when she slowed and made a right turn on a fire-route county road and headed west.

This road led to his cabin, and he had thought only a couple of people knew about its location. Finally, however, the driver stopped right in front of his gate, and she smiled at Noah. "Hope you enjoyed your ride."

He thanked her, retrieved the duffel bag and waved as Candice drove off. Noah unlocked the gate and closed it behind him before he walked the quarter-mile to the cabin. He couldn't see any recent signs of a vehicle on the trail.

He quickly grew warm from carrying the twenty-pound bag. The ballistic vest didn't breathe and reflected the body heat.

When Noah finally came to the small clearing, he dropped the bag and conducted a full walkaround. The A-frame building looked the same, and he couldn't see anything out of place.

At the front door, he unlocked it and stepped inside, dropping the bag on the couch. The alarm system wasn't on. Right in the middle of the kitchen table sat a burner cell phone.

Once he went through the menu, Noah found one pre-programmed number. He pushed the call button and waited.

*****

Angie crouched beside the stream, washed the blood off her hand, and assessed the damage from the rope cuts. The skin was peeled back almost two inches, the tissue underneath raw, and blood slowly seeped out. The swelling went past the wrist and the second knuckle of the thumb. Every movement was painful and stiff. If that were the price for her freedom, Angie would take it every time.

The cool water from the stream felt good, and she wished there was time to stay and soak her hand, but even the brief stop was too long of a delay.

With cupped hands, she took a few sips of the cold water then stood. The creek was only three feet wide and shallow, only a few inches deep. Large dry rocks sat in the middle.

She stepped in the wet mud at the edge and pressed down on the flat rock with the toe of her running shoe.

Once she stepped back, the wet smear of a toe print was visible on the rock. Angie slipped off her damp running shoe, and instead of crossing the stream, she moved farther north along the creek bed—from flat rock to flat rock.

After twenty feet, she confirmed there wasn't a trail, so she stepped back into the shelter of the trees and put her shoe back on. Finally, another twenty feet inside the woods, she found something that would work.

An old white pine had fallen with the root structure intact across another tree. She got to her knees and had moved a few branches out of the way. Then she crawled under the thick trunk and pushed the leaves and soil to the side, creating a small shelter.

It wasn't a perfect cover, there were a few gaps where she could see the immediate area, but it was the best opportunity to hide she had seen since she entered the woods.

She made a small pillow with the rope to keep her head off the soil and waited. It took effort not to let the circumstances get to her. She had to rely on her training and determination to help get her through this. Her heart rate slowed, and she started to relax and take stock of the situation.

Jeans, a T-shirt, and running shoes with a length of nylon rope were her only items. Her pockets were empty, and besides bruises and scrapes from the branches and her injured left wrist, she was in good condition. After a few minutes, she realized one problem.

Ants.

There were dozens of large black ants crawling over her, and she felt a few as they made their way inside her pantleg. She was about to brush them off her arms when she froze.

A cell phone rang. It was *very* close.

She could hear some muffled cursing, and then the former police lieutenant spoke.

"I'll contact you shortly for the next part. Stay in position."

Angie lifted her head to peer through the branches. Zane Piekenbrock stood fifteen feet away. A .300 Win Mag lay across his left shoulder with a cell phone to his right ear.

She couldn't hear the response, but she guessed it was Noah on the other end.

"Yes, she is fine." He paused, then he turned to her hiding place and held out the phone. "Tell Detective Hunter you're still alive. I have work to do."

Chapter 56

The helicopter landed in a far farmer's field, half a mile from the target location. They flew the distance in forty-five minutes before they hovered one foot off the ground, and it held steady against the eastern winds. The HRT spread out and stuck to the wood line, H&K 416 rifles at the ready. The pilot lifted the Black Hawk and, with a one-hundred and eighty-degree turn, moved two miles east to wait for exfiltration.

The GPS coordinates led them to an area northeast of Rock Springs. The higher altitude and rocky ground limited farming to low-laying canyons. When the team came within three hundred yards of the farmhouse and barn, they could easily see the whole property from the elevated position.

Agent Brent Madison dropped into the prone position and looked through the telescopic sight on his weapon. He scanned the ground and windows of the property. There wasn't any sign of movement.

The two-story home had a large, covered porch on the south side, and the barn was smaller than what he expected. It resembled a three-car garage with an elevated roof. The bay door was large enough to drive a tractor inside. The barn looked freshly painted red with white trim around the doors and one window.

The long driveway was empty of vehicles.

Madison pointed to two men and gave them the thumbs-up. They kept low and circled the property to provide the team with an elevated coverage when they approached.

The remaining six men did a secondary equipment check, and then everyone studied the ground and the property while they waited.

After he felt the vibration in his chest, he pulled out the cell phone and confirmed they had a copy of the electronic warrant.

"We are greenlit. Confirm once in position."

Twenty minutes later, they received confirmation from the sniper team, and they spread out and crossed the field in a diamond-head formation with Madison on point.

He stayed low with the butt of the rifle into his shoulder as they continually scanned the area to their front and sides. Their black tactical outfits blended into the terrain. Only from behind were the white letters FBI across their shoulders were visible. That separated them from a special operations division of the military, and it was also legally required that they were identified.

At twenty feet from the home, they spread out in an extended line, and two men on the end moved to the barn while the four moved to the front door on the porch. With their backs to the wall, the last man stepped forward and dropped his backpack to remove a small-shaped charge.

Madison held up his hand, and they paused when he reached out and tested the door handle. It was unlocked.

Soon as he felt the hand on his shoulder, he entered the home and swept the corners while the remainder of the team followed him in. The sharp sound of glass breaking in the kitchen could be heard throughout as two more of the team breached the old farm door.

Two men went up the narrow, steep stairs to the bedrooms while two more went down into the cellar. Nine seconds after entry, the "all clear" was heard throughout the home.

Over his headset, the team heard the two men who went to the barn report it was empty.

A secondary search of the home showed that an elderly couple lived there with no obvious signs of Piekenbrock or a hostage.

As the team left, a business card was stuck in the front door for the homeowner to call the local field office in Cheyenne.

The Black Hawk was called into the nearest field for extraction, and a few minutes later, the HRT flew back to Arrow Point. All eight agents failed to notice the cell phone underneath a small solar panel on the roof of the home. The solar panel powered a relay/repeater digital box, and the cell phone was out of the elements. It acted as a small cellular base station and could forward calls and boost a signal. Bought and sold off Amazon for under eighty dollars and easy to install. Especially in the dead of night, without the homeowner's permission or knowledge.

*****

Noah waited the full sixty minutes after he heard from Piekenbrock, then he followed the instructions.

He left the duffel bag on the kitchen table and made his way to the gate. Every step felt like a defeat, but there were little to no choices left. If there was a chance to save Dickinson, he had to take it.

Instead of turning left to walk out to the Interstate, he turned right. His property was over fifty acres of forested countryside with a swamp dividing his property and the next on the north. He had never seen either neighbor to the sides. When he went to the cabin, he went there for privacy and to relax.

As he walked along the gravel road, he looked for signs that he was going the right way. After ten minutes, he found a farm gate on the south side of the road with a pink ribbon tied around the top.

He checked the Glock in the holster for the tenth time while scanning the tree line. He was alone with no one else in the area. Noah wasn't sure if it was a trap or a real exchange. He didn't know the value that Piekenbrock placed on the bones.

First kill, first trophy? Most likely.

Regardless, he had to take the chance for Angie's sake. As he climbed over the gate, he couldn't help but think of how they tied in to the case and their importance to Piekenbrock.

The gravel road turned into a worn trail through the grass, and he saw recent tracks that had pressed the grass down flat. He followed the path for twenty minutes as it wound across an old field and through a set of woods before a meadow opened on the other side of the trees.

An old barn sat fifty yards out in the open. It looked as if it hadn't been used in decades. Boards had fallen off the sides, and the tin roof had long since rusted away. The exposed beams and wooden framing looked solid. One of the barn doors had fallen, and it resembled a drawbridge across a moat that beckoned him inside.

He drew his pistol and took a deep breath while he brought it into the ready position. With the muzzle leading, he stepped inside.

Chapter 57

The rifle was slung over his shoulder, and the Beretta tucked into the waistband of his lower back. The gray sweatshirt was pulled over the top of the pistol. Unless he was frisked, it remained hidden. Not that he was worried. If anyone was close enough to identify him, odds are they would be shooting first.

The trail he had followed went through old fields and various sections of woods. After crossing the small creek, he stopped the ATV and began the short walk through the thick brush. He had completed this route twice before when he scouted it out, and Piekenbrock had no problems.

A small clearing with a utility shed appeared before him, and he paused. Zane had wondered a few times about the structure. It was set back into the trees and was almost hidden from the cabin. He wasn't the only one with secrets. Noah was hiding something.

However, he knew that time was precious if he had to stick to the plan. Once passed the shed, he stood beside the outhouse and peeked around the corner. The back of the A-framed cabin had two windows for the kitchen and back door. There was also a small window in the loft that overlooked the woods.

A glance at his watch confirmed he had a few minutes. One thing he knew about Noah Hunter was that he would follow the instructions to the letter. He wouldn't want to risk Dickinson's life.

The world is a big place, and he could've been anywhere by now, safe, and undetected. However, he couldn't leave without that bag. It helped drive and motivate him.

When the cabin's front door closed, he waited another minute before he stepped around the outhouse and moved to the side. Noah walked away in his tactical uniform, heading down the driveway where he turned the corner and moved out of view.

Back at the rear door, Piekenbrock reached above the ledge and pulled down the spare key. Seconds later, he had the duffel bag over one shoulder. He locked the door behind him and replaced the key. From the angle and reach required, he was certain that Noah had no idea it was there. Keep him wondering.

Piekenbrock abandoned stealth for speed as he jogged back to the ATV. He strapped the duffel bag to the front before he started across the old trail. The truck was ten minutes away, and he was ready to disappear and lay low for a while.

*****

The mid-morning sun shone throughout the old barn, and Noah could see old, rusted equipment stacked along one side and a row of horse stalls on the left. Above in the rafters, a flock of pigeons tilted their head and stared at him as he tried to detect any movement or danger.

In the third stall, Noah found Angie underneath a blue plastic tarp. As he drew closer, his footsteps caused her to struggle, and he heard a muffled scream. He holstered the Glock, pulled the tarp aside, and threw it over a short wooden wall. Her hands were tied behind her back, and the noose stretched about her neck was secured to her ankles. If she made a move to straighten her legs, it would choke her.

Jesus Christ.

Soon as Angie saw her rescuer, tears trickled down her cheeks, and a few sobs of relief escaped her lips. Noah made quick work of the ropes and removed the gag. He frowned when he saw the multiple scratch marks on her face and arms and the wound around her wrist.

"Are you okay?"

"Yeah, just tired and sore in places that I shouldn't be."

Once she stood and brushed her hands clean, she gave him a bear hug. If he hadn't been wearing his vest, Noah was sure his ribs would have cracked.

"It's okay now."

He patted her back and reassured her everything would be fine. It took a few moments for her to regain her composure, then she wiped her eyes, twisted and stretched. Noah saw her wince as her right shoulder moved, and her left hand was swollen.

He quickly caught her up on what had happened, and she was shocked to find out they were only a thirty-minute walk from his cabin property.

He pulled out the burner phone—no signal in the barn.

"Let's head back to my cabin. There's food and water there, and the reception is better. I'll call in for help."

"A coffee and an ice pack would be amazing. Do you know where Piekenbrock is? How are we going to get him now?"

Noah just smiled at her questions. "I'll explain on the way."

After ten minutes, Angie laughed when she heard everything. Her mood had instantly changed. "I can't wait. I *will* be there when we nail him."

Noah doubted he could have stopped her, and he'd be glad to have her there. She had more than earned it.

Chapter 58

Jessica Ross slipped on her white lab coat and clipped the identification tag to the large pocket as she turned on the equipment in her laboratory. The FSL building had just reopened, and the county sheriff's office finished supervising the clean-up crew before anyone could enter.

Her specialty was DNA extraction, and recently she had branched her research into genealogy. In her mind, it was a natural progression.

The separator beeped when she finished the last button on her coat, and she realized it had been a full eighteen hours since she had run the program.

She lifted the glass lid, removed the sample, and sat at her stainless-steel workbench. Jessica added the sodium-ion solution to neutralize the mixture. It caused the DNA to lose any negative charge, and it made the sample more stable. With a dropper, she added the isopropanol to help separate the unwanted cellular material. Then she connected the purified sample to another machine that would rinse and extract the DNA for analysis.

The final purification stage only took twenty minutes, then Jessica closed her emails and began to upload the data.

The national database for the United States was the Combined DNA Index System (CODIS), and it operated on three different levels—local, state, and nationwide. Immediately, she uploaded the sequencing into the program, and then the DNA was sent to her genealogy partners at MyFamilyTree.

Sometimes, the process could take hours, weeks, or months before a family tree with descendants was established. In this case, it took less than forty-five minutes for her to see an emerging family tree. When she compared the CODIS results, at first, Jessica was confused. It took a solid hour to confirm and clarify the data. It was made easier when the DoD approved her query.

Her analytical mind worked overtime to solve the puzzle. Finally, when she figured out the answer, she stood fast enough to knock her stool over. She searched her desk while her hands shook in excitement. Jessica eventually found the business card in her lab coat and called the detective.

*****

Noah walked into the command center along with John Gaston from the highway patrol. He headed to the coffee machine and poured himself a cup while several waited in anticipation.

He took a sip, then smiled at everyone. "It worked."

Marshal Sedore immediately turned to his computer system and activated the map overlay while they waited for the program to sync. The red dot pulsed, and Daryl zoomed in. They saw it proceed north along Interstate 90. His large finger tapped the screen. "He'll be in Montana in a few minutes, heading north."

Noah looked at the map. "Canadian border?"

The Marshal remained focused. "It's possible."

Noah began the coordination with the FBI, and he saw that Special Agent Madison was already on the phone with his supervisor, and he picked up his phone to call Lieutenant Bydal. The Montana Highway Patrol would need to move quickly, but everyone was motivated and ready.

The Billings FBI field office couldn't deploy where Interstate 90 entered Montana in time. However, the state police had no problems when it came to setting up a traffic control point. The ramps were monitored, and each vehicle was checked. With the recent issues around the state prison, they were ready to deploy and cordon off the area within fourteen minutes of receiving the call.

Marshal Sedore stayed on the phone with the patrol captain, and when the GPS drew within a mile, the state police were ready.

Barriers were erected across the Interstate, and spike strips were stretched across all lanes, north and southbound. Traffic began to back up as each driver was checked and allowed through individually.

"Quarter mile and slowly closing."

Sedore remained calm as he relayed the information, and Noah stood behind his right shoulder. He tapped his foot and fought the urge to pace.

"The signal is on top of your location."

Over the speaker, Noah heard shouting and officers yelling. The highway patrol captain must have run to the vehicle. The wind noise and his harsh breath sounded through the phone.

It was only a moment later when they heard muffled cursing from the officers.

Noah leaned over and spoke. "What's going on, Captain?"

"The vehicle in question is a 2015 Dodge Caravan, and there's a family of four inside. No sign of Piekenbrock."

"Is there a large green duffel bag?"

"Wait one."

Car doors slammed over the speaker, and the captain ordered a trooper to search the vehicle. It didn't take long for him to reply. "I have one green duffel bag in the roof rack with the family's sports equipment. The driver said it wasn't his. He doesn't know anything about it."

Noah felt his hopes plummet. "What's inside the bag?"

"Nothing. It's empty."

Fuck.

"Roger. Stand down the blockade. Thank you for your assistance."

Noah sat on the nearest chair and placed his cold coffee on the table. The trackers placed in the duffel bag had worked, but Piekenbrock was a step ahead of them. Again.

Shoulders slumped, the mood in the command center was somber. Their last solid chance had slipped through their fingers like a smoke-ring against an errant breeze.

Noah drummed his fingers on the table while he thought of the next step. Old fashioned police work. They would have to go back through all the evidence from the first body found and chase down each lead.

When his cell phone rang, he saw *FSL* on display, and a flicker of hope rose through his chest. When he heard Jessica Ross talk and her excitement, he couldn't help but grin. The game had just changed yet again.

Chapter 59

Jessica had time to go over the information and called in a few more favors with the Department of Defense. Her dark-rimmed glasses were low on her nose as she bent over the table and flipped through the folder. She absently tucked her hair behind her ear. Noah sat on the opposite side of the conference table in the station. He had the command center stand down and disassembled. The next phase of the operation would be restricted to a few key players.

"Zane Piekenbrock, born 14 August 1962, to Edward and Anne Marie Piekenbrock, in Mercer, Ohio. This information is from his first deployment in 1982 to Lebanon, with the 1st Calvary Division and covered through until his last tour in Saudi Arabia in 1991."

She spun the pers file around, and Noah saw a standard picture that most military members had taken. A much younger Zane Piekenbrock stood on a slight angle in full dress uniform in front of the flag with a blue background. Noah had almost the same picture from his military days.

"Because of the soldiers that were taken as hostages, the DoD had started a DNA identification process. It was the only way they could identify bodies sometimes, once recovered. With the current sample obtained from the skeleton, we have a positive match. The larger proof at this time is fingerprints. The set on record with the military doesn't match the current prints on file for APPD. When he joined the police force, there would have been no reason to compare."

Noah looked at the probability chart. There was a 99.999% chance that there was a match. Good enough for the courts, good enough for him.

"So, if the remains are that of Zane Piekenbrock, who did I work with for almost twenty years?"

Jessica pulled out a secondary chart with a family tree and a copy of a birth certificate, dated 2 October 1964, along with a census record from Mercer, Ohio, from the following year.

"Anne Marie Piekenbrock had a second son, Robert Charles Piekenbrock. If I could get a DNA sample, I could compare it with the first sample to confirm. However, with the similarities there is almost no doubt."

Noah thought about all the items he collected from the apartment—from toothbrushes to a comb. "I think we can get you a sample for testing and comparison. Very soon, in fact."

He tapped the picture of Captain Piekenbrock on the military document. The Piekenbrock he knew looked like this picture. Enough that he couldn't tell the difference. If thirty years were added to the photo, it would be almost the same.

Noah sat back in the chair and looked at the information in front of him. He couldn't argue against the science. For some reason, Robert Charles Piekenbrock assumed his brother's life and turned into a serial killer. Before or after he joined the Arrow Point Police Department, Noah wasn't sure. If he assumed that the first kill was his brother, then everything else happened after.

"As to his reasonings for assuming his identity, I just don't know. I deal with the DNA. Everything else is in your area of expertise."

Noah thanked her for driving out to Arrow Point and briefing him. As of yet, he didn't know how this information would help him locate Piekenbrock. But now, he had a greater insight into the driving force behind the former LT. It was a step forward and not back. That alone inspired hope.

Jessica packed everything up in a folder and handed it over to Noah. "If you need anything, let me know. Glad I could help."

After she left, Noah sat alone in the conference room and again went over all the material. He may not have all the answers right now, but he was getting close. One thing was certain. The next step wasn't in Wyoming.

*****

Piekenbrock drummed his fingers on the steering wheel of the Chevy truck. He had to lay low. Preferably for the next thirty years. With his safehouse burned down, the apartment raided, and his other house under observation, he was low on options. The tremor in his left hand had disappeared. About time.

In the truck's backseat, a large blue Rubbermaid container with a Snap-On lid rested on the bench seat. It didn't take twenty seconds of searching to confirm a GPS tracker was placed at the bottom of the bag, mixed in with the dirt and another in the handle. A large container was needed to sift through the duffel bag contents. In the Walmart parking lot, it was easy to find an out-of-state vehicle that looked loaded for a drive as a decoy.

"Just you and me again. If you have any ideas, now's the time to let me know."

Robert pulled a baseball cap low on his head while going through the drive-through at the donut shop downtown Casper. As he reached for cash in his pocket, he noticed the other wallet from the former owner on the floor.

There was quite a bit of cash inside, and he used it to pay for the food and coffee. As he drove away, he tapped the wallet on the steering wheel while he whistled. The ideal safe location just appeared in his lap. With a chuckle, he headed south to the Interstate ramp.

Chapter 60

Police Chief Birch sat in stunned silence along with several others as Noah finished the briefing. LT Bydal shook his head at the situation, and the rest of the room echoed it. The FBI liaison officer leaned over to look at the reports, then muttered something.

Constable Dickinson stood at the back of the conference room. She wore her jeans and T-shirt, along with a Glock 19 at her hip. Her left wrist was in a brace, and the swelling had begun to recede. The white bandage stood out against her tanned skin.

"Chief, one recommendation until this is over. All patrols and members that are on duty double up in pairs."

The chief tapped his pen on a notepad while he thought. "Off duty?"

"All we can do is have everyone report in every four hours. I can't see this lasting long."

Birch nodded and wrote a few points.

"I also want to send someone to Mercer, Ohio. We may learn more on the background of Piekenbrock and the motives that are driving him."

At this, the chief shook his head. "That would be out of our jurisdiction. However, the FBI could handle it. Agent Courtice?"

The liaison officer nodded. "I'll ensure this gets priority. The field office in Columbus will head this up. Some great investigators work out of there. So, if anything is to be found, they will find it."

The chief thanked him, and Noah cleaned up the paperwork in front of him and placed it into different folders. "Are there any questions?"

"Detective Hunter?" Special Agent Courtice kept his eyes on the reports. "Robert Piekenbrock has proven resourceful and planned for various contingencies. My best guess is that we will have to get lucky to find him. You'd previously stated that you don't think this will last long. Why's that?"

Noah looked across the table and met Marshal Sedore's eyes, and they both grinned.

*****

After the forty-minute drive south of Casper, Piekenbrock pulled the truck over to the side of the road and confirmed the address on the driver's license. The steep driveway had two large wooden posts on either side and was over a hundred yards until it reached the home.

The two-story building overlooked one of the many canyons in the area, and the sand-colored walls blended into the landscape. The second floor would have a perfect elevated view. However, there seemed to be one potential problem.

Above the home, rugged terrain peaked higher than the roof, which prevented anyone from approaching in that direction, and to the east was a canyon. The drop-off was quite steep, stopping anyone from that approach. The only entry and exit would be the driveway. Again, perfectly defensible, but also, it could be a trap.

After all the years in the police department, he knew the attention span of the law enforcement officers would last three days, maximum. After that, budget concerns would cause the workforce to slacken, roadblocks to cease, and normal cases would pile up. Then, after a week, it would fade from memory as life resumed.

Robert ran his hand over his face while he thought of the risk factor. The stubble had come in mostly white to match his hair, with a dark patch on his chin. A few days holed up would give the beard time to grow, and it would help stop him from being recognized. It was all in the details.

With that in mind, he placed the truck in drive and headed toward the home.

After knocking on the front door, an older woman answered. She glanced over Piekenbrock's shoulder at the truck. "Oh my God! You've found my husband?"

By the time she looked back, her eyes had watered in hope. He pulled out his wallet and flashed the golden APPD badge. "Mind if I come in so we can talk, Mrs. Mason?"

Betty nodded and led him to a living room just off the kitchen. The house was neat and tidy and filled with pictures of their family. She didn't question why a police officer was dressed in jeans, tactical boots, a gray hooded sweatshirt and baseball cap.

"Have you found John? Where is he?"

Piekenbrock looked out the rear window of the home. The backyard ended one hundred feet out, and the drop-off for the canyon began. He was fairly sure a goat wouldn't be able to climb from that angle.

She sat on the couch and waited while he looked around. Finally, he pulled out the wallet from his front pocket and handed it to her as he stepped back. "He wanted you to have this."

Betty looked down at her husband's wallet, confused. When she looked up, the officer reached behind his lower back. She would see her husband sooner than later.

~

Piekenbrock finished his lunch, left the dishes in the sink, and smiled at the body on the couch. "I'll clean these later if that's okay?"

One benefit to the secluded home is that there were no neighbors to hear the two shots. He chuckled to himself as he went to the truck and moved a few things inside. The .300 Win Mag and a black backpack of mixed ammo were set up in the master bedroom. It had a perfect view down the long driveway. He slipped his arms through a small green backpack of clothes on the second trip, and he carried the rubber storage container into the kitchen.

As he set the blue bin down, he frowned. Piekenbrock lifted it up and down as if he were doing biceps curls. He did not like to disturb his brother more than necessary, but something seemed wrong. Robert lifted the lid and looked at the contents. There were seven or eight inches of dry soil that he had dug from the old cellar, and the remains of Zane were mixed in.

While at the shopping center parking lot, he didn't have time to go through the duffel bag, but he knew enough that it would have been bugged and a second tracker would be buried in with the dirt. It's what he would have done.

Now he turned his attention to the bones themselves. They looked too clean and different. The skull rested on top of the dirt, and he picked it up and hefted the weight in his right hand.

Piekenbrock opened the cutlery drawer, pulled out a steak knife, and dug the tip into the skull. It slipped easily through the bone. He dusted some of the dirt away, and saw small letters inside that were written in gold.

Made in China.

Small holes at the base of the skull where the vertebrae connected were uncovered, and he found another set of small holes where the remainder of the skeleton would connect.

When he threw the skull across the kitchen, it bounced off the refrigerator and rolled on the tiled floor. It was made of plastic.

He had seen this skeleton many times in the coroner's office. It had hung on the stand in the corner wearing a white lab coat.

Mr. Bones.

Chapter 61

Three cars covered every possible access to the Natrona coroner's office, and chase cars were parked on the ramps to the Interstate. In the fields that surrounded the building, police officers were hidden in camouflaged blinds. With the sun going down in an hour, they were almost invisible. They had lost their air support and HRT from the FBI. They were needed elsewhere.

All the staff were absent, and Noah sat behind George's desk with Lieutenant Bydal and Marshal Sedore. All the men were dressed for tactical operations, and they had enough weapons loaded to give a biker gang serious pause.

Noah's cell phone was plugged into the StingRay and a laptop, ready to track and trace. They waited two hours before the screen lit up with an incoming call, and *Private Number* was displayed.

He placed it on speaker. Piekenbrock started to swear immediately. "Listen here, you motherfu—"

"Call back when you're in a better mood. I'm busy."

Noah disconnected the call. Sedore looked at the display and shook his head. Bydal sat on the edge of the desk and grinned. "How did that feel?"

"Pretty good, actually." He moved a shotgun to the side and folded his hands on the desk. "That's why I'm not on the FBI negotiation team."

One minute later, the phone rang again, and he let it ring a few extra seconds before he pressed the button. "Are you in a better mood now?"

The three men smirked when they heard silence on the other end. "You'll pay for what you did. I have nothing but time."

Noah leaned forward. "I don't think so. The only *time* you are going to have is waiting on death row, Robert."

There was no response, then Piekenbrock let out a short bark of laughter. "Good job, Noah. Of course, it doesn't change anything, but good job."

Lieutenant Bydal moved to stand behind Sedore, looking at the results of the search. The signal originated from the same location, the farmhouse in the southwestern area of Wyoming.

"We have the real Zane Piekenbrock, and we will have you—"

Noah smiled when he wasn't one to disconnect the call. He turned to Sedore. "Tell me we have something more substantial this time?"

"That signal is definitely coming from that cell tower. Origins are that same farm. I think they must have missed something last time."

Bydal opened his phone and scrolled through a long document before he showed them. "The warrant for that address is still valid for the next forty-eight hours."

Noah leaned back in the desk chair and drummed his fingers on the desk while he thought. "I would suggest moving the bones to the APPD secure lockup and keeping this place empty for a few days. In case of retaliation."

Bydal nodded. "Sounds good. I'll contact the chief and the feds and get a team to revisit the farmhouse property." He turned to the marshal. "I'd like you there as well if you're up for it?"

Sedore grinned. "I wouldn't miss it."

Noah pulled the handheld radio unit off his vest. "All call signs, stand down."

While the two men restored the office to how they found it and packed the equipment, Noah went farther into the building and entered the refrigeration storage. The short black body bag didn't weigh more than twenty pounds. He carried it with him when they left the building.

Back at the APPD, Noah conducted the after-action meeting, and Lieutenant Bydal put together a team that would work alongside the FBI and the US Marshals. In addition, the county sheriff would have groups in the area on alert to act as backup, if required.

The farmhouse was almost a three-hour drive from Arrow Point, and they didn't have use of a helicopter. Bydal planned on them leaving by three o'clock in the morning. That would give them enough time to set up and execute the warrant when the sun began to rise.

Noah looked at his watch after the meeting. He could still get a solid four hours of sleep. He was about to head home when Bydal pulled him off to the side.

"Noah, I want you to stay here at the station in case there's a problem. I know you can handle it."

He started to object, then he remembered his promise to respect his friend's rank and decisions, so he simply nodded.

Bydal squeezed his shoulder. "Thanks. We're light on senior officers, and despite this being a priority case, we have other problems that arise. I asked you to stay because I can trust you."

"No problem. You will keep me informed of everything?"

"Promise. Okay, I need a couple hours' sleep, and so do you. We need to stay sharp. Be back here in four."

Within twenty minutes, they headed home, and Noah almost fell asleep soon as he laid down. His Glock was loaded and rested under the pillow, and he had another pistol on the nightstand. Despite the exhaustion, his eyes opened with every creak of the house as the wind picked up. He wouldn't be caught unaware again.

Chapter 62

Despite the restless sleep and his mind constantly going over facts, Noah felt recharged after four hours. He was back at the station just before sunrise.

The team had arrived at the farmhouse, and Lieutenant Bydal briefed him before they began a more detailed search. The homeowners were an elderly couple, and they were not aware of anything on their property, and they had no connection to Piekenbrock. They had cooperated fully.

Frustrated, Noah turned his energy into paperwork, and he finished several reports. There was another identification on a missing person from nine years ago. They had managed a DNA match from one of the bodies recovered at the graveyard. Jessica had pulled through again on the research.

He forwarded the information to the Denver Police Department with his regrets for the family and his assurance that they would do their best to close the case. Hopefully, the family would gain some closure.

At this time of the morning, the cube was a hub of activity as the night shift finished and the day shift took over. Staff Sergeant Steve Hutchings had reported back to work. It had taken him a few days to recover in the hospital, and the wound had healed enough for him to move with his arm in a sling. "It will take more than almost dying, not to help out when I can." He wouldn't be working a full shift for a while, but he said he couldn't just sit at home. If the chief didn't like it, too bad.

Noah couldn't blame him, and he was glad his friend expected a full recovery.

Constable Dickinson walked into the cube with a large stack of paperwork and her reports and statements filled out. She had taken off the brace from her left wrist since the swelling had gone down. Besides the bandage, she appeared to be fine. She was dressed the same as Noah, in a full tactical uniform with a vest. Angie had also replaced her baton with a Taser.

It was noon before he realized the time and a quick check in his locker showed he was out of protein bars.

"Did you want to grab lunch across the street?"

She looked up from the computer screen and yawned. "I could use a stretch. Any word from the LT?"

"Nothing yet. If there were anything significant, he would have called. I'm assuming it's a dead end."

The coffee shop across the street was fairly busy, and by the time they got a sandwich and coffee, they decided to eat back at their desks.

After he logged in, Noah noticed a new report on top of a stack of paperwork. Someone had dropped it off and wrote, *Follow up* across the top in black pen, underlined.

The first page was a missing persons report for John Mason from his wife, Betty. They were south of Alcova in Natrona County and the make and model of the vehicle he was last seen driving was a 2015 black Chevy Silverado, king-cab with short box.

The second report was from the coroner's office with details on the unidentified male found shot in the backseat of Piekenbrock's police cruiser on the day he went missing. The same day Noah had found Hutchings.

Noah read the two reports and then showed them to Dickinson. "Did you leave these on my desk?"

She read them quickly, then shook her head. "Not me." Angie read the description of the truck once again, and then she held one finger in the air. "Give me a second to print this out."

Once she returned and handed her latest report over, Dickinson grinned. She described the vehicle that Piekenbrock had her in, matching the missing persons truck.

Excited, Noah immediately called dispatch with the particulars of the truck's year and make. Within five minutes, all law enforcement within the state would be on the lookout for the black Chevy.

Noah asked around, and no one in the area had seen anyone drop off the reports when he was away. At this point, he didn't care.

"Do you think he's still driving the same truck?"

Angie shrugged. "Not sure, but it's Wyoming. It seems every other vehicle here is a pickup truck of some kind."

Noah couldn't help but agree. "I'm driving one as well."

It didn't take long for them to catch up on the reports. He sent a text message to LT Bydal at the farmhouse, but they didn't respond. They could be finished and on their way back, or they were busy. If they were busy, it could mean they had found something.

Noah called the forensic lab. However, they hadn't completed any further work. His eyes landed on the report once again, and he shrugged. "There are no problems at the station. How about a quick road trip?"

Angie stood and smiled. "Ready."

*****

Piekenbrock stood in the backyard and stared out at the countryside from the elevated view. He could see for miles. He knew his days in Wyoming were finished. It was time to leave and start a new life. Robert had started over before, and he could do so again.

This time he would be more careful.

When he turned back to the house, he caught his reflection in the glass door, and one thing jumped out at him. He had kept his hair short in a military-style crew cut for the last two decades. It was expected with the job.

However, one thing had happened over the years, something that he couldn't change. Ten years ago, his hair began to turn white. Not gray or silver, but pure white. It had never been a problem before, but now it would be a beacon, and law enforcement would spot it easily, even if most of it were under a ballcap.

He rubbed a hand through his hair and over the weeklong stubble on his face and thought of options. Shaving it would be temporary and not something he wanted to do. He headed back inside the house to search the bathrooms.

Time to look younger.

Chapter 63

Alcova was too small to be considered a town or a village, with less than one hundred people living there full time. There was a small set of stores that sold the essentials. A drug store doubled as the post office, and Melanie's Diner on the corner catered for the travelers. The busiest place was the Liquor Depot next to the grocery store for those on a camping trip or a day on the water. They didn't have a streetlight, but there were a few signs that suggested people were to yield to oncoming traffic.

The population moved into the thousands once the tourists came through. The Alcova Reservoir was the main attraction, and many drove the thirty miles from Casper just to be on the man-made lake. The fishing was a mix of trout and large-mouth bass that would draw more with boats and personal watercraft. Even sailboats were seen out on the water during the day.

A large RV park on the western shore was considered the nicest in the state, and it drew people from all over. Without the reservoir, the small area was too arid for farmland, and it would have been just empty countryside.

Piekenbrock's search in the home turned up empty, and he yelled at the corpse on the couch. Then he had a good look at the older woman. Her hair was a uniform gray, explaining why he couldn't find any dye or coloring in the bathrooms.

He found the woman's purse on the table by the front door, and he took her cash and headed into town, the truck was built for the rugged roads, and the tires easily found traction on the gravel.

The Mason's home lay west of the reservoir off an old dirt road. Had they built the house on the other side, they would have had a distant view of the water. However, they had preferred the scenery where they could overlook the canyon.

Piekenbrock had timed it so he could be in the drug store soon as they opened, and it would limit the number of people out on the street shopping. He would be on the road by noon, head to the west coast, and eventually make his way to Alaska. He knew a man could disappear there for years and be comfortable.

The chimes rang as he opened the door, and he kept his head down in case of a security camera, ballcap pulled low. His thoughts were on hunting elk and a few other possibilities, and he failed to see the Ford police cruiser as it drove past. The bright gold APPD logo and letters stood out against the black vehicle and caught the morning sun.

*****

The drive from Arrow Point to Alcova took a full hour, and they would have been there sooner, except there was one problem. Everyone slowed in front of them on the Interstate. Soon as other drivers saw the cruiser in their rearview mirror, they hit the brakes. After it happened a dozen times, Noah stopped counting but remained frustrated, while Angie just laughed.

"We're helping the Highway Patrol, apparently."

Early on a Saturday morning, the traffic south of Casper picked up, and when they drove into the area, they were both ready to stretch their legs. The RV park was packed with a line of campers that were arriving.

As they drove through the downtown area, Angie continued to run plates on the data terminal. They had passed several trucks along the way, and it helped pass the time. Thirty feet on the other side of the gas station, Angie typed in another plate, and as they drove by the truck, Noah took his foot off the gas. He almost turned fully in his seat as he watched the sidewalk.

His foot hit the brakes at the same time Angie yelled. "Positive match!"

"Good, because I thought I saw Piekenbrock enter the store."

They slipped off their seatbelts as Noah pulled into the next parking space, fifty feet ahead of the truck.

He grabbed the handset. "Dispatch, 4417 requesting state backup in Alcova. Positive ID on Piekenbrock. Hunter out."

Noah and Angie didn't wait for the response. They slammed the doors shut and moved onto the sidewalk.

"I want you to circle around back, and I'll take the front. Do not hesitate once you have a positive ID. If he twitches, shoot to kill. Are you okay with that?"

Angie grinned and kept her hand on her sidearm. "Very good."

Noah opened the trunk and pulled out two communications sets. They hooked them into their belts and attached the mic and handset on their left shoulder with the cord under their vest. Before he closed the trunk, they each grabbed a shotgun.

"Keep your head on a swivel. Let's end this."

At the sight of two fully armed police officers on the sidewalk, people began to notice across the street. When a teenager walked out of the drug store and turned in their direction, Noah waved him away and directed him to cross the street.

When they came to the alley, Angie moved to the rear of the building while Noah ducked in to remain hidden until she was in position.

With his back to the wall, he concentrated on his breathing and attempted to slow down his heart rate. He couldn't afford to panic, and he knew with Piekenbrock, he would only get one chance.

Seconds later, Dickinson whispered over the radio, "In position. Ready."

"On the count of one," he took a deep breath. "Moving in five, four, three …."

Chapter 64

There were not too many options in the store. It was either red, black, or a chestnut brown. He chose a few more essential things he would need and paid cash. The girl behind the counter never looked up. She was more concerned with her phone than the customer. For the first time, Piekenbrock was good with that type of service.

She placed his items in a small white paper bag and mumbled something that had the word "day" in the sentence. The chimes rang again as he stepped outside. Then he froze.

A police cruiser was parked along the sidewalk ahead of the truck. The LED light bar stood out, and despite the new low profile, he spotted it right away. He had recommended the purchase for the APPD several years ago.

Piekenbrock switched the paper bag to his left hand, and his right snuck around to the small of his back and found the grip of the Beretta tucked into his waistband.

Out of the corner of his eye, he could see the pickup truck. The keys were in his front pocket. He doubted there would be enough time to make it.

He took several steps backward, and when Hunter burst around the corner of the drug store, he stepped into Melanie's Diner and drew his gun.

*****

Noah couldn't have been more surprised when he stepped out of the alley. As he brought the muzzle of the shotgun up, Piekenbrock smirked and stepped sideways into the diner on the corner.

His left hand pressed the toggle switch on the handset. "He's in the diner on the corner. Moving."

Dickinson's voice cracked through the speaker. "Roger."

Noah stepped forward to the edge of the window for the restaurant and looked inside. He jerked his head back in time to avoid a bullet. The shot echoed in the street, and screams of the patrons within quickly followed it. Shards of glass bounced on the sidewalk after a golf-ball-sized hole was punched through the front window, right where his head had been.

The front door burst open, and a family of four ran down the street away from Noah. The woman screamed and clutched her two small children, while her husband fumbled for his car keys and tried to keep up.

Noah kept the butt of the shotgun tight into his shoulder, leaned toward the window and yelled. "It's over. Lay down your weapon, Piekenbrock."

There were muffled screams from inside the diner, and then a single shot fired. The cries grew louder.

Noah took a quick look inside to see the situation before pulling his head back.

There was a low counter with stools on the left-hand side and a long wall of booths along the right. The kitchen was at the rear of the diner. Piekenbrock had a waitress in front of him with the pistol pointed at her head, and the other hand was tight across her mouth. A figure dressed in a white chef's coat lay face down on the floor by the cash register, blood stained his back where he had been shot.

Jesus Christ.

"Robert, let her go." Noah heard him laugh, and it sent a chill down his back.

"Not a chance, unless you wish to take her place? It'll be like old times, Hunter. Come on in."

He couldn't rush in. The woman acted as a shield, and Piekenbrock would not hesitate to fire. Noah whispered into the handset. "Are you in position?"

Dickinson answered by hitting the toggle switch once. There was a slight crackle over the speaker. Affirmative.

Angie couldn't answer verbally, which meant she was close. Noah was about to bet his life on that assumption.

He raised the shotgun over his head. He stepped in front of the window and stopped at the door. Piekenbrock had moved back and placed the counter between them. The older waitress was bent back, his hand firm across her mouth. Robert hunched down to present less of a target of himself.

Noah used his left hand to open the door while the right held the gun off to the side. "Take me, and you let her go. That's the deal."

"Step inside and unload the shotgun. Then place it on the first table."

He followed the instructions. The pool of blood grew in a circle around the chef on the floor and filled the grout between the tiles like small rivers.

Noah lowered the shotgun, pressed the magazine release in with his thumb, and cycled through with the forestock. Four shells ejected and rolled under a far table.

Noah left the action open and turned it to show that it was empty before placing it on the table. "Now, let her go."

"Drop your Glock on the ground and kick it over."

Soon as his hands curled around the polymer grip, the swinging door from the kitchen opened. Angie stepped forward and aimed her pistol at the back of his head. "Drop your gun!"

Piekenbrock's knees buckled, and he dropped to the ground. He pulled the waitress on top of him all in one move. The Beretta moved from her temple, and aimed at Dickinson. He pulled the trigger twice.

Angie flew backward through the kitchen door while Noah stared in shock. When they dropped to the floor, they fell behind the counter, and Noah didn't have a shot. He drew his pistol in an automatic reflex and aimed at the counter. He didn't have a target, but he would soon as Piekenbrock moved.

With her mouth free, the waitress screamed and thrashed on top of her captor. After a dull thud, the waitress fell silent. As he shifted to the side to look over the counter, the kitchen door opened and Piekenbrock crawled into the kitchen.

Noah couldn't see Dickinson, and he couldn't fire blindly into the kitchen. He moved behind the counter. The waitress was unconscious, a small cut on her temple.

He stepped forward, kicked the kitchen door, and moved inside.

Chapter 65

Noah tried not to notice Dickinson as she lay on her back, ten feet inside. Her arms were spread out to her sides, and she was still.

The kitchen had a long stainless-steel counter through the middle, and on the right was a grill and deep fryers, next to a gas stove. The rear wall had a red steel exit door and to the right was a walk-in pantry.

Noah held his Glock straight out at shoulder height and swept the room. As he leaned over to see the other side of the counter, Piekenbrock edged out of the pantry and fired.

Soon as he saw the movement, it was his turn to drop to the floor, and the round passed overhead into the wall. The shot echoed in the small area, and his ears rang.

He moved forward on his knees toward the stove and when he looked around the corner. Piekenbrock was doing the same movement on the other side of the kitchen island.

Noah didn't have time to aim when he fired his Glock and ducked back. After a glance at the footings, he braced himself against the wall and put his shoulder into the counter, then pushed hard.

The fifteen-foot stainless-steel counter squealed on the tiled floor and slid toward the pantry.

He heard a thump, stood, and fired toward the end of the counter. There was a groan of pain, but it didn't come from Piekenbrock—it was Angie. When he looked over the other side to see if she was okay, the counter slid across the floor *back* at him and knocked him into the wall.

As he started to fall, Piekenbrock stood and fired his Beretta. The first round hit him in the center of his chest, and it flung him into the wall as if a horse kicked him. The second round hit the wall, two inches beside his ear and above his shoulder.

Pain radiated across his torso, and he fought to remain conscious and breathe. He sunk to the floor. The ballistic vest prevented the round from penetrating, but it couldn't do anything about the force generated—except spread it out over a larger area. As he struggled, Noah felt the pressure on his ribs and he knew at least one was broken.

Piekenbrock walked around the counter. He stood six feet away, his gun raised. Noah squinted through the pain, and he raised his gun when another shot was fired.

The former police lieutenant staggered forward then fell back on top of Dickinson. The Beretta dropped from his hands, slid across the counter, and landed on the floor.

Angie had shot him from behind but had only grazed his right leg. As Noah struggled to his feet, he made a decision that he would regret for the rest of his life. With both of them on the floor and Piekenbrock unarmed, he couldn't bring himself to shoot. The risk was too high against his partner.

He left the Glock on the ground and leaped forward. All his weight dropped on top of Piekenbrock as he tried to twist his arm and flip him over. Noah weighed over two hundred pounds with his vest and gear, and when he landed, it knocked the air out of Piekenbrock and Dickinson's lungs.

Angie screamed and fought to bring her gun into play, but with the amount of weight on top, it pinned her arm to the floor. Noah found he had little strength after being shot. It was coming back quickly, but not soon enough. White stars of pain exploded across his vision as his rib throbbed.

Piekenbrock brought his right hand over in a hammer-fist and struck Noah several times on top of his head. He couldn't keep up to the onslaught, so he let go of the man's wrist and brought his fist across in a right hook into Piekenbrock's jaw.

Dickinson lay in shock as four hundred pounds rocked on top of her cracked ribs and lungs. The gap between them widened enough for Robert to get a knee inside and kick out his left leg. Noah flew into the shelving unit filled with white plates and bowls. Several dishes rained down on him, and one clipped him behind the right ear.

As he struggled to his feet, Piekenbrock stood and kicked him hard on the right side. The vest continued to protect him, but the pain levels caused him to see spots—the same place as the broken rib. On instinct, Noah lunged and knocked Piekenbrock back against the counter before he could strike again. He absently noted the person screaming was himself. Rage, fear, anger and pain fought a battle and he operated on pure instinct and reflexes. The end of the fight was almost in sight.

The weight caused the island to skid and slide tight against the stove and grill. They both noticed Dickinson's Glock on the floor beside her. Noah screamed and dove for the pistol.

Piekenbrock spun to the side, reached for the wooden block on the counter, and pulled out a fourteen-inch carving knife. As Noah's fingertips brushed against the grip, he felt a searing flash of pain across the outside of his left leg.

The knife had only grazed his leg, but it had buried deep into the top of Angie's thigh. Noah rolled off to the side as Piekenbrock jumped over them and, in four large steps, hit the crash bar on the rear exit and bolted.

Dickinson had trouble breathing, and her hands wrapped around her upper leg as blood ran through her fingers and on the tiles.

Things had just gone from bad to worse. Hopes of finishing this, were becoming less likely.

Chapter 66

Piekenbrock tried to ignore the burning in the side of his leg and crashed through the door at the rear of the diner. To the right was a secondary road and the sidewalk went around to the front of the building. To his left were large dumpsters and the back of another store.

He turned right, dug the keys out of his front pocket, and favored his leg as he ran around the outside of the diner. The truck was parked outside the drug store. He hit the remote and unlocked it before he slid behind the wheel. The engine roared to life.

He had a split-second to make a critical decision.

Drive calmly away and disappear or head back to the house and his other weapons and cash, *then* vanish. When he pulled out of the parking spot and drove away, he noticed the street was empty, except for a few that were brave enough to look through a window or around the corners of the building across the street.

He couldn't leave his brother in Wyoming.

Robert was the reason Zane had died. He could still picture the day they got into that stupid fight. Over a woman of all things. Every night when he closed his eyes, that day replayed over and over.

Robert worked at the veterinary clinic for almost a year and was about to close for the night when Zane had stormed in. That was when the fight began. Robert didn't know his brother had started to date and was interested in their mutual friend.

He had asked Donna out himself. In reality, all this was *her* fault, for she had gladly dated them both for weeks until Zane caught her.

The fight had turned physical, and despite all his years of training with the army, Zane had been knocked out by a rogue punch. Robert had looked for a way to keep him unconscious and injected him with a drug the vet had used earlier in the day.

He had brought his brother home, and he locked him in the basement, chained to the post. Only until they could talk about this reasonably. That was a bad choice and a deep regret, but he couldn't change the past.

Things had gotten worse, and after another heated argument, he left his brother downstairs for a few days to calm down. However, when he returned, it was too late. Zane Piekenbrock, his only brother, had died.

A switch flicked in his head. He'd held his brother for days and cried, but it didn't change anything.

One month later, a police officer came to the door and inquired as to the whereabouts of Robert Piekenbrock. The owner of the clinic was worried and kept trying to locate him. Doctor Kyle Hammond also called the police. His intentions were good. Robert had introduced himself as Zane, and when the officer looked at the Ohio driver's license and military ID, he was satisfied. Despite the three-year age difference, they could have been twins.

He told the cop that his brother had moved, and he didn't know where. After that moment, he knew it was safer to *be* his brother than to be Robert. So, he simply cut his hair in a short military style and wore collared dress shirts and dress pants. No one had noticed the difference. Not even Donna.

As he drove along the highway, he recalled how long she screamed and pleaded with him to let her go, but he just turned the music up to drown her out. She lasted much longer, chained to the post in the basement, than his brother. Which was good. She paid the price for her actions.

That brief moment with the police officer had sparked an idea. There would be no better place than to hide in plain sight.

For two decades, he fought down and repressed the memories. However, four years ago, the headaches and nightmares forced his hand. When he accidentally clipped a vagrant with his Jeep, the old desire reared its ugly head. He was *not* about to go to jail or be charged for someone else's incompetence. The killing was easy. Disposing of the bodies took some time, but he had a plan. After that, it became a game. Robert never lost, and he would come out on top.

The throbbing pain brought him back into the present as he glanced down at the wound on his leg. He had to clean it soon. The blood had trickled down his leg into his tactical boot. He whistled as he sped along the road and thought ahead of the next task. Noah Hunter was easily dismissed from his mind.

He suspected that the remains would be with the coroner's office. If he were going to tackle that, he would need some firepower and resources. Right now, he had neither. The police station had a fully-stocked armory, and he knew enough tricks that emptying it would not be an issue. Collateral damage would occur, but he wouldn't miss any sleep over it.

He slowed the truck and turned south on Kortes Road. A few vehicles were in his way, and he easily passed them as the large engine hummed with power.

Ten minutes later, he stayed to the right at the Y-junction and began to head north on the gravel road to the Mason's home. Before he made the right turn onto Fremont Canyon Road, he caught a flash of movement out of the rearview mirror. In reflex, he stepped on the accelerator, and the truck leaped in response.

Chapter 67

Dickinson struggled to breathe and shifted onto her side as Noah moved. Her eyes rolled back in her head from the pain, and a low groan came from her throat.

"Hold on, hold tight." Noah searched the shelving unit and found a stack of clean white hand towels. He left the knife in the top of her leg and wrapped the lengths of cloth above and below the wound to stabilize it.

He grabbed a few more towels and tucked them under her head, then forced her to lay down. "I need you to relax and breathe slowly. Can you do that?"

Angie nodded. Noah felt like he had been run over, but he winced and forgot about his injuries after one quick look at how far the knife went into her leg.

"I'm going to check on the waitress. Will you be okay for a second?"

She ground her teeth together, and her eyes squinted closed. "I'll be good. Go."

Behind the counter, Noah checked on the unconscious woman. Her pulse was strong. She seemed to be breathing fine. He rolled her into the recovery position.

A few poked their head around the corner and looked in the window.

"You and you, get in here and help."

Noah pointed to an older man with his teenage grandson. They looked confused for a moment. "Yes, both of you. I'm a police officer, and I need your help."

They came through the door, and Noah had the young man stay with the waitress while he brought the other into the back room.

"Help is on the way. I need you to stay here and keep pressure on her leg, just above the wound. Can you do that?"

The older gentleman nodded. "It's been a while, but I know what to do."

Noah picked up the three pistols on the floor. He placed his back in the holster, and held the other two. "Dickinson, I'm going to find him. Are you okay if I leave?"

She opened her eyes and grinned through the pain. "You better get your ass out of here and get him. I'll be fine."

He ran through the kitchen's rear door, picked up Dickinson's shotgun and kept going. With a hostage, the shotgun was not effective with a scattershot. She had made the right call. Moments later, he threw the weapons on the front seat of the cruiser as he hit the flashers and siren before he peeled away from the curb.

Noah placed a call to dispatch. "4417, suspect heading north on Fremont Canyon Road, officer down, but stable at Melanie's Diner in Alcova. Send an ambulance. Civilians injured or dead. I'm in pursuit. Send backup."

The traffic was sparse, but anyone in his way saw the flashing lights and pulled over long before it became a problem. Dispatch read his broadcast back. He tuned it out and focused on the road. On the straightaway, he pushed the Ford police cruiser hard enough that the lines on the road began to look like dots.

There were a few side roads along this stretch. However, Noah knew the general area and location of where the owner of the truck lived. There was only one reason for Piekenbrock to be out here. He had to be using the home as a base of operations.

At one point, Noah grew uncomfortable with the speed, and he pulled the seatbelt across his front and locked it in tight. However, he didn't slow until he approached a large gentle curve in the road.

Two hundred yards farther up, a black truck turned right, then disappeared from view. An outcropping of rock kept it hidden, but the plume of dust marked its path. He turned off the flashers and sircn.

"Got you, asshole," he whispered under his breath. He turned right at the gravel road, and the back end skidded a few feet before the tires gripped, and he shot forward once again.

The cruiser almost ended up in a ditch twice as the narrow road dipped and turned. Noah was forced to slow.

The truck's rear soon came into sight through the dust cloud, and he realized that as bad as it was to drive through it, it also hid him from Piekenbrock.

He stepped on the gas, and despite the steep slope of the gravel and the lack of proper traction, Noah closed the distance.

He shifted to the left lane hoping to clip the rear bumper, but the truck swerved in front and hit the brakes. He was forced to brake, but the traction on the gravel road was tenuous. Noah could not avoid the collision. The front bull-bar on the cruiser crunched the rear bumper before Piekenbrock shot forward. The four-wheel drive made the truck accelerate as if it were on flat pavement.

Noah quickly recovered and closed the distance once again. This time he didn't slow down—he just collided with the back end. The impact slammed him forward in his seatbelt, but he wasn't prepared for the shock of pain that took his breath. His ribs seemed on fire and he had to breathe shallowly or it would catch.

He didn't have enough speed to hinder the Chevy, but he did manage to hit it on enough of an angle that it fishtailed. Encouraged, Noah moved to the other lane, and instead of trying to pass and sideswipe, he used the front right bumper of the cruiser to aim for the left rear of the truck.

He had used the pursuit intervention technique (PIT maneuver) once in his career. When done correctly, the pursuing vehicle forces the fleeing car to turn sideways, and the driver loses control and is forced to stop.

It had worked properly on the suspect's car, but that was a small four-door Toyota, and this was a full-sized pickup truck. When the two vehicles collided, the truck's back end swung to the right.

Piekenbrock knew how to recover, and he spun the steering wheel to the left and right, steering *into* each skid, and within a few lengths of the vehicle, it had straightened out.

Then the former police lieutenant made a mistake.

The truck moved to the left-hand lane and began the bend into the driveway of the Mason's home. Soon as the tires turned, Noah floored the accelerator, and he kept it pinned as the Ford's 318 horse-powered engine caused the cruiser to leap forward. The bull-bar embedded into the right side of the truck, and he braced himself as things got worse.

Chapter 68

Piekenbrock knew it was too late to turn properly, but he thought the cruiser wouldn't have as much traction on the gravel as the truck did. When Noah collided on the right side, he tried to make the turn, but he had too much speed.

On either side of the driveway were two large decorative wooden posts to mark the property, and they were as thick as a telephone pole and buried deep into the ground.

The cruiser hit the truck enough to lift the tires a few inches, and then he lost all control. The driver's side impacted the wooden pole with enough speed that he cracked the side of his head and shoulder against the door and window. The airbag from the steering wheel exploded in his face.

It was like being punched in the head and upper torso, and he was slammed back into the driver's seat. Robert was sure that his nose was broken as a result.

The driver's door had crumpled around the post, and it sounded like a gunshot as the windshield cracked across its length. Piekenbrock tried to shake off the collision. He floored the gas pedal, but the truck only lurched a few inches before shutting down.

Hunter didn't waste any time. He reversed the cruiser and shot forward, slamming into the truck's right side again. He had time to see it coming, and he braced himself for impact.

The windows on the left side exploded inward and showered him with glass. The collision was loud enough in the cab that he thought he was deaf. The cruiser had enough, and the airbags deployed, then the engine shut down.

When he sat up enough to see, glass cascaded around him. The bull bars of the cruiser crumpled the passenger side of the truck, and he knew that the doors wouldn't open. Seconds later, he went out the passenger window feet first, off the cruiser's hood and ran toward the home. Noah opened the door, and spilled out onto the dirt and dry heaved.

Perfect.

By the time he hit the front door, Hunter had fired at his back, but he was fairly safe at that distance, and he didn't look. Although, when he closed the front door behind him, one round clipped the top of the frame. Lucky shot.

He twisted the deadbolt and ran upstairs to the master bedroom where he flung open the curtains. He had a perfect view of the driveway and the two vehicles. Hunter had just switched magazines and had the Glock propped on top of the cruiser as he scanned the front of the home.

Without looking, he grabbed the black ammunition backpack and opened the front zipper. Another Beretta Hi-Power was slipped into the waistband of his pants.

Next item was the .300 Win Mag rifle leaning against the wall. He opened the window enough to poke the muzzle through the screen window, then took aim.

Hunter wouldn't charge the house. Noah was too good a cop and couldn't be sure if there were hostages or not. He would stay there like a well-behaved puppy. The range of the 9mm pistol could not compete with the rifle, especially at one hundred yards.

His right thumb clicked the safety. He took a deep breath and slowly exhaled. Halfway through the exhale, he held his breath, ignored the tremor in his left hand, and slowly squeezed the trigger.

Piekenbrock wasn't sure how bad Noah was hurt, but the 180-grain 7.62mm round had hit. Hunter flew back as if punched and fell behind the police cruiser.

He calmly slid the bolt to the rear, ejected the spent casing, and then loaded another round into the chamber while he smiled. There was no other way to approach the house. It was only a matter of time.

*****

Noah didn't realize he was screaming in rage as he threw the cruiser into reverse and then rammed the side of the black pickup truck again. The collision slammed him forward against the seatbelt at the same time the airbag deployed. The pain from his ribs made his eyes roll back as he struggled.

He was pressed back into the seat fast enough that it felt like he had yet another accident. The air bag worked. It took a few seconds for him to find the seatbelt release, and he opened the car door and fell outside onto his hands and knees. The queasiness in his stomach caused him to dry wretch as he struggled to catch his breath.

Noah still felt uneasy when he stood and drew his Glock. Piekenbrock had a solid limp, but he still ran up the driveway faster than most could run normally.

The driveway was over one hundred yards in length, and he knew it wasn't likely to hit, but he still leaned on the roof of the cruiser and took aim.

Seconds later, he emptied the magazine at the target, but nothing landed. He hit the release, the magazine dropped, and he reached into his utility belt and automatically reloaded. By then, Piekenbrock was already through the front door of the home.

Fuck!

A quick look at the terrain showed that he was trapped, and with the truck out of commission, Noah knew he had him. He was about to shift behind the larger truck for coverage when pain exploded in his left shoulder, and he was flung back onto the ground.

He never heard the bullet that hit him until it was too late.

Chapter 69

Noah lay flat on his back and blinked against the pain. White fluffy clouds crossed the sky as reality began to sink in. He wasn't dead. But the pain in his left shoulder almost made him wish he were.

He struggled to sit with his back against the side of the cruiser as he examined the damage. The vest was only two inches wide and the round hit on the outside edge. It didn't go through his shoulder, but it grazed across the top and left a jagged furrow, half an inch deep and four inches long.

He couldn't tell if it was a direct hit or the result of a ricochet off the car. However, he knew how good of a shot Piekenbrock was, and he leaned toward a direct hit. Noah knew he would have been dead from a head shot had Robert not been injured and in good physical shape.

When he rolled the shoulder in a small circle, the intense pain made him grind his teeth, but he could still move. Noah glanced inside the cruiser. He was about to open the trunk for the first-aid kit when he realized Piekenbrock might not know if he was dead or not. If he opened the trunk, he may as well put up a banner that said that he had missed. On his utility belt, he pulled out a small lock-blade knife and cut the bottom three inches off a pantleg. Then he folded it into a makeshift bandage and tucked it under his shirt and vest, pressing it against the wound.

As his heartrate slowed, he assessed his other injuries. The cut on his leg had stopped bleeding, and his face felt like he'd been beaten with a baseball bat. One of the swings was a home run. He worked his jaw back and forth and concluded that he would be fine with a month's rest. Loose teeth were not important at the moment.

He holstered his pistol, kept low on his hands and knees, and moved down the road before standing. Noah crouched behind a large outcrop of rock and studied the terrain.

Piekenbrock had to have been on the second floor, which gave him full coverage of the driveway and the eastern slope. That didn't leave too many options. And he wasn't sure if Mrs. Mason was alive or not. Even though he was confident that Piekenbrock had killed her, he couldn't assume she was dead. There was enough death surrounding the former police officer, and he didn't need to add to it, even if the chance were minimal.

The ditch on the south side of the road dropped twelve feet. He slid down it on his behind. It was a matter of time until backup arrived, but it could be ten minutes or an hour or longer. He would use that time to try and get in a better position. If an opportunity to take him out came up, he wouldn't hesitate.

The world would be a better place without Robert Piekenbrock.

He ground his teeth against the aches and pains and shuffled along the ditch, then into a canyon. He must have hit his head and wasn't thinking right when he came up with a twisted idea.

If he could do it, it would give him an edge and end this whole disaster. "Does luck favor the bold?"

He would find out shortly.

*****

Angie cried out as she was lifted onto the stretcher and the older man patted her shoulder. "You're doing good, dear. You're going to be fine."

"Thank you for staying with me."

"Not a problem."

The county sheriff and the highway patrol arrived on scene at the same time, fifteen minutes after the first shot was fired. For such a remote location, they made good time.

It had taken thirty minutes for an ambulance to arrive from Casper, and the paramedics quickly assessed the situation and stabilized her. The waitress had woken and was also treated, but they couldn't do anything to help the cook. He was dead before he hit the floor.

This certainly was the most action to happen in Alcova in recorded history. Dickinson tried to raise Detective Hunter on the radio, but there was no answer. So, either he was out of range, or …

She hoped it was the former.

The troopers from the highway patrol knew the general area, and once the diner was secured and the county sheriffs agreed, their two cruisers sped south to try and find the location and Detective Hunter.

As she was loaded into the ambulance, Angie looked at her watch. Noah has been gone for forty-five minutes, and that also meant backup was that far behind him.

Frustrated, she couldn't help. She did something she hadn't done in twenty-six years.

Pray.

Chapter 70

Noah shifted the bandage under his shirt and holstered the Glock as he assessed the challenge. The vertical climb stretched over two hundred yards, and with the amount of rock piled at the bottom, he would have to test each handhold and maintain three points of contact at all times. With the wound on his left shoulder, ribs and cut leg, the degree of difficulty increased.

He didn't want to know the angle of the slope. At times it appeared to be over ninety degrees. Although they were not the same as the gloves he used to climb, he hoped his police tactical gloves would hold up.

He had enjoyed all the previous rock-climbing adventures with his brother many years ago. But they had used lines and harnesses. Iain had insisted they were always to use the appropriate safety gear.

"I could use your help right now, brother."

After a glance at his watch, Noah hoped that he could be in position before others arrived. There did not have to be any more casualties, and this approach should remedy that.

He didn't have any difficulty for the first thirty feet, but then a small boulder the size of a watermelon gave way under his right foot. He maintained his grip, but slammed his knee off a large rock.

Just add that to the list of injuries. Keep moving.

The burn that came off his legs intensified in his right knee the longer he climbed. The common mistake most made when climbing was to use their hands and arms to lift them. The leg muscles were larger and stronger, and they could do most of the work. The bullet graze on his left shoulder didn't slow him but, he could feel a trickle of blood as it ran down inside his shirt.

Noah was pleasantly surprised at the tactical boots. The vibe-sole seemed to cling to the rock, and he could dig the toes in the cracks fairly well. When he arrived at the halfway mark, the route ended at a sheer rock wall stretched twelve feet above his head.

A glance over his shoulder revealed a view from where he started the climb and how far he had come. Unfortunately, if he slipped on this next part, there would be no recovery. There was no other route to the sides.

A thin crack ran through the middle of the large rock was just over three inches wide. Just enough of a gap for Noah to slide a hand inside. With his fingers straight, he cupped his hand and forced the back of his hand tight against the rock while he pressed hard with his fingertips. The jam-hand technique had never been a favorite of his, but he knew how to do it.

The gap wasn't wide enough to allow him to do the technique with the gloves on, and if they slipped, even a fraction of an inch, it would mean death. So, he peeled them off and placed them in his cargo pocket before he resumed his efforts. Noah reached up with his left hand, wedged it in the crack, and stepped against the rockface with his right foot.

Soon as his weight settled, the wound in his left shoulder tore, and a new flow of blood trickled down. The makeshift bandage was saturated, and his shirt did little to absorb the blood.

Noah ground his teeth as he slipped his right hand between the rock, and his left foot moved into position. If he were fully rested and not injured, he figured that the climb wouldn't be a problem. Now that he was totally suspended, he noticed a tremor in his left arm as the pain increased.

When rock climbing, there was a balance between safety and not being rushed. Regardless, you have to move with a sense of urgency. Muscle fatigue and over-confidence could send a climber to their death or result in serious injury, amongst several other factors.

Although, he didn't have the strength or endurance to play it safe. Soon as his weight settled on his right hand, he reached with his left and jammed it in the crack. The large flat rock was only twelve feet tall, but it felt like he had climbed Mount Everest when he pulled himself over the edge and collapsed. Noah struggled to breathe and calm the tremors in his arms and legs with his feet over the side.

His hands throbbed in time with his pulse. His knuckles had ripped open and there was a cut along his right palm. Though, he couldn't feel it. There was no time for rest.

There weren't any challenges for the last eighty feet. It was like a ladder in comparison to the first half. At the edge, he regained control of his breathing before he peeked over the side.

The rear of the house had a covered porch with several chairs and a swing. It would be a perfect place to sit and watch the sunset over the canyon. Unfortunately, the Mason family would no longer be able to do so. Noah had no illusions that John's wife had survived despite the faint glimmer of hope. Piekenbrock had gone off the deep end, and he seemed determined to leave a swath of death in his wake.

The second-floor windows were empty. Noah couldn't see any signs of movement. With a burst of energy, he ran the one-hundred feet to the rear porch. His right hand drew the Glock from the holster, and he brought it to the ready position, his left hand cupped around his right. The cuts and scrapes were ignored, and his grip was steady despite the blood.

Noah glanced through the rear door. Inside was a large modern kitchen that opened into a living room with a wide hallway on the far side. The other door off the kitchen led to a small dining room.

There was no movement. He couldn't hear anything when he tried the door handle.

It was unlocked.

That caused Noah to pause. A small detail overlooked by Piekenbrock is a rarity, and he felt he was about to walk into a trap. After a deep breath, Noah turned the handle and slipped inside the kitchen.

Chapter 71

Noah was about to step farther into the home when the sound of glass shattering echoed all around him. He froze until he could identify where it came from. While it sounded like it came from inside the house, he realized the glass broke behind him—outside.

In the kitchen doorway, Noah looked up at the side of the house. The muzzle of a rifle swept glass out of the window frame as shards littered the back porch. Piekenbrock was using the rear window of the home to gain a clear vantage point over the backyard and down into the canyon. Had he been three minutes slower, he would have been shot.

From the second floor, anyone approaching the front of the home or the rear would be dead. However, only one side could be covered at one time.

Noah had gained entry in time to avoid detection, but when the hostage team arrived, they would just rappel in from a helicopter. He hoped this would be long over before they were required. It had moved into a personal goal to take him down long ago.

Besides a barbeque and patio furniture, the immediate area was empty. In the back corner of the yard stood a small cedar shed with a tin roof. It probably contained yard maintenance or garden equipment. The idea of taking him out from a covered vantage point ran through his mind, but with the Glock as his only weapon, it wasn't likely. He would need a rifle to make that work, and some distance.

Noah turned back to the kitchen. He had the best weapon for close encounters. It would have to do.

As he stepped forward, someone grunted and an aluminum baseball bat swung around the corner. It struck him in the middle of his chest. The vest took most of the energy from the weapon, but it hit hard enough that he flew backward, his right heel catching the edge of the kitchen door. As he fell into the backyard, Piekenbrock stepped around the corner, wide-eyed, his face set in a permanent scowl.

Noah used the energy to continue the movement, rolled to the side, brought up his Glock, and fired at the open doorway. The three-round burst landed in the stainless-steel Samsung refrigerator.

Piekenbrock had disappeared.

Noah slowly climbed to his feet and moved closer to the side of the home. His adrenaline spiked and did nothing to calm the tremor in his hands. Robert should not have been able to move silently from the second floor in time to strike him. But the bruising on his chest said otherwise. A burning sensation radiated throughout his torso. Another rib may have cracked and it made his eyes water.

There was no point in trying to be quiet now. Robert knew he was here. Time to draw him out instead of playing into his ambush.

Noah side-stepped around the perimeter and made his way to the front door. Both vehicles still blocked the end of the driveway so he ruled out that direction. Twenty yards north, at the end of a garden, was a three-foot-tall stone wall.

If Piekenbrock were focused on the rear or anyone approaching, he would have a clear shot from the side. At that range, the pistol would be perfect, and the stone would offer protection. As much as he wanted to finish this himself, he could use some help.

In a dozen steps, he dove behind the wall and waited.

Crawling forward, he raised one eye above the wall. The muzzle of the rifle protruded from the window at an angle. It was resting and unmanned. Piekenbrock must be at the rear.

Kneeling, Noah used the stones to take steady aim at the opening as he waited. The cell phone vibrated in his pocket, but he ignored it. There may only be one chance, and he was not going to miss it.

Five minutes passed, then ten.

Nothing.

"You aren't making this easy, are you." Noah spit to the side and waited another two minutes before deciding to go after him. "Ready or not, here I come."

Chapter 72

After trying the locked front door, Noah was left with no choice. He had to go around to the back. Soon as he stepped inside, he heard a muffled *click* from the other side of the house, then silence.

Noah raised his heel and rocked forward along the outside edge of his foot. His steps were measured and deliberate as he made his way through the home. One rogue floorboard could give his position away, and he would lose the element of surprise.

His senses were wired and stretched to the utmost. Noah knew he was running on fumes and adrenaline. Long as he kept moving, it didn't matter what the fuel was.

Twelve feet into the kitchen, he identified a familiar scent, and the faint sound of the buzzing of flies gave away the location. Stretched out on the long couch in the living room, Betty Mason lay on her back with two gunshot wounds to her chest. Blood had pooled on the floor and the area rug. Her left arm hung off the side with her fingertips resting on the blood-soaked carpet. The gray pallor of death covered her features.

Noah crept down the hall, past the wall of framed family pictures, and stopped. Inside the front door, an empty syringe lay on the hardwood floor, the orange plastic protective cap beside it. To the left of the foyer was a set of stairs. Above the front door, the ceiling was over eighteen feet tall, and it opened up to the second floor.

He stepped to the bottom of the stairs and looked up in shock. "Son of a bitch."

Robert Piekenbrock's tactical boots were a few inches above the ceiling, and they moved back and forth as the body swayed like a wound-down pendulum.

Noah took the stairs three at a time to the second floor and stood in shock at the railing. A small stool had toppled over, and a long orange extension cord was tied off to the banister before looping over a thick beam in the ceiling.

He absently noted that the line was wrapped in a perfect hangman's noose with thirteen coils revealed, and it cut deep into Piekenbrock's neck.

Five minutes earlier …

However, if he had arrived any sooner, he would have hung Robert himself. At least this way he won't go to jail for murder. A glance in the master bedroom showed how Piekenbrock had it set up as a sniper's perch. The two nightstands were pushed to the window, and the screen was torn for the barrel of the .300 Win Mag to fire. His left shoulder ached, not just from the climb but from the memory of how close he had come to death. A black backpack of ammunition lay open beside the bed.

Noah slid the Glock into his holster and walked downstairs. The realization that this was finally over had started to sink in, and he was unsure how to deal with it. Everything Hunter guessed on how Piekenbrock would have reacted was wrong. He had thought that he would go down, guns blazing.

He opened the front door and stepped outside into the sunlight. He tilted his head back and closed his eyes, letting the late-afternoon heat soak in.

Noah pulled out his cell and was about to call Bydal and the chief to let them know it was all over when he got a chill, and he spun around. His right hand automatically rested on the grip of his pistol, ready to draw.

The front door had slowly closed behind him with a muffled *click*. The same noise that he heard when entering the house from the kitchen.

As his adrenaline spiked once more, Noah limped down the long driveway, past the police cruiser and pickup truck, and looked in all directions. A faint hint of dust settled on the gravel road and rose with a slight breeze. He wasn't sure if it was from a recent car or the wind.

Noah turned in all directions as his heart pounded in his ears.

He was positive the door was locked when he tried it. But right now, Noah was alone.

Chapter 73

Noah sat on the lawn chair in his shorts and T-shirt and opened the cooler in front of him before he placed his feet on top as a footstool and settled back. The Eagles sang "Life in the Fast Lane" on the radio while he gave serious thought about dinner.

The last three days were a whirlwind of activity, interviews, and statements. Despite his injuries, he still had paperwork that needed to be completed. His left shoulder was the most serious, but the dull ache had receded. It would be many weeks before the bruises and small cuts healed, but he would listen to the doctor's advice and take it easy, for now.

He had just finished texting with Dickinson. She was doing good and recovering. She still couldn't place any weight on her leg without running the risk of further injury. They were both going slightly stir-crazy while they were forced to rest.

For now, he would make the best of it and just enjoy the moment as he cracked another beer.

"Can anyone join you, or do I need an invitation?"

George Hall from the coroner's office smiled as he walked into the backyard.

"Come on in!" Noah started to get up, but he was waved back down. George pulled over another chair. Noah opened the cooler and handed him an ice-cold beer.

"I won't say no to that. Thanks."

Noah took another sip, then looked down at the folder George carried in his left hand.

"I'm guessing this isn't a social visit."

George loosened his tie and slipped off his jacket. He hung it over the back of the chair. "I'm afraid not."

Noah turned down the music, and they both had a few sips before George opened the folder and passed a sheaf of papers over.

The hand-written notes were on the autopsy and information found for Robert Charles Piekenbrock. Noah read a dozen pages twice and started to get an idea of the technical and medical language used.

"If you could simplify this just a little for me."

Noah handed the folder back, and George pulled a pen from his breast pocket and used that as a pointer for the diagrams. "First, there is a reason I'm coming to you for this. Right now, you are the only one who has a copy of *this* report."

Noah took his feet off the cooler and sat up straight. George had his full attention. "I understand. Go on."

George pushed his glasses back on his nose before he began. "Piekenbrock was injected with etorphine hydrochloride (M99) at a dosage powerful enough to sedate a rhino in full charge."

Noah nodded. "That was the drug he had used previously. His prints were on the syringe found at the Mason house. He self-injected."

George ignored his comment and continued. "There are two types of hanging. A high-velocity, long drop or a low-velocity, low drop. Low drops are just strangulation while the victim's weight tightens the noose and they slowly suffocate. A high drop hanging has slack in the line, so when the body's weight comes down, it acts as a whip, and most times, it will break the neck. That's why they used the trap doors for public hangings. Someone thought it was more humane."

He was in full teaching mode, and he turned the pages to the diagram of the body. Notes were in the margins with arrows that connected to specific locations. After another sip, George pointed with the pen. "Piekenbrock's hyoid bone was broken, and there were signs of torn thyroid cartilage. If the victim was elderly, this type of damage could be caused by either method of hanging. Piekenbrock wasn't even sixty-years old, and the likelihood that it could happen from a low-velocity fall would be almost zero."

Noah's heart pounded hard, and his breath seemed to catch as the information was quickly processed. Finally, the inconsistencies started to make sense.

George closed the folder and passed it back to Noah. "It appears he was injected, then strangled, prior to being hung. I knew of the suspicions you had about a member of the police department being the killer. However, I think there may have been a second person involved."

Both men finished their beer in silence, and Noah automatically reached into the cooler and grabbed them another. He suddenly felt the urge to drink a few more.

"If you had handed the report into the station …."

"I could have easily handed it to his accomplice. Right now, besides myself, you are the only one to know. Your work isn't done yet, Detective. For now, it would be better if I handed in a formal report. One that would wrap up things nicely, to keep up appearances."

Noah went over all the facts and information of the case in his head.

What did I miss?

One thing for sure, the other person believed they had gotten away with it and would make a mistake in time.

Was it someone from the APPD or another police force?

Noah leaned back in the lawn chair and shifted the cooler to the side so they could both rest their feet on top. He thought about the various possibilities, and not for the first time in his life, Noah wondered how he would deal with what waited for him in the future.

When a Merle Haggard song came on the radio, he smiled and let out a little chuckle as the answer was obvious.

One day at a time.

Preview for

Course of Action

The Noah Hunter Series: Book Three

(Forthcoming June 2022)

Chapter 1

Noah stood beside the front door in full tactical gear, with his Glock 17 ready. When he nodded to the US Marshal, he counted down, "Breach in three, two …."

On *one*, Sedore swung the battering ram, and it collided with the door just under the locking mechanism. The thirty-five-pound Enforcer shattered the wooden frame and bent the dead-bolt—it didn't stand a chance against the four tons of force generated.

Noah threw the flash-bang grenade and leaned away from the opening. The loud explosion resonated throughout the house, and despite the fact he was around the corner, Noah's ears rang from the concussive wave. Anyone inside would stagger from the noise and be blinded temporarily from the light, which gave them an advantage.

A plume of smoke shot out the door and began to fill the room. Angie Dickinson took a deep breath and tapped her hand on his left shoulder, and they entered the small home in a rush.

Noah cleared the left corner while his partner swept the living room's right side, "Clear."

His ears rang from the grenade; however, he could still hear a young baby shriek down the hall.

Dickinson stepped to the side at the doorway to the kitchen, brought her Glock 19 to shoulder height, and fired two rounds at the older man with the knife.

When the blade hit the floor, Noah crouched and peered around the corner, "Covering."

"Moving." Angie stayed to the right with her back to the kitchen wall, barrel trained to the man's head. Her shots hit an inch apart, dead center of his chest.

"Clear."

Smoke filtered into the remainder of the home as Noah moved through the kitchen and down the hall. The sound of the child crying grew more substantial, and he gestured to the first bedroom on the right. Angie stood at his back and covered the two closed doors down the hall, "Ready."

When detective Hunter opened the door, he didn't hesitate when he saw the shotgun. A three-round burst from his pistol hit the woman in the head, and she crashed into the curtains, then fell across the nightstand. The baby continued to scream on the bed as the sound of small-arms fire filled the bedroom.

"Clear!"

No time to deal with the infant as they turned down the hall, Dickinson in the lead. When the door at the end flung open, Angie fired at the same time as she reeled from a hit to her shoulder. Her shot went wide and into the top of the door frame. The large man wore a balaclava and had withdrawn into the room while she swore and fell against the wall.

"Stay here." Noah stepped around his partner and tried to slow down his heart rate and not let the excitement impair his judgment. When a figure leaned around the open doorway in the last bedroom, Noah squeezed the trigger in reflex, and his Glock jumped in his hands with the recoil.

By then, it was too late.

The woman in the grey dress slumped to the floor, the warning klaxon sounded, and the bright overhead lights came on.

Noah couldn't help but groan, and Angie swore under her breath as she regained her feet.

"It's okay. Everyone falls for the switch with the first run through here."

The US Marshal had followed several steps behind and punched him in the shoulder as they turned and filed out of the training house. Angie kicked the mannequin in the kitchen as she walked past and holstered her pistol. The exhaust fans turned on while the crew prepared for the next team.

They had received permission to train at the Federal Law Enforcement Training Center (FLETC) in Glynco, Georgia. Over the ten-day session, they took advanced evasive and defensive driving techniques classes and electronic countermeasures and enhanced communications lectures. Noah had recognized Marshal Daryl Sedore, who volunteered to work with them for the house clearing (CQB) drills. FLETC was also home for the US Marshal's training center, and Daryl had taken them under his wing.

"Hunter and Dickinson, briefing room Charlie."

Noah saw their instructor as he leaned over the observation platform and pointed at the set of offices at the far end of the warehouse. Noah gave him the thumbs-up.

"Good luck. Will I see you for dinner?"

"Sounds good." Sedore nodded and removed the training vest and glasses before he went to the storeroom. It had been half a year since they worked with him in Arrow Point. His knowledge and expertise were essential to their last case. They had almost captured the serial killer before a hangman's noose solved the issue of a trial.

"I should have covered the door better." Sergeant Dickinson was the most demanding critic of her performance.

"You were fine. I was the one to shoot the hostage. I didn't verify my target."

Angie nodded, but Noah could tell she wasn't too thrilled. The debriefing room had several desks that faced a large display monitor where the instructor would play back and analyze their last session. The Arrow Point Police Department lacked a tactical division or a quick reaction force where this training type would be standard. Long as the budget allowed, the Chief would authorize cross-training of this nature.

Noah had done such room-clearing drills while in the military as part of his work-up training before deployment. It's been over twenty years; however, the techniques they used hadn't changed.

Angie collapsed behind a desk and pulled out her notebook to go over the two-person room-clearing drills, yet again.

When Noah's phone vibrated, he answered when he saw Steve Hutchings name on the screen. They talked for a minute when Noah abruptly stood, and the chair tipped over onto the floor.

"You have to be kidding me …."

He couldn't help but grin at the news and scratched his short dark beard that had started to grow in. Angie closed her manual and waited. When Noah was excited about something, it would be interesting.

Hunter looked at his watch, "Give me sixty minutes, and then I'll be at the airport and back in Wyoming soon. You better wait for me. We've waited eighteen years for this, and a few more hours won't kill you."

After he disconnected the call, Noah closed his eyes and took a few deep breaths.

Angie placed the manual off to the side and smiled, "So, are you going to let me in on this, or will I have to guess?"

He couldn't help but grin, "New information on an old abduction cold-case. The first investigation I worked on, actually."

Noah had been a rookie and only with the Arrow Point police department for two weeks when the call came in. They hadn't found the little girl that went missing, and despite the eighteen years that passed, he had never forgotten.

Angie took off her training gear, "There isn't a chance I'll be staying here. They better have room for us both on this flight."

Noah gave her a wink and immediately called the airline while his right foot tapped as he waited to connect. Dickinson left to find their instructor and turn in the gear. His mind spun with the possibilities, and he was ready to re-open the case. This time he would find answers, and the likelihood the little girl could still be alive fueled hope.

After eighteen years, he knew Angela's parents hadn't given up on finding their daughter, and neither will he.

Chapter 2

The next flight from Georgia to Cheyenne wasn't until the following morning; however, Noah found a direct flight to Denver International Airport that same afternoon. There wasn't a chance he wanted to wait until the next day. Noah tried to rest during the three-hour flight and remember all the details from the missing child case.

"I was only gone for a minute! When I turned around, my daughter was missing." Sergeant Steve Hutchings and constable Noah Hunter heard the mother scream when they first arrived at the motel. Unfortunately, that wasn't the last time Noah listened to a similar statement from a parent. However, those words and that moment in time still resonated eighteen years later.

The Taylor family were on holiday and passed through on their way to Yellowstone National Park. They stopped at the Travel Resort motel in Arrow Point and would continue their drive the next morning. Leslie Taylor brought in the luggage had let her daughter Angela sleep in the car while her husband, Joe, went to the motel office.

Leslie had thrown the suitcases on the bed, and when she returned to the car, the door was wide open, and her daughter was missing. The four-year-old couldn't reach to unbuckle the harness from the car seat, which only left one option. Someone had taken her.

They had quickly set up a perimeter search, and the Highway Patrol and the county Sherriff's arrived on the scene within thirty minutes; the FBI as well. After several days of searching, they slowly called personal away for other tasks due to the lack of viable leads. The various statements from the witness in the area and the road drivers didn't provide any credible information. Leslie and Joe Taylor eventually returned to Washington DC, heartbroken. Their life and hearts had shattered; regardless, there wasn't anything the police could do without new information.

Noah opened his eyes when the flight attendant asked him to raise his seat fully. They began their descent into Denver, and he looked out the small window at the countryside. The early fall weather had turned the trees a brilliant orange and yellow shade, and winter would not be far away. The farmer's fields were bare and ready for spring planting.

Georgia was humid and warm, but they had to wear a light jacket when they got off the plane. The autumn weather was well underway in Colorado.

In a rental vehicle, they drove north on interstate twenty-five from Denver. Construction outside of the city slowed them down, but he relied on his badge to get him out of trouble if it came to it, and he quickly made up the time.

Two-and-a-half hours after they left, Noah could almost hear the Chevy Equinox sigh in relief when he closed the car door. "Much better than a four-hour drive."

Angie stepped out of the car and stretched while she listened to the engine tick as it cooled, "I think you have set a new record."

She stood two inches taller than Noah at six-foot-one, and had recently cut her long brown hair to shoulder length. Despite being twenty-eight, Angie looked eight years younger and had a few problems with her apparent youth. After four years with the APPD, she was the youngest officer promoted to sergeant. Despite her misgivings, she had scored perfect on her exam, and was excellent at her job. Noah didn't hesitate to choose her as a partner, a decision he never regretted.

Eight hours after he received the phone call, Noah walked through the police department's doors, eager to find answers.

~

The FD-258 fingerprint card was standard with the FBI for background checks through any government agency. Noah remembered the process as part of his application for the police department background check.

He held the form up to the light and tried to read the blacked-out, redacted text.

"Have we verified this with the Feds? Why would that information be left out?"

Staff Sergeant Steve Hutchings took the form, held it up to the light, and squinted, but he couldn't see anything. He sighed, "This didn't arrive through the regular channels. Someone wanted us to see this."

The top half of the fingerprint sheet had an area for name, address, aliases, etc. There was only two pieces of information not redacted: the gender, marked as female and the state of Florida.

It arrived with the daily mail to the police station, care of Noah Hunter with no return address. Since 9/11, the staff sergeant processes all incoming mail and packages as a security precaution. Hutchings ran the prints in their system and got a match within minutes.

"Do you think it is real?" Noah handed the form over to Dickinson as he sat behind the conference room table.

The staff sergeant nodded. "Without a doubt."

The prints matched those of Angela Taylor, but as an adult. They had dusted and found a full set of fingerprints from the four-year-old at the scene, but nothing else. The abductor must have worn gloves.

"Who do you think sent this? They must have known I worked the case."

Hutchings shook his head, "Not sure, but the good news she is alive."

"Do you still have the envelope it came in?" Angie slid the prints across the table and took out her notebook, while Hutchings removed the large manila envelope from a folder.

She looked at the corner, "This didn't run through the post office. There isn't a postal meter on this; it didn't go through the system. Hand-delivered?"

Hutchings ran a hand through his short white hair and shook his head, "No. It was in the pile of mail early this morning."

"What about this?" Only one end gaped opened, the other sealed by the sender. "Any chance of prints on the inside?"

"We can send this to the lab to look for trace, but I wouldn't put much hope in it. However, more importantly, this is a solid lead. Review the files, go over the evidence. Start from square one."

Angie looked at Noah and grinned, "Maybe your new girlfriend can help?"

"We're just friends."

Even Hutchings smirked at this.

Noah stared at them both and realized he wouldn't get anywhere with them, "A couple of dates, but that is it. First, I need to sign out the evidence and go over the files."

Steve moved to the door, "I will have the FBI run the prints through their system. It's their form; they should know more. I want to put this one to bed before I retire. Get crackin' Rookie."

After he left, Angie asked, "How much longer is he going to call you that?"

Noah chuckled, "Rest of my career, most likely."

Despite the long day and drive, he was anxious and filled with energy, "I'm going to need my own office before we begin. We won't be able to work in the general area properly."

The second floor's main workspace had a large open area filled with desks, which all the officers shared. The only rooms on this floor were the captain's office and the conference room.

Captain Haslam preferred to work the night shift, and lieutenant Bydal worked days, rarely was there a problem sharing an office. It has been done this way for decades due to lack of space.

Angie frowned, "Not too sure where you want to set up. Not much free room left."

Noah stood, "How many times have we used all three holding cells at once?"

She laughed, "You want to have an office in lockup? There is a definite odor there." Angie tapped her pen on the table while she thought, "How about the travel trailer in the parking lot?"

The twenty-eight-foot trailer was a mobile command unit, and it's rarely used, except for a recruitment information center at Casper College this last spring.

"At least it wouldn't smell like disinfectant. I think it will work. Call Bruce and have him set up a phone and at least two computers. I have some more driving to do tonight."

Noah wanted to get to work right away; however, he still had to drive to Cheyenne Regional Airport to get his truck and return the rental. With a quick look at his watch, he figured he would be lucky to get a few hours of sleep. After eighteen years, a night without rest would be a small price to pay.

Chapter 3

By three o'clock the next afternoon, Noah was on his fifth black coffee as he toured Dickinson around the Travel Resort Motel property. He used to wear a suit while he worked, but it wasn't practical in the end. His default uniform was now jeans, running shoes, a dress shirt, and a suit jacket. The shoulder harness was replaced with a holster for the Glock 17 on his right hip. Since Angie's promotion to sergeant, she had worn much the same clothing, opting for comfort and practicality.

He passed her the photos and the AS-32(a) report (initial form including sketches and distances) as they stood in front of the motel room.

"The Taylor family arrived at 18:53 hours on August third and checked in with the office. Joe Taylor moved their vehicle and parked in front of room eight, ten minutes later."

Angie looked at the eight-by-ten pictures, then at the building, "Not much has changed."

The motel's shape resembled a long L, with twenty-four rooms that faced the parking lot. The office was next to the road, with ice and vending machines underneath the overhang—the sign on the road advertised air-conditioning and free wi-fi with each room. The red sheet-metal roof had faded with time, and it gave the building a worn-down look.

"Why did Joe go back to the office after he parked the car?" Angie looked across the parking lot. The office was one hundred feet away at the end of the building.

Noah looked at the reports typed from his notes, "The couple in room nine was loud, and he wanted to see if there was another room available."

The rooms were in order. and room nine shared the same wall as room eight.

"Do you think we can see inside?"

"Let's see if the room is vacant, just to have a quick peek."

Despite the interior pictures, it doesn't compare with seeing it in person, if possible. When they walked into the office, a bell rang off the door hinge to announce a customer.

A chest-height check-in counter stood next to a display filled with pamphlets of local attractions and restaurants on the right-side—large windows gave a view of the interstate on one side, and the parking lot on the opposite filled the office with light.

Noah eyed the coffee maker and took a step forward but was interrupted when a young woman came out of the offices. Two minutes later, they walked across the parking lot with a white security key-card.

Inside the room, two double beds were on the north wall with a nightstand between them. A large dresser filled the opposite wall, with a flat-screen television next to a small coffee maker. A small pedestal table and chairs were just inside the door, in front of the window.

Noah headed to the small closet next to the bathroom door, "This is where Leslie Taylor placed the bags, then washed her hands. When she returned to the car, she found the rear door open, and Angela was missing. The call came in at 19:04 hours, and we were on scene within six minutes."

Dickinson opened the closet door and then inspected the standard motel bathroom, "Are the curtains open all the time, or would they be closed when she first walked into the room?"

Noah flipped through the typed notes and reports. The half-inch stack was freshly printed. "Not recorded. Hold on."

There was only one other car in the parking lot. He walked under the overhang and checked a few different rooms before he came back.

"It looks like the vacant rooms have the curtains drawn. But, I'm not sure how they were eighteen years ago."

Noah wasn't sure of the paperwork versus his memory. He wasn't sure if the minor details had faded, or mis-remembered. Angie opened the drapes above the small table and stood in front of the closet. Noah could see her reflection in the mirrored door.

"If I'm standing here, with the curtains open, I can see where they parked. Same as the bathroom."

Straight ahead inside the bathroom, the sink and counter with a large mirror were along the far wall.

Noah stood at the sink, "I can see straight through the window. They would have had a full visual and even partial sight if the door was left open from this angle."

"Stay there for a second, and I'll move the cruiser." Noah left the door and curtains open. Seconds later, he stood at the vehicle's rear door and left it open. He could see straight into the bathroom from that location, and when Dickinson stood near the closet, he could see her through the window.

As he stood outside, Noah looked around the parking lot and at the front office. He could see the young woman behind the counter as she watched. There were no blinds or curtains in the office. Anyone behind or in front of the counter would have a full view of the parking lot.

Angie joined him beside the cruiser, "Unless things have changed in the last eighteen years, they should have seen everything."

Noah slowly nodded. He should have noticed this eighteen years ago, and the fact that the girl's parents didn't mention they had line-of-sight to their vehicle raised a red flag. The sense of unease steadily grew.

"Let's head back to the station and start going through the full file, step by step."

*****

The dress shoes clicked against the polished stone floor as she strode around the older man with the red dust broom and his veteran's ballcap.

"Sorry, Andy."

"No problem, ma'am."

He had kept the lobby clean for over thirty years, and everyone knew Andy. However, she didn't have time to talk. The woman smoothed her grey dress suit and tucked the file folder under her left arm as she continued.

She passed the one-hundred and thirty-three stars engraved into the marble wall, as well as the black book encased in a display of steel and glass. Her passing caused the American flag to stir as she reached for the myriad of security passes and identifications that hung around her neck.

Next to the staircase, the black security door had a card reader and a biometric scanner, and it took the woman a few seconds to find the correct card before she was through.

The long hallway ended at a large door with a wooden plaque. The Latin motto was engraved in large letters, *Tertia Optio*. Directly translated, 'A third alternative,' more commonly known as 'the third option.'

Yet another security card opened the door, and she walked into the small set of offices. She took a moment to look in the mirror behind the display cabinet and fixed her hair. The stress of the job had aged her. Despite being sixty-five years old, the woman could have passed for seventy. Her once long blonde hair was now short, streaked with grey, and cut over her ears. The lines on her face had deepened over the years, and her oval glasses would slide down her nose when she bent forward. She would always stand with her shoulders back and head held high to avoid this.

She knocked on the middle office door, looked up at the wall and ceiling corner, and waited. It was hard to see the camera inside the black housing, but she knew it was there.

The lock clicked, and she stepped inside.

"It's been a while since you've been here, Miriam. To what do I owe the pleasure?"

The large office hadn't changed in over two decades, and it still resembled a 1940s cigar lounge with dark leather chairs. Law books and encyclopedias filled the floor-to-ceiling shelves. TV screens filled the south wall and a small mahogany bar-cart beside the sizeable executive desk's right side.

She thought this was the only office in the entire building with a twenty-by-twenty-foot area rug. Somehow it seemed to fit.

The gentleman stood when she entered, walked around the desk to give her a brief hug, and gestured to take a seat.

He was in his late seventies and wore his usual dark slacks and a blue golf shirt, and his short white hair resembled a military brush-cut.

"Is the room secure, Walter?"

He held a finger in the air and sat behind his desk, and flicked a switch inside the top drawer before he nodded, "We're good."

All electronic communication now ended at the walls. Nothing could be broadcasted nor be received. There wasn't anything they could do about internal recording devices, but a crew swept the room once a week.

Miriam relaxed into the comfortable leather chair while Walter sat across from her. He gestured to the bar, and she shook her head, "I only have a few minutes before I have to go."

She handed him the file folder while he pulled a pair of reading glasses out of his breast pocket and studied the reports.

When he frowned, the lines on his forehead deepened. Miriam knew he had finished the first-page summary.

Once he completed the remainder, he folded his glasses and rubbed his eyes, "How many others know this information?"

"Including us, only four."

Walter slowly nodded before he passed over the paperwork, "All roads will lead to a dead end. I'll make sure the Florida field office acts accordingly."

Miriam stood, "I thought you should be aware."

"I appreciate the heads-up. It's been a while. Dinner sometime?"

Walter gave her another brief hug after they stood. A sheet of paper fell out of the folder and landed at his feet. He picked up the FD-258 form and handed it over.

"I'll give you a call if there is any new information. No need to wait for our next meeting." With a half-smile, she left without a response to his question. Some things she wasn't willing to forget.

However, Miriam could not see the cold, deadpan look that overcame Walter's face as he watched her leave. Not looking back would cost her dearly.

About the Author

David grew up in a small town east of Toronto, Canada. He has had many interests throughout the years, including the military, martial arts, playing guitar, reading, and in his own mind, he is quite an excellent fisherman. David is married and has one daughter, and misses his chocolate lab daily.

Feel free to write to David at:

author.david.darling@gmail.com